The Bootlegger's Widow

Keith McClellan

ISBN-13: 978-1500807504
ISBN-10: 1500807508

ACKNOWLEDGMENTS

I am grateful to The History Press for permission to publish extracts from two folk songs in **Folklore of Cornwall** by Tony Deane and Tony Shaw.

I would also like to thank Amanda Leigh, Sara Banerji, Imogen Matthews, Sheila Johnson and Peter Perugia for their advice and support.

For Carol, whose love of Cornwall was too infectious to resist

CONTENTS

PART 1

Martha could see the lantern swaying as it moved along the cliff top. There was no moon. A mix of lowering cloud and windborne spray carried over the cliffs from the waves crashing onto the beach below. She closed the door and pulled her shawl around her, wincing as the rough cloth rubbed across her battered arm. Still seething with fury and frustration, she moved towards the three-legged stools scattered across the bare earthen floor. One seat had parted from its legs; he had used the leg of another to attack her, its socket splintered by his raging violence. Wood smoke puthering from the fireplace, driven down the rudimentary smoke stack by the gale, forced her, coughing and spluttering, towards the shuttered window.

She thought she heard the sound of shouting and returned to the door, not daring to open a shutter for fear of the wind. A line of lanterns was moving swiftly towards the cliff top. Revenue men! Now he was for it, the obstinate brute. She'd tried to warn him; the whisperings along the moorings had been most particular. She looked at her arm as her shawl flapped in the wind. That's all I get for my pains, she thought. If they take him now I'm lost: lost with him, lost without him.

The smell of sea salt and gorse filled her nose and mouth, the salt stung her arm as she re-entered the cottage to warm herself. She threw the offending stool leg on the fire, careless of the need to replace it. The fire spat sparks and flared up, filling the room with a bright flickering light. Behind a smoke-stained woollen drape was the truckle bed she dreaded to share. At its foot a chest fitted exactly into the remaining space. He kept it locked with a heavy iron key.

In an adjoining curtained recess were the kitchen utensils: knives, pewter plates and tankards, water jugs and, on the floor, a few empty brandy kegs, his percentage as he called them: a part of each consignment paid for but withheld for his personal use. The one in current use stood on a low shelf. She struggled to roll an empty keg out to the main room and set it upright as a stool. The low crunch of a musket shot penetrated the buffeting of the wind, followed moments later by another, and another, and then a series of them, not quite regular enough to be a firecracker, but showing a determination to disable their quarry. She sat still, nursing her arm in the flickering firelight, suspended between hope and despair.

Knocking and rattling at the door disturbed her reverie. She rose and moved slowly towards the sound. The door rattled again, loudly and impatiently. He wouldn't have knocked, so who could it be? She opened it enough to see who was there but it was thrust wide, sending her reeling into the rough limed wall. Her arm dragged across a ridge. She gasped and cried out, a mix of surprise, pain and fear. As the intruder raised his lantern to inspect her, she saw a thickset, unshaven face below a battered tricorn hat.

"Where is it?" he shouted into her face, "where's the liquor?"

Three more men crashed through the door. They filled the room. They shook the water from their cloaks like dogs. The fire stirred and spat. Smoke swirled between them, making them cough and splutter.

"God's eyes! Shut the door, damn you, before we all choke to death," shouted the leader. The last of the men turned to obey and became aware of Martha cowering in the far corner.

"Ahoy there, my lovely," he leered, "aren't you the lucky one?"

"Leave her, Rawdon, we've liquor business to finish. Let's search this place nook and cranny."

"Won't take many minutes to clear this smoky hovel, will it, my dear?" said Rawdon, still looking at Martha.

"Have, er ... , have you seen my, my man, my husband?"

"Name, lass, what's his name?" asked the leader, straightening up and looking towards her.

"Baines, Sir, Will'm Baines."

The other two men continued searching, rolling empty kegs towards the door. Before the leader could reply, Rawdon, whose attention had been fixed on Martha throughout, laughed.

"Seen him, my little beauty, we done more than that. He won't trouble us no more, nor you for that matter. You'll be all alone in that there bed from now on, unless o'course I decide different."

Martha sank to the floor, her body heaving with silent sobs as she drew her shawl around her.

"Leave her, Rawdon, we've got work to do," shouted the leader.

"Just about finished here, Cap'n, nothing much left, must've been expecting a big top-up tonight," said the shortest of the men, rolling an empty keg towards the door with his foot, "these are the evidence you wanted, eh?"

"Rawdon, get that trunk out from next to the bed. Bound to be something useful in that, statements, letters, papers. I'll give you a hand," said the Captain, approaching the bed. He and Rawdon dragged the chest out.

"Uncommon heavy, strong lock by the looks. Where's the key, Mrs?" Martha was speechless, quaking with shock and fear. Rawdon bent and grabbed her under the armpits. She screamed as he dragged her up and pressed her against the wall.

"Key, my dear, we need the key," his yellow teeth leered an inch from her face. Tears left rivulets through the encrusted dust on her cheeks as she drew in deep gasping breaths.

"Leave her, Rawdon, she's lost her mind for the moment. Help me get this outside. Then you can carry it up to the hut," said the Captain as he pulled his end of the chest and caused Rawdon to lurch away from Martha who slid noiselessly to the floor.

"A health unto the revenue men!" shouted the short man. Rawdon and the Captain turned to see him holding a pewter tankard aloft. The fourth man at his shoulder had the same.

"I'll join ye with that," shouted Rawdon, abandoning the chest and crossing to see what they had found. The Captain sighed, put down his end of the chest, stretched and wiped a sleeve across his face. The two men with tankards sat on the chest and Rawdon appeared with a small pewter jug and took a long draught from between handle and spout. The Captain ignored their invitation and positioned himself to shield Martha from their sight. He judged the moment when they would follow him without argument and ordered them outside. Rawdon turned to Martha,

"Don't worry, my lovely, you shall not lay cold and alone too many nights before I return."

II

The tide was out, exposing a wide crescent of sand to the wintry sun. The shadow of the cliffs shortened as the sun rose towards its midday height. On the far side of the bay lay a series of rock pools, rising towards a shallow cave in the limestone cliff. A lone figure was balancing and stooping among the pools. She carried a worn leather bucket with an inch or two of seawater as she plucked mussels from the exposed rocks, scooped the occasional small fish as she waded into the deeper pools and dragged strands of edible seaweed from the tangled mass on the tide line.

Sensing the tide turn, as the breeze freshened, Martha made her way to the track at the base of the cliff. She wound a strand of rope, picked up from a previous visit, around the pile of driftwood she had collected earlier and heaved it onto her back. There was enough rope to go over her shoulders so that she could hold the ends as she clasped the leather bucket to her chest. She walked steadily up the zigzagging track, pausing briefly to gather her strength. Back at her hut she released the wood and lowered herself down to sit for a few minutes. Placing the bucket beside her, she looked out across the still dormant bracken and heather to the village on the far side of the bay. The sea was calm today.

News of a wreck had come in yesterday after the storm. It was too far down the coast for her. Others had set off in the early hours with various carts drawn by horse, donkey or hand. It was a long way to go and she knew there would be brawling with the local people unless it was an impossibly large haul. Without Will'm she had no protection. She could easily be robbed once her cart was laden. She stood, picked up her bucket and turned to enter the hut. There was a note pinned to the door.

Inside the hut she broke the red wax seal. She recognised the Cornish chough in the crest of Sir Oliver Trewarren. It was proudly displayed on the newly installed iron gates to the manor house drive and on the coach that took Sir Oliver and Lady Elizabeth down to the harbour where their schooner was moored. Why would the lord of the manor write to her? She wondered. Perhaps it was not him but a mean jester who knew of her troubles and had access to Sir Oliver's desk. For a moment she feared the worst, it must be that terrible brute. He had threatened to return: a threat that had given her nightmares ever since that terrifying night. She must have it read, but who could she trust? Few people in the parish had the schooling. There were letter writers down at the harbour but they would demand payment. Nor could they be trusted to keep what they knew to themselves.

She could think of no one who'd had schooling. Except, of course, why hadn't she thought of it before? The Rector, the Reverend Francis Trewarren, younger brother of Sir Oliver. He at least was kindly and if he mentioned the letter to anyone it would be to his brother. If it were a jest Sir Oliver would be made aware. She brought in the wood and stacked it by the chimneystack to dry. The bucket with its fish and mussels she drained of seawater and poured in some fresh from a wooden basin. She rinsed the mussels, scraped them, and placed them in an old copper cauldron. She rinsed the seaweed, combed it, and chopped it into small pieces. It would eke out her remaining flour to make bread.

The rectory was an imposing building next to the church; ivy clung to its walls, reaching almost to the top of the eaves. It was half a mile from the centre of the village, overlooking the bay. As she approached it, Martha paused and glanced back across the cliffs. A rising twist of smoke suggested her own small hut. It lay in a dip in the moorland which rose towards the great headland. She had been to the rectory once before when she came with her father and Will'm to arrange her marriage. She pulled the bell cord tentatively and, hearing nothing, tugged it more vigorously. A maid appeared.

"You're a forward young hussy. It's not your place to show impatience. The rector is not impressed by such ignorant behaviour. State your name and the purpose of your visit." She stood with arms folded, blocking the doorway. She's about my age, approaching five and twenty, thought Martha, yet her skin has not weathered.

"I'm very sorry. The rector can be sure I would do nothing of a purpose to disturb him." She bowed her head.

"Yes, yes, but who are you and what do you purpose troubling him like this?"

"Who is it, Sarah? Can I not be left to my sermon? The Sabbath is all but upon us," called a voice from the depths of the house.

"Now, you see, you have disturbed him. He's busy on important work. Be off with you." She moved to close the door.

"Wait." Martha surprised herself by her own firmness as

she stepped forward. "Martha Baines is my name. I'm but a poor widow from beyond the village. I beg you let me speak to the rector. I need his help. He is the only one as can help me." She now stood just inside the door.

"Sarah?"

"It's a Martha Baines, Sir. A widow. Says she must speak to you, Sir. You are her only hope, she says. I'll send her away, Sir." She pushed Martha towards the door.

"No, no, let her in. She's shown some courage getting this far. I have a duty to the poor of the parish. Show her through." Martha was shown into a book-lined study where the rector rose from his desk, took off his spectacles and came towards her. Ignorant of the etiquette required she made a small curtsey. The rector smiled.

"What can I do for you, Mrs Baines is it?"

"If you please, Sir, would you be so kind as to read this letter for me, being as how I've not had the schooling, Sir?" She reached under her shawl and drew out the letter.

"Of course, my dear, of course. Why don't you sit for a moment?" He indicated a wooden-backed chair by the desk with one hand and took the letter in the other. Martha sat stiffly with her hands folded in her lap as the rector read the letter.

"It's from Sir Oliver. He understands you have recently been widowed?" He looked at her inquiringly.

"I have, Sir, yes Sir."

"Yes, of course you have, my dear; I do beg your pardon. We buried your husband not three months back. I recognise you now. I thought the name was familiar." He looked back at the letter.

"Says he likes to help when he can; needs someone in service just at present. Will see you on Monday. See if you are suited. Eleven o'clock sharp." He smiled down at her.

"Well there," he said, passing the letter back, "very handsome of him, very handsome indeed. You are a lucky young woman, Mrs Baines, a lucky young woman."

"Yes, Sir, thank you, Sir." Martha was taken aback. It was difficult to take in.

"A bit of advice before you go," added the rector as she stood up. "Wear your best clothes. Likes a smart woman, Sir Oliver does, and his housekeeper, well, ahem, she's not too easy to please, if you understand me."

"Best clothes, Sir? These are me only clothes. I'm only a poor widow, Sir."

His eye ran down from her grey linen frock under a woollen shawl to the hessian apron from waist to ankle.

"He'll ask me for a reference too, Mrs Baines, regular at church and so on. God-fearing man is Sir Oliver."

"I comes when I can, Sir, but it ain't always easy, what with the weather out there on the headland." It must sound a feeble excuse to a man like the rector, she thought.

"I wish you well, Mrs Baines. Good day to you now." He led her to the door.

III

As she made her way back towards the centre of the village, a string of packhorses approached from the track along the coast. Behind them a couple of carts, mud caked around their wheels, were lumbering along, their horses snorting and lowering their heads with the effort. Martha remembered the wreck; it looked like a good haul. Out along the bay in the opposite direction smoke still rose from her chimney. From this angle it was possible to discern the origin of the hut, the upturned stern of a lugger, much adapted by Will'm's father and by Will'm himself. He'd been a good man when not in drink, but he'd taken the brandy more often of late: the cause of her miscarriage.

"Well, dang me if it's not Widow Baines," the shout broke through her thoughts. "How are you, my lovely?" Rawdon was grinning down at her. "I'll come and visit you, my dear. You must be frightful lonely. Three months is allowance enough, I think, grievin' for that drunkard of yours." He sat astride his horse in his heavy felted coat and tricorn hat. She could see his yellow teeth, irregular and lined with black. Spittle appeared in the corner of his mouth. He moved his tongue across his lips, cleared his throat and spat a stream of brown tobacco onto the track. "I'll not forget you, never fear." He nudged his horse and moved off, calling over his shoulder, "I'll see you anon, my lovely."

The sun was low over the sea as, head down, she pulled her shawl more tightly around her and hurried round the bay, panic rising in her breast. What could she do? Should she stay away? But where could she go? She must be at her best on Monday; it was her one chance to escape a lifetime of poverty. Perhaps he wouldn't come before Monday, perhaps he wouldn't come at all, was just trying to frighten her. She let herself in, saw to the fire and began to prepare her supper. The cauldron with her mussels she hung over the fire. She gutted the fish, speared them onto an iron spar and wedged them over the fire, turning them slowly. The smell at least was pleasant.

She had no rushes and no fish oil for the lamp. She went outside. A three-quarter moon was rising over the privy as she walked the few yards there and back. She ate her supper by the flickering fire light. Then, sliding a wooden pole through the latch to secure the door, she lay down on the bed. She dozed fitfully; the day's events would not leave her.

A loud crash shocked her fully awake. Another. She sat up, relieved that the pole was holding. A third crash, a splintering and the door swung open. She slid off the bed and raised her hand to her mouth. Rawdon stood there grinning.

"Ahoy there, my lovely, time you had a man in the house. I do hope you have not entertained while I have stayed away in consideration of your grievin'? Well?" She was unable to speak. "I trust you are pleased to see me. I shall not neglect my duty to relieve your loneliness and service your needs." He dropped his coat and hat to the floor and levered off his boots. He took a pace towards her, seized her round the waist and threw her onto the bed. A wave of fury coursed through her body.

"Get off me, you brute, leave me be," she shouted repeatedly into his face. She struggled, kicking his legs, punching and scratching his head and biting any part of him that came close to her mouth as he pushed her skirt above her waist, and climbed on top of her.

"Feisty ,eh? You're a lively one to be sure." His strength overpowered her. He had his way until, sated, he slid away from her and put his feet on the floor. She lay with her eyes closed, bruised and sore. A pale shaft of moonlight angled through the window, lighting the side of his face as he sat.

"Now listen, my lovely, and listen well. Young widows are worth as much silk as comes my way in a year. You were very lively there at the start, enough to fire a man up. You will do very well when you adjust to my ways. I had a good day, today, my lovely, a very good day, what with taxes gathered and confiscations from those as chose not to pay." He turned and smiled at her, but her eyes were closed. He reached for his boots and forced them on against the bed frame. "You learn my ways, my lovely, and you will live like you never dreamed with that double-crossing sot of a man you married. I'll bring you a silk dress next evening, a beauty it is I warrant. If you are more accommodating to my ways, you may try it for a fit." He pulled on his coat and the battered tricorn hat and turned towards her.

"Get out, you brute, and leave me be, I beg you, leave me be." Her eyes were open now. He grinned once more, turned

17

and strode out.

"Leave me be," she said. "Pray God you leave me be."

IV

She closed her eyes and lay still. Waking suddenly, she sat up, registering the soreness between her thighs. A slight greyness showed from the doorway. The fire was out. She shivered and stood up. She must have gone to sleep and left the door open all night. At the privy she doused herself to remove all traces of Rawdon's presence. Back in the hut, she drank some water and chewed on a remnant of dried fish suspended from its hook in front of the fireplace. She felt better.

I must do something, she thought. I been scraping around like some scavengin' pauper. I been livin' under the fear of Will'm so long, with his drinkin' and beatin'. I'll have it all over again if I don't have a care. That Rawdon is worse. Least I were wife to poor Will'm; he weren't all bad, he did his best to provide for us, when he weren't in drink.

I'm a self-respecting widow, still young enough, still in me prime, you could say. I needs to support myself. If I finds another man, so be it. I s'll take more care in the choosing of him, whoever he be. I needs a bit of independence, I reckon, a bit of wherewithal, sommat to keep me from the parish paupers' list. Must make the most of me chances in service at the manor house. I ain't the wherewithal to be a baker, and I'd be lucky to find work guttin' pilchards down in the harbour. Family work that is. I'm no more'n your average needlewoman, so it's service or a bit o launderin', which there ain't much call for in these parts. But enough of this brooding.

Martha collected the remaining firewood, took some kindling from the alcove and built a new fire. It soon took light and its heat began to spread across the room. She stood straight, brushed her hands against her hessian apron and tried a smile of satisfaction. It was a strange but welcome sensation. She set to work sorting the ingredients for a loaf of bread. She could just about have it ready to leave with the baking lady on her way to church, she reckoned.

Martha was kneading dough when Molly arrived with her basket.

"I've brought you some bread and some salted fish."

"Thank you, Molly, I'm sure, but I'm not seeking your charity." Martha continued her kneading.

"For the sake of our Good Lord in heaven! What can we do with the woman? We're family Martha, sisters, and never mind if our men had their foolish quarrels. With Will'm dead and gone, you need your family. Now take this food and make us some tea. Have you any left? I'll bring you some if there's need."

Martha took a cloth and wiped the floury dough from her hands. She felt into the recess in the alcove and drew out a pot. She turned and smiled at Molly.

"I still have a little, from Will'm's last dealing. We'll have a nice brew, the two of us."

Over tea, Martha revealed her troubles. Molly listened

without interrupting as Martha told of her struggle since Will'm had been shot: the re-emergence of Rawdon and her hopes of better times in service with Sir Oliver.

"I'm minded to say something to you, Martha, my dear, maybe not to your liking."

"Say what you will; I feel better for the unburdening, much better. You've been kindness itself to hear my troubles." Martha smiled.

"'Well then, I think it's time you finished with your grieving. Think of the future stretching before you. Seize the chance that Sir Oliver offers."

"I do aim to, Molly, really I do."

"But more than that, stand tall for yourself, don't let this Rawdon have his way with you. Or if his strength is so great, find ways to use him. Every man has a price. You owe no man your virtue."

"I don't have the strength, Molly, not as yet. I'm striving for it, mind." said Martha.

"There's sommat else, you'll not welcome me sayin', but 'tes right to raise it. You'll not want a babby now; not in your present state. It'd be the end of you, Martha, as you know full well."

"So what are you saying?" said Martha.

"You needs a preventer. If that Rawdon carries on he'll not want a babby neither. Have you some linen and some pilchard oil?" said Molly.

"I don't rightly know. I have heard of such things, but never had need."

"Well think on it. You have need now. That Rawdon will have his way, leastways till he tires. But I'm thinking he has bigger plans for a comely widow. Best have a preventer to hand whenever he comes for you."

"I'll think on it, Molly, I will," she added at Molly's doubting expression.

"A widow is a gift to a man like that, especially one so pretty as you could be. Let me tidy you a little, clean the dust from your face and neck, put some wild heather in your hair, comb it out for you." She delved into one of the bags she had brought and drew out a wooden comb.

"'Oh I don't rightly know. It seems such a betrayal. I promised the rector." She paused.

"Promised him what? That you'd go to church regular, I'll be bound. 'Tes easy to do, yet make the most of your charms. Let me see to that hair."

In the afternoon, Martha walked across to the church, leaving the loaf she had made at the baking house on the way. After the service, the rector shook her hand as she left, praised her attendance and complimented her on her appearance.

"Sir Oliver will appreciate your efforts. He understands your poverty. So your attempt to look presentable will please him. Well done, my dear Martha, well done."

She walked back, feeling uplifted that he had noticed. She stood tall and straight and smiled to herself, surprised at how much better she felt.

Back in the hut, she could no longer put off thoughts of Rawdon. He would be here within the hour. In the back of her mind was a fragment of conversation. Something he had said. Something had broken through the closed mind with which she had resisted him. A dress? He would bring a dress. A dress would help her so much to please Sir Oliver tomorrow. A preventer, she said to herself, I need a preventer. Linen, where can I find linen? She had none spare save her own few clothes. Will'm's shirts she remembered, with sudden inspiration. He had two linen shirts. She dragged one out and tore a strip from the sleeve, dipped it in a jug of pilchard oil and shaped it as best she could. It'll have to do, she decided.

Rawdon swept into the hut without knocking, made her a mock courtly bow, and dropped a bundle at her feet.

"I see my little widow has prettied herself in my honour. That is pleasing indeed, and not a little surprising." He moved towards her with arms raised to seize her waist but she spun away, smiling over her shoulder.

"Oh, Mr Rawdon, Sir, will you not take a cup of tea with me?"

"I am truly astonished," he said. "You will offer conversation next, but to business." He moved towards her and grasped her waist.

"Oh, Mr Rawdon, Sir." She slid her arms around his neck and took hold of his hair. His wig came away in her hand and her giggle was genuine. He threw her onto the bed. She pummelled his shoulders and back with her clenched fists.

"Take me gently, Sir, I beg you, or I must fight for my honour."

"Honour? There is no honour for the likes of you. I shall enjoy you just as I fancy." Yet he was less rough than he had been. She suppressed her revulsion, allowed him his will, and gave fulsome praise to his manhood. He rolled away gasping with exhaustion.

Later he took out the dress and insisted she put it on. It had a high-necked collar, narrow waist and full skirt. She loved the rich red colour from the French dye. She spun round, in a move she could not have imagined only a day before.

"Perfect, my little widow, perfect. You shall keep it. Wear it for me next week. You are stronger today and more easy in your ways. I may grow quite fond."

Martha shivered at this but smiled as he left her. Tomorrow another fate awaited her.

V

Martha swished up the gravel drive to the Manor House. She held her head up and her shoulders back in spite of the cold clammy air and the threatening cloud. She stood in front of the house, uncertain what to do. She was sure the grand front door in the portico above the wide stone steps was not for the likes of her. There must be an entrance for servants and trades people but she could not see where it was. As she stood there, a rider on horseback crunched across the gravel behind her. She turned to see Sir Oliver himself trotting from the drive towards the stables at the far side of the house. A groom appeared and held the reins while Sir Oliver dismounted. Martha thought to wait until Sir Oliver had gone inside before asking the groom where she should present herself.

"Mrs Baines?" She looked round. Sir Oliver was addressing her. In confusion she tried to turn and curtsey at the same time. She slipped onto one knee. She recovered in time to note Sir Oliver's smile and obeyed his gestured invitation to approach.

"A pleasure to meet you, Baines. We'll go inside and discuss terms and duties." She followed him up the steps and through the great oak door, which opened at Sir Oliver's approach. The maid curtseyed to Sir Oliver, but could not hide her astonishment at Martha's entry.

"Show Baines into the library, Constance. I'll be with her shortly."

"Yes, Sir. Wait in here, Baines," she said, still unable to conceal her disbelief. Not trusting herself to speak, Martha followed the maid into the library. Her mouth fell open as she gazed around. The maid left her without another word. There was a fire blazing in the huge granite fireplace. A large, brass-edged, leather box of logs stood to the edge of the hearth. Giant brass firedogs stood either side, with fire irons to match. A number of portraits hung on the walls, previous lords of the manor, she supposed. What struck her most was the sheer number of books. She had never seen so many together. She had seen one bookcase full in the rector's study when she had sought his help with the letter, otherwise there was only the great bible, chained to the lectern in church. She approached the shelves and ran her finger over the ridged backs of the leather bindings. Further along, what had looked like a case of books turned out to be a smooth wooden painting of books on shelves. Why would anyone do that? she wondered.

"Now, Baines, why don't you come over here to my desk?" She turned to see Sir Oliver smartly dressed in a morning suit. "The housekeeper usually deals with servant matters but, in your case, I wanted a few words with you myself." She said nothing so he continued, "Baines, how aware are you of your husband's, what shall I say? Work? Activities? Yes, that's more appropriate: your husband's activities?"

"Well, Sir." She played for time as she struggled to think what she could reveal. "He were not one to talk a great deal on that, Sir. He never 'ad no boat of his own, Sir, but he were crew for others in time of need. He knew the sea and the fishing, Sir. Or he might help out with carting the fish to the pilchard cellars. It's the women as gutted and salted, as you know, Sir."

"Yes indeed, Baines, and hard work it is too, I'm sure. Now did William bring much in the way of luxuries, supplies I might call them, back to the house?"

"Well, we was never short on tea, Sir, and o'course there was the drink. That were the death of him in the end, least that's my belief. He couldn't keep off it, you see, Sir; rum or brandy

25

mostly."

"'No luxuries then? I see that you are wearing a very elegant dress this morning. Is that the gift of a devoted husband, Baines?"

"I was advised to look me best by the Rector, Sir. The Reverend Trewarren advised me of that, Sir."

"I'm sure he did, Baines, but that does not explain how you came by it. You would have to travel to Exeter at the very least for such finery, if not the capital itself. It may be presumptuous of me to say so, but I do not think you or your late husband would have had the means for such an expedition."

Martha said nothing.

"Very well, we shall not discuss it further at present," continued Sir Oliver, after a pause. "The maid will show you to the servants' quarters, where you will wait upon the housekeeper's summons to go through your duties." He rang a little brass bell on the desk.

"Thank you, Sir," she said, relief flowing through her.

"One more thing, Baines." She looked up at him, as the maid reappeared. "Keep the dress at home; I don't expect to see it again."

VI

After a dinner during which she had conversed little with her husband, Lady Trewarren retired to the drawing room, settled in her chair by the fire, and took up her embroidery. She held the frame up at an angle to the lamp she had had placed to give maximum light to her endeavours. Sir Oliver, meanwhile, was enjoying a cigar and a glass of brandy in the library, which doubled as his study and smoking room. The brandy was rough to his palette. He examined the bottle closely. He was not impressed. He suspected a surreptitious exchange had taken place. He warmed the bowl of the glass in his hand, swirling the amber liquid round. The taste did not improve and neither did his temper.

"Elizabeth, my dear, I'll join you if I may. There are some matters I wish to discuss." He walked across to a wing-backed armchair opposite his wife, drew the tails of his jacket under him, and lowered himself into the chair. His wife glanced across at him and resumed her embroidery.

"You said nothing at dinner, Oliver. Has something happened in the meantime?"

He looked across at her sharply but her head was bent over her sewing.

"In one case, yes, and in another, no," he said, ignoring her ironic tone.

"Then pray enlighten me." She smiled, and placed her embroidery in her lap. "I am all attention."

"The brandy has been switched," he said. "It's a household matter. I would like my displeasure made known to the persons concerned, with a clear understanding as to what is to follow unless recompense is made. First have the consignment checked. Let us see how many bottles are involved."

"Is this a permanent adjustment to household responsibilities, my lord, or simply a temporary convenience? I should be grateful if you would clarify this point for me before I am embarrassed in front of the servants."

Her attitude saddened him, so different from the early days of their marriage. She had not recovered her early devotion to wifely duties since the loss of their daughters, both in the same year. Emmeline, barely into her sixth year, lost to the smallpox, and Lizzy, fast growing into a marriageable beauty, thrown from that wild hunter she was so fond of; her skull shattered against the gnarled trunk of the old oak at the bottom of the meadow.

"I do wish we could avoid such petty differences and concentrate on the serious matter in hand. I can, if circumstances demand, tolerate an inferior brandy. That is not the point at issue. One moment my dear," he added, raising a hand to stem her interruption. "If you would be so kind as to curb your impatience for one moment, my concern is that someone who has access to our source of supply is bold

28

enough to exchange high quality brandy, which will fetch a far higher price, for this rough young sample that would not match that which it has replaced were it to be racked in the cellar for thirty years. The insult to my discerning taste is as nothing compared to the unknown threat posed to our enterprises until it is exposed and removed."

"I know little and care to know even less of your enterprises," replied his wife. "Yet I accept that it could pose a threat to our income and our social standing. It is fortunate indeed that Widow Baines is now in our employ."

"My next point exactly. How astute you are, my dear, when our mutual interests are at risk. How is our new serving wench settling?"

"That dress she wore this morning was most inappropriate, Oliver, as I made clear. There were whisperings between the maids, much giggling and muttering of 'scarlet woman'. However she settled in, as I hope you observed when she carried the food in for dinner. You did notice, I suppose?" Sir Oliver nodded. "She will need a deal of training in the ways of domestic service. We need say nothing directly of other concerns. She has accepted the need for regular church attendance on Sundays. Francis will warn her of the Wesleyites. That will be most appropriate."

"Indeed it will, we are of a mind on that at least. I too warned her about the dress. She will not wear it here again. She was not forthcoming on how she came by it."

"We shall learn that in due course, I've no doubt. Elspeth will befriend her."

"Good, my dear, good. I shall look forward to her report on the matter."

They sat in silence for a while. Oliver looked across at her again. Did she blame him for the girls' deaths; surely not. Perhaps it was young Richard's profligate behaviour in London. He knew she felt he should have reined the young man in long before his debts had grown so large. He was profligate with women no less than with money. He had disqualified himself from marriage into any respectable family in society. Elizabeth seemed to Oliver to blame him for what she termed the loss of hope for her children's future. Thus she put distance between them not only over his enterprises, but over their most intimate relations also. When he came to her bed she admitted him on sufferance, and then but rarely. These thoughts were interrupted by a tap on the door as Elspeth entered.

"I came to discover if you have any further needs this evening, ma'am," she said.

"No thank you, Elspeth, you may retire when your duties below are fulfilled."

"Thank you, ma'am, Sir Oliver. I bid you good night."

"I shall need a word in the morning, Elspeth."

"Yes ma'am, thank you, ma'am." She bent her knee in deference and left the room.

VII

The cloud lay low over the sea as Martha hurried along the cliff towards the church. She could see only a few yards ahead. A good day to fetch the crop, she thought, no wind to power the revenue cutters. The wet from the mist settled and ran down her cheek. She pulled her shawl more tightly around her in an effort to absorb the moisture before it set her whole body shivering. The church would not feel warm today.

"Mrs Baines, Martha." She looked up in surprise.

"Why Elspeth, I thought to meet you in church; 'tes a cold damp morning and no mistake."

"I thought I should walk with you this first time."

"But Elspeth, I am no stranger to the church; I married and buried my Will'm there. Besides, I owe my position at the Manor to the Rector. Indeed my conscience is troubled if I miss my communion on the Sabbath." She smiled.

"Of course, but 'tes your first time to sit with the servants. If you entered uncertain and alone, it would start the young maids giggling. They are of an age to laugh at any excuse." Elspeth returned the smile.

"You are most kind, Elspeth. You have been a great comfort to me in face of my tormentors."

"Oh come, Martha, you must not take it so hard. 'Tes only the fooling of silly girls. Were you not the same at thirteen years?"

They quickened their pace as they came amongst others making their way to the church. Martha felt Elspeth take her arm and guide her to the manor servants' pew. Looking across the nave, she caught the ghost of a smile on Lady Trewarren's face as she turned towards her brother-in-law, who stood at the altar. He glanced towards Martha and she fancied he gave a barely perceptible nod towards Lady Trewarren before welcoming the congregation and beginning the service. The Rector had always seemed a rather distant, kindly figure to Martha. He had rarely delivered his sermons with passion. This morning, however, he spoke at length and with feeling about the one true path, castigating those who would deny the Lord the honour of robe and surplice, leading worship in the plain dress of the everyday; those who would have their church as plain as their dress; who would class as sin any means by which the humble poor may relieve their misery.

As they left the church the Rector was his usual friendly, smiling self. He had warm words for Sir Oliver and his wife, and a kindly smile for the servants.

"You took the meaning from my sermon, I trust?" he said to Martha, holding her eye.

"Thank you, Sir," she replied in confusion as they passed out into the damp air.

"You are privileged to have a special word spoken, Martha. I hope you take the meaning of it," smiled Elspeth.

Walking back along the cliff, Martha pondered over the service. It was kind of Elspeth to meet her, of course. She had taken her under her wing from the beginning, or almost so, but the remark as they left the church was out of character, or was it her imagination? The Rector, too, seemed to single her out, but perhaps it was just the newness of her situation. She could hear the sea below the cliff; the tide had turned. She glanced out across the bay. She could make out the indistinct shapes of ships moored in the Roads, but Falmouth itself was still shrouded in mist.

She took most of her meals at the Manor now, and took good care to keep hunger at bay. The remains of a loaf with some pilchard pickled in vinegar would suffice today. She might allow herself a glass of the cloudy cider from Molly. Take the edge off Rawdon's visit, she thought, the better to act the temptress. She smiled at her own guile. She looked up as the black-tarred wall of the cottage emerged from the mist. There was movement to the side. Through screwed up eyes she detected the tossing of a horse's head. A large well-groomed mare moved restlessly against the hitching post. Martha stopped. Fear coursed through her body, surging through her chest, causing her to gasp for breath.

The swish of the wet grass and the crunch of the stones would give her away, she was sure. The mist was her best hope of escape. As she approached the mare turned and whinnied, raising its head. The rope, tight on the hitching

33

post, jerked the mare's head down increasing its anger. Its neck swung sideways, bending the hitching post like a primed long bow. Martha paused, undecided but ready to run.

The house door flew open. Rawdon moved to the mare to quieten it, but it swung its hindquarters at his approach and its kick caught him in the groin. He was wearing the thick pleated woollen coat of His Majesty's Excise, but fell to his knees nonetheless. He crawled out of range and threaded an exploratory hand through the folds of his coat. His tricorn hat lay abandoned at the edge of the track.

"God's eyes, Silver, is that what you think of me?" He tried to force himself up, but gasped with the pain, "I'll bring my whip to you, be sure of that." He was still on his knees. He sat back on his heels until he was breathing more steadily. Martha watched, unseen, as he staggered to his feet and leaned on the wall of the house.

Should she make herself known, and offer him help, or evaporate into the mist and return towards dusk? She turned to retreat and caught her foot on a stone, which rolled a few yards down the track. The mare swung its head round and fixed her with a malevolent stare.

"Ahoy my little widow, just in time to treat my wound with a noggin from La Belle France." His smile twisted in the effort to hide his pain.

There was no escape, she thought, as she moved forward. Yet his injury should dampen his lust. He reached for her shoulder and stumbled against her. She fought to retain her balance.

"God's eyes, you clumsy whore!" His face twisted with pain.

She regained her footing and led him the few steps to the door. She paused to work out how best to manoeuvre him into the house, but her thoughts were interrupted.

"Rawdon, you old rascal, where's this flighty whore of yours? I'm getting impatient!"

VIII

"Damn fine sermon, if I may say so, Francis. Didn't know you had it in you."

"Really, Oliver, Francis has delivered nothing less since devoting his life to Our Lord at his ordination."

"Why thank you, Elizabeth, you flatter me indeed. Do I detect a subtle trace of irony in your comment? Aha, your smile confirms it." Francis tilted his head with a wry smile of his own. He dabbed his lips and chin with his napkin and leaned back.

Oliver sat at the head of the table, with Francis to his right and Elizabeth to the left. The table stretched away in front of him, bare beyond their immediate places.

"I'm lost in the web of your subtleties," said Oliver. "Talking of which, did you catch a comforting word with our pretty little widow?"

"Indeed, I did, though she was quite pink with confusion."

"I am sure Elspeth will perform her duties in the matter," said Oliver, with a glance at his wife. He refilled his glass with claret and raised it: "To free trade and the Church of England."

"To the Church of England and free trade," said Francis, more quietly. He and Elizabeth raised their glasses in unison, smiling at each other across the table.

"Let us enjoy the benefits of our investment: we have some fine cognac and cigars freshly arrived, Francis. I'm sure you will join me?" he glanced at Elizabeth, who rose slowly.

"I shall withdraw, gentlemen, reluctant though I am to deny myself the delights of your uplifting conversation." She smiled at them both, and swept out of the room.

The steward brought the brandy decanter and glasses' first to Francis and then to Oliver and, having served them, placed the decanter at Oliver's elbow. He returned with the box of cigars, clipped each man's choice, lit a spill from a candle and gave each smoker a light.

"That's all. Thank you, Pollard."

"Thank you, Sir." Pollard bowed his head and left the room, glad to get to the kitchen to enjoy his own lunch.

"Don't you find it ironic that the Wesleyites, who claim they serve the poor, attack the practice of free trade which benefits the poor in so many ways?" said Oliver.

"Indeed I do, yet they gain such a grip on simple minds. They have taken a firm hold of the tin miners of Scorrier and now Gwennap. I hear they number poor fishermen among their converts. It is causing some alarm, as my sermon implied."

"Surely the death of Wesley himself will see them wither away? Do they have other rabble rousers among their number?"

"Locally down in Pendean, I believe, and up in the north of the country. It is hard to say what effect Wesley's death will have. He has truly planted a seed; t'would be foolish to deny it," said Francis.

"More cognac?" Oliver held the decanter.

"Thank you, just a taste." Francis watched his brother pour and held up his hand as the liquid reached the full width of the glass. He raised it to his nose, swirled the glass around and caught the rich fumes in his nostrils. "Mmmm, a fine crop, chosen with refined taste."

"You will not credit this but, only last week, I had a serious apprehension over interference with the consignment. A most inferior sample was served. Indeed I strongly suspected foul play."

"May the Good Lord preserve us! Were you not alarmed?"

"I was, I admit, deeply concerned. I discussed the situation with Elizabeth, who shared my fears. We interviewed the housekeeper together and, as you have so courteously indicated, the matter is resolved for the present." He held up the decanter as if to emphasise the truth of his statement.

"I am very relieved to hear that," said the Rector, as he watched his brother serve himself. "Speaking of Elizabeth, does she not enjoy a sip now and again?"

"She is not over fond of spirits, It is no a drink for a lady, or so she tells me."

"Perhaps the incident explains my feeling that she has not been happy in herself these past months. It's such a pity, a lady of her beauty and intelligence."

"She is worried concerning young Richard. He is quite the profligate in town, I'm sorry to say. She expects his return in the next day or two, and is collecting her thoughts on how to convey her displeasure without driving him back to the iniquities of the city."

"There has been no improvement then?" Francis sipped his brandy and stubbed out his cigar. "Excellent," he added, hastily pointing to the cigar as he saw his brother's puzzled expression. "If I can be of any assistance: perhaps a quiet talk about his Christian duty?"

"Let us join Elizabeth in the drawing room," said Oliver,

standing as he stubbed out his own cigar. "She may well appreciate your offer." He indicated with his arm and led the way out of the room.

IX

"So this is your juicy whore, Rawdon? Your taste has truly improved, by God. It is a pity you'll not enjoy her for a week or two," the young man laughed. "An injury most inopportune, is it not, you rogue? It is most fortunate I am here to service her."

Rawdon lay against the wall, propped up on his elbow, hand moving gingerly within the fold of his heavy coat. He glanced up with a sneering grimace.

"Indeed, a young widow needs regular pleasuring to keep her in condition, is that not so, my pretty young whore?"

Martha turned her attention to the visitor. He was barely twenty by her reckoning. He wore no wig but his fair hair hung over his collar and, unsmoothed since he removed his hat, had a windblown look to it. His coat, which hung open, was well cut and revealed a white shirt of the finest silk under an extravagantly embroidered waistcoat.

"My first duty is to Mr Rawdon, Sir. He has suffered injury, as you see." She turned back to the groaning figure. "What will you take to ease your pain, Mr Rawdon?"

"Grog, you little whore, fetch me grog, fetch it now."

In the alcove, Martha scrabbled desperately in the hope

39

that some dregs had survived the raid all those months before. To her surprise, she came upon two full half kegs pushed clumsily behind a threadbare blanket draped over a pair of stools. She raised one to a shelf, took up a wooden tap and a mallet and drove the tap into place. As she reached up towards a pewter tankard she felt two hands on her waist.

"Come, little temptress, I have the impatience of a young stud. Deny me no longer."

"I must serve poor Mr Rawdon his brandy, Sir." Martha swung round, the tankard in her hand, to find herself face to face with her assailant. His grip on her waist tightened as he drew her to him; she smelt a mix of perfume and male sweat.

"I must serve Mr Rawdon, Sir." She sidestepped and, taken by surprise, he released her.

Swiftly she moved to the brandy and began to fill the tankard. He reached for her again but a rough voice intruded.

"Grog, whore! Grog or I'll flog you the moment I'm able."

"Coming Mr Rawdon, Sir." She eyed her young attacker. "The keg were not yet tapped, but 'tes pouring nicely now, Sir." She turned off the tap and pushed past the young man. "Here you are, Sir. May it aid your recovery, I pray, Sir." She bent low to place the tankard by his hand, and felt her wrist grasped in an iron grip, holding her down. She felt the brush of stubble and the damp spittle in her ear as he whispered, "Serve him well, whore, or we shall both suffer." He released her and raised the tankard to his lips. Trembling, she stood and turned.

"Truly, you wicked little witch, you play the role of temptress too well. But I am sure you do it only to improve the power of my thrusting." His smile was ugly as he reached out and snatched her to him. "Is that not so?"

"Satisfy your purpose, Trewarren, and get me out of this hovel." Rawdon's voice was developing an ugly slur. Martha, caught off guard by the unexpected familiarity of the name, cried out as the young man tossed her towards the bed. She stumbled and pulled herself upright against the bed, her back to her tormentor. She felt her skirts lifted from the back and thrown over her head. A strong hand in the small of her back forced her face down over the foot of the bed.

"Stay, little trollop, stay." His hands, smoother than any she had known, slid down the inside of her thighs to the knee. With sudden, brutal strength her legs were forced apart and he entered her from behind. She gasped in pain and surprise but found she could do nothing to fend him off. Unlike Rawdon, he took pleasure from pleasing the women he seduced: those young girls in society at least. Thus his performance was more sophisticated than his language. Once she was over the initial shock, the experience was not physically unpleasant. If this was to be her new life, this young gallant was preferable to the revolting wreck of a man drunkenly ranting on the floor by the wall. She stood, smoothed down her skirt and gave him a wan smile.

After a tot of brandy, Trewarren bent over Rawdon, took his arm and wrapped it round his neck. Rawdon belched and spat down the wall as his head fell forward. Easing him up between them, they staggered out to the horse. Martha held the bridle and calmed the creature, while Trewarren mounted and hauled Rawdon up to a side saddle position. They rode off without looking back. Martha doused herself thoroughly from a bucket of seawater drawn from a barrel. Back inside, she lit an oil lamp in the gathering gloom, took the remaining bread and filled the tankard with the last of the cloudy cider. She added a log to the fire and enjoyed her meal in the cosy comfort of solitude. She turned her thoughts to the afternoon. Rawdon shouldn't trouble her for a week or two but young Trewarren would be back, no doubt. Was that name a coincidence, she wondered, or was he related to Sir Oliver?

***

Next morning, Martha emerged from the darkness into the warmth of the manor house kitchen. The servants were sitting at table over their porridge.

"Come, Martha, porridge is prepared, take your bowl and join us." Elspeth was welcoming as ever. The others all but ignored her, so engaged were they in their conversation.

"It was so late last night, I was fast asleep, but I knew it was him, I just knew," said Constance, her face alive with excitement.

"How did you know? Was it your business? Decent girls are abed at that hour, and not only abed but asleep." Mrs. Crabbe wanted no scurrilous talk in the household.

"I peeked out my door." She caught Mrs. Crabbe's eye. "I heard the noise, Mrs. Crabbe. I thought I might be required below stairs here."

"I am the one who decides that, my girl, you'll need all your strength for the day. Besides, no member of the family or their guests can be seen from the servants' rooms."

"I know it was him." A sullen look displaced her excitement.

"Who are they talking about?" whispered Martha, resting her spoon in the empty bowl.

"'Tes Master Richard come home, by Constance's reckoning," said Elspeth at her side. "But Mrs Crabbe will have none of it."

"Master Richard?"

"Aye, the son and heir, in London for the season, if three year make a season. The handsome bachelor seeking a wife. Ain't the half of it though, by all accounts."

"To your duties, everyone. You are not paid to sit about and gossip." Mrs. Crabbe stood away from the table. Her frown was directed at each in turn as they scrambled up and set about their duties.

"Martha, help Constance clear the kitchen. Then the both of you up to prepare the breakfast room." She and Cook went through to the scullery for their morning conference on the needs of the day ahead.

Martha collected bowls from her side of the table. Constance came in with a bowl of water from the pump in the yard. As they leaned over the bowl, their heads close together, Constance whispered, "He was so handsome,

43

Martha, his eyes so blue and sparkling."

"You saw him?" She stood up and stared at Constance.

"Yes, he spoke to me, Martha." Her eyes blazed at the memory. "He touched my face." She blushed and looked down. Martha said nothing, puzzled by this sudden burst of confidence. Constance had always been quick to taunt until now.

"I'll up to the breakfast room, Connie. Join me when you have emptied the bowl." She made her way up the back stairs and through to the breakfast end of the dining room. As she turned the corner to enter, she was seized from behind, her scream cut off by a hand across her mouth.

"Why if it's not my pretty little whore. How boldly you seek your pleasures, my temptress."

X

Molly was scrubbing down the bench when Martha walked in. Fish scales, stuck in the knife scorings, obstinately resisted the bristles for all Molly's vigour. The wooden tub brimmed with skeletal fish: ribbed spines with heads and tails swam in gut-infested, bloody saltwater. Molly ran the scrubber against the inside of the rim, replaced it on the table, pushed unconsciously at her sleeves and smiled at her sister-in-law. Her hands were a raw, angry red, chapped and ridged by long exposure to cold seawater.

"Martha, my dear, welcome! We so rarely see you of late."

"I hope I do find you good and well, Molly. I see you are busy. I must not take you from your duties." Martha caught the surprise on Molly's face. "But forgive me. I greet you most warmly as sister and friend." She moved towards her sister-in-law and put her arms around her.

"Sit you down, my dear. Here." Molly gestured to a stool, as she removed a stack of empty pilchard boxes. "I sense a need in you. You are burdened, I think."

Martha held her dress behind her knees and lowered herself onto the stool. Feeling secure, she sat up, straightened her back and smiled at Molly, who pulled forward an upturned box. She perched on its edge and returned Martha's smile.

"I thought to thank you kindly for the wise words you spoke when last we met. I am the stronger for them."

"All is well at the Manor? I am sure your hard work is pleasing to your patrons?"

"You know me well," Martha smiled shyly, "and you are wise indeed. For though my work is passing fair, my fellow servants kind enough, I am sorely troubled, Molly, sorely troubled." She looked down at the earthen floor and brushed away a wisp of hair released by the removal of her bonnet. Molly could not restrain a grunt of satisfaction as she heard of Rawdon's accident.

"That will keep him ill-disposed to call on you for a week or two." Glancing at Martha's face, she added, "It is his returning capabilities you are so afeard of. A man can vent his anger at long denial of his desires, whatever be the cause."

"For sure, you warn me of another danger I had not thought on. My fear has quite another cause. This young man with Rawdon do mount me like a dog do mount a bitch on heat and, being young and strong, his stiffness soon return so he do twice or thrice of an afternoon, when Rawdon ain't about."

"I have heard of such doings among the most depraved of privileged class; who was your young abuser?"

"I knew not who he was that first time but, Molly, I should've understood from the strange smoothness of his hands, to say nothing of his speech. He were no less than Richard, son and heir of Sir Oliver himself!" Worldly-wise Molly gasped in shock.

"You are truly sure 'tes so?" she said. Martha nodded.

"He's at the Manor now; he has no money. Sir Oliver and Lady Elizabeth despair of him so it's said below stairs. You see my situation, Molly. If I do refuse his needs he'll see me banished, yet if do I give in and it be discovered …"

"The scoundrel! His reputation goes before and now he proves its truth! One thing you must ensure, my dear. He must not get you with child. All would be lost; likely your very life in such a case." Molly took Martha's arm.

"My life? But surely banishment, disgrace, no midwife to my aid, perchance a weak and sickly child."

"The dangers of childbirth are well known but Rawdon's services would be engaged. He rides on both sides of the saddle, much to your Will'm's cost."

"Do I mistake your meaning?" asked Martha, alerted by mention of Will'm.

"Will knew more than was good for Rawdon's safety. Surely you knew that he must be silenced? How many carriers are killed like Will was, shot like a dog. Most are taken by the revenue and fined or such. Will was more than just a carrier, make no mistake."

XI

Martha sat looking out over the restless sea. At the head of the promontory, the chair-shaped rock, where she and Will'm had so often sat during their courtship, was sheltered from the wind and from prying eyes. In her rare moments free and alone she liked to enjoy the tranquility of the place. She lifted off her bonnet and shook her hair free to be stirred in the slight breeze. Below, the tops of the wavelets were white-crested where the sea was more exposed. It was, perhaps, the first day of warm sunshine after a cold winter. In London the Thames was almost free of ice. Here by the sea there had been little snow, but the wind had been numbingly cold.

She mulled over Molly's words. How much did she know? Would Will'm tell his sister more than his wife? She could feel Will'm's arm along her shoulder. Dark hairs curled the length of his deeply tanned forearm, reaching to the backs of his scarred fingers, which lay lightly across her shoulder. She closed her eyes and leaned back against the rock. It must have been this very month, already five years past.

"Martha, I ain't a man o' words, saving when I'm out in the galley, but thou knows I have looked to thee much these last months." She opened her eyes and stared down at the spot she had stared at when the words had been uttered. A gorse branch had crept along the ground and now hid the chipped rock that lay there.

"We share a great sadness, Martha." His fingers tightened on her shoulder. "We both lost our fathers, we're both alone. I have a duty to thee, Martha, I feel it most powerful."

"But you ain't alone, Will'm, you have Molly and Thomas in your home, and Molly been carrying awhile, her time must be near." A brief smile crossed his face in response.

She remembered those months in the house with them all. Will'm and Thomas, hiring out when they could; their galley lost in the storm when their fathers were drowned. Molly, newly wed now she was with child, and glad of her company. Molly's time had come soon enough. Martha had stood to help the midwife, but Molly was strong and her milk had flowed well for the first weeks. Times had been hard till the summer pilchard seining. Molly had shown her the gutting and smoking, but Martha could never match the speed of her knife. With the pilchards all done, the nights long and dark, half tubs of brandy appeared. A full tea chest stood by the fireplace for a few days. Molly filled coarse bags with the tea and sold them under cover of darkness.

One night, as spring approached, shouting and banging from below woke Martha. The baby was roaring, gasping for breath and roaring again. Will'm was not beside her. She felt her way to the steps and descended backwards, turning as she reached the beaten earth floor. Will'm and Thomas staggered about, streaks of blood on their faces, teeth bared in misshapen grimaces. Molly clung to the screaming child; the raging men stumbled and lashed drunkenly at each other in the flickering firelight.

"Will'm!" she'd shouted, as Thomas, distracted by her movement, caught Will'm's wild punch squarely on the jaw and fell, slithering to the floor.

That was the moment, she thought, opening her eyes to gaze at the sea. That's when things changed, for he had turned and smashed her across the face, his fist sticky with blood, so that she had crashed into the stair rail and slumped to the ground. She'd been his common law wife for almost a year, and fancied she could feel the weight of his child in her belly. They'd agreed they would marry if she should carry his child. He was mortified next day. He swore on oath he'd not hit her again. The child had driven him mad, he had said, with its incessant roaring. They had moved up to her father's upturned shell of a boat to be away from the child.

Out at sea, an excise cutter, sails billowing, was returning to Falmouth. They'd had no more contact with Thomas and Molly. Will'm, she knew, had been a carrier when the galleys came in but, jealous of Thomas and in constant fear of betrayal, he had sought to weave a web of protection about himself. Who did he know and what did he know? Martha no longer followed the threads.

The angle of the sun, seen between high white clouds,

suggested she should return to her hut. She stood, stretched, recovered her bonnet and eased her hair back under its restraint. As she approached her hut she saw that a horse was tethered nearby. It was a horse she recognised.

XII

"So Richard, what are your plans now that you have exhausted London society?" Sir Oliver swirled the remains of his claret in the bowl of his glass, raised his head and smiled at his son.

"The season draws to a close, Father. I came home to escape the everlasting cold of the city and irritation at the cluster of invitations to visit the most boorish of hosts. Men whose daughters, desperate for marriage, were so lacking in character, charm and taste that no dowry could compensate for such a sacrifice." Richard eased back in his chair, swirled his own glass, threw back his head and swallowed the remaining wine.

"It must come as a great relief to you, dear Richard, that you are still so much in demand. We were clearly mistaken in thinking your credit exhausted." His mother smiled, ignoring her husband's warning frown. "If it is warmth you seek, I am very much afraid it will be different in nature from the sophistications of the city."

"I thought I might ride a little, hunt a little perhaps, before the end of the season; look up old acquaintances, make a few new ones. Perhaps even rally to the cause of free trade; I know it is close to your heart, Father." He placed his glass on the table. "Which brings to mind your magnificent cognac and Cuban cigars, Pollard! Oblige me by supplying me with prime samples of both." He leaned back in his chair and turned towards the steward.

Elizabeth looked directly at Pollard, who hurried to hold her chair as she rose. With the briefest of nods, she grasped her skirts with her left hand and, head high, she swept from the room. Pollard moved towards the decanters on the dresser but Sir Oliver held up his hand, halting the steward.

"Mother plays the empress even better than I remember." Richard had not adjusted his position, though his smile had tightened.

"Wait, Pollard. Is it or is it not the prerogative of the Head of the House, to offer a digestive?"

"Indeed, it is. I do humbly beg your pardon, Sir Oliver." Pollard lowered his head in a contrite bow.

"Come Father, do we need to stand on such ceremony while the two of us dine alone?"

"Indeed we do, Richard, standards must be maintained. Pollard, you may serve the cognac."

Pollard reached for the decanter, taking great care in serving Sir Oliver to pour exactly his usual measure, and to serve Richard slightly but perceptibly less. Grateful for the slight nod from Sir Oliver, which he took to be both approval and dismissal, Pollard retreated to the ill-lit corner at the far end of the dining room.

"And cigars?" asked Richard. Pollard took half a pace forward but drew back and waited for Sir Oliver's response.

"Not tonight, Richard. Before you luxuriate too greatly in your homecoming, I wish to understand your intentions." Sir Oliver warmed his brandy with cupped hands, raised the glass to his nose, drew in the rich aroma and, satisfied by the quality, savoured a mouthful. Catching Richard's quizzical look, he smiled, "One can never be too careful where cognac is concerned."

"One is talking of the free-trade vintage?"

"One is indeed, Richard, one is indeed." He sat back contentedly. "Pollard, perhaps we'll have that cigar after all." They puffed in quiet companionship for a while, Sir Oliver's sharpness forgotten for the moment.

"I thought that might come into my future plans at some point, Father: a better understanding of the free-trade process."

"The principles and practices of free trade as they operate at present require discipline, discretion and a delicacy of touch, Richard; qualities I have yet to be convinced you have developed with sufficient consistency." Sir Oliver watched his son register this rejection. His young face was puffy, his eyes glazed with over-indulgence. The impact of his father's words reddened his flesh, and the sudden intake of cigar smoke forced him to suppress a sputtering cough, which reddened him further. With a supreme effort, he leaned back and, with a wan smile, placed the cigar on the ashtray.

"Then I must find a way to prove myself to you, Father."

"Shall we join your mother?" Sir Oliver rose and turned to the door. Richard got to his feet, grasped the back of his chair, steadied himself and followed his father towards the drawing room.

***

Lady Elizabeth's head was bent over her sampler as she stitched with great care. The candle lamp directed the light and focused it on her needle, picking out the name, Emmeline, under a cherubic figure, as she had done several times before, sometimes combining with Elizabeth, sometimes on its own. She preferred her own company, her own thoughts. She pined for her daughters still, remembering them as they were when they died: children, suffering in fear and incomprehension. They would have been lively young beauties by now, both of them married, she was sure. Instead, there was Richard, a difficult son to be proud of however strong a mother's love.

"May we join you, my dear?" Sir Oliver did not wait for an answer but eased himself into his favourite chair, moving it slightly to conceal a sudden eruption of flatulence. Elizabeth did not look up. He glanced at the great granite fireplace with the Trewarren crest above the mantelshelf. Every maid knew to keep the candles well towards the end of the shelf. Candle soot on the family crest would lead to a severe warning, if not dismissal. Yet the walls still showed the original grey stone and mortar behind the occasional picture. There was a small tapestry, which had lost much of its vibrancy, on the far wall; heavy curtains in rich plum velvet covered the casements.

"Richard, give the fire a stir, there's a good chap." He shrugged as his son poked at the logs with exaggerated disdain. He attempted a winning smile at his wife, on whom it was wasted.

"I see we have a new maid, Mother. I do admire your taste. She's not resident here at the manor, I understand?" He stood with his back to the fire, hands behind his back and, distracted by a sudden movement, was just in time to see his father, scratching under his grey wig, flick off a crawler.

"When did you last powder your wig, Father?" Sir Oliver ignored his son.

"It was none of my doing," said Elizabeth, without looking up. "It was your father's choice."

"Standards must be maintained, eh Father?" A smirk hovered on Richard's face.

"It was a charitable act to aid a helpless young woman, widowed through no fault of her own." Sir Oliver's jowls quivered with righteous distain. "She is not without experience in domestic duties." He paused. "Of a housekeeping nature," he added, seeing his son's smile broaden. "And I know you will have enough of the gentleman not to think of taking any liberties with her whilst she is in our employ."

"Those standards again, Father, you do work them hard." He walked over to the harpsichord, flicked through the music on the stand, and pressed a group of keys. A discordant sound expressed his frustration. He sat down in an armchair facing the fire.

After some minutes of silence, Sir Oliver began to snore. Lady Elizabeth glanced across at him. "The intellectual stimulation is too much for my simple female mind, I shall retire for the night." She swept from the room without a backward glance. Richard followed her from the room shortly afterwards, without waking his father. It was remarkable, he thought, how his father had been transformed from an alert, astute landowner, exemplar of his class, to this bumbling figure, snoring and flatulent, over the course of a hearty three-hour meal. He felt a new flicker of sympathy for his long-suffering mother.

He did not follow her example and retire, however. It was rumoured that a cockfight was to be held in Truro. The night was still young; he could be there in under the hour with a fresh mount, and the betting might be profitable. He needed some excitement, some contact with the more rakish elements in the city, whose star was on the rise. He leaned low over Caesar, reached back with the whip, and let the wind blow his depressing thoughts away.

XIII

That mare be tethered too tight, thought Martha, as she stepped across the track to the cover of a gorse hedge on the seaward side. A dislodged stone bounced against a rock as it slid into a rut. The horse paused in tossing its head against the rail and stared intently in her direction. Shielded partly by the gorse and partly by a broad flat-topped rock, she paused.

"If he come out and chastise yer, give 'im the same again, my beauty, aint no more'n he deserves," she muttered. The sea was now no more than a murmur; she could no longer see the shore, only the greyish green stillness against the distant line of The Lizard fading away towards the horizon. Gulls screamed urgently as they circled overhead. Martha slid to the ground and leaned back against the rock. Time was short. If she walked back round the headland and took the track from the next bay over to the manor, it would take over an hour and she would likely be late for evening duty. I could never stand in front of Mrs Crabbe like this, she thought, yet if I go down to the hut to tidy myself he'll detain me and I'll not have the strength to deny him.

I must end it, I can't live me life in such fear and trouble. I ain't like Molly, kind though she be. She brought me out from the shadow of my grief and I thank her for it; from the bottom of my heart I thank her. But I can't play the trollop like she say I should; it ain't in me nature. I feel his dirt on me, through me, not just me body, through me very soul, may God forgive me. She closed her eyes and looked to heaven, praying silently. A loud neighing broke the spell. She turned and raised herself on her knees to look over the flat grey rock. There he was. Perhaps her prayers had been answered, she thought, perhaps he was leaving. He stood, calming the horse with whispers and a comforting hand on her mane. He's learnt something then, she told herself, he's uncommon kindly to his poor mare, respectful more like.

Something about the figure caught her eye. Even from this distance he looked slimmer, taller; a trimmer figure altogether. His tricorn hat was set less rakishly and his movement more athletic. I thought that were not like him, she told herself, showing kindly to the horse. Indeed it ain't him, it ain't him any ways at all. Unknowingly she had revealed her presence, distracted by the unexpected turn of events.

"Widow Baines?"

Too late, Martha ducked down behind the gorse, disturbing some yellow flowers and releasing an invisible cloud of musk-like scent.

"Widow Baines, is that you, my good woman?" The voice was much nearer. Martha stood reluctantly, and brushed dust and tiny yellow petals from her dress. He was more than halfway towards her. She stood out on the track. He wore a coat and hat as formal and heavy as Rawdon's but brushed and tight-fitting; brass buttons polished.

"There you are, woman, I despaired of finding you, in truth I did, but the Lord has smiled as he is wont to do when we despair." He gave the slightest of bows as he smiled also. Martha said nothing. "Captain Carter, Josiah Carter, ex-Purser in His Majesty's Royal Navy, now Captain, supervisor of the Revenue from St Just in Roseland to Portscatho." She nodded, unable to speak.

"Shall we?" He stood to the side and swung his arm low in the direction of the hut. She did not move.

"Come now, you shall come to no harm, you have my word on it." His arm swung again indicating the track. After a further pause, she began to walk towards the hut. He walked a pace or two behind her.

"One of my riders, an officer by the name of Rawdon, suffered injury in the course of duty. In his absence, I patrol his area as part of my own duties. I understand he offered you particular protection. As such, I thought I should call to reassure you that he will return to full duties shortly, by the turn of the month I would estimate." He was seated on a chair brought over to her by Molly's Thomas: a tree trunk with a right-angled wedge cut out to provide seat and back. "Well, my good woman, what do you say to that? You are much relieved, I'll warrant."

"I thank you for informing me, Sir, it is most kind." She broke her silence at last. "But t'were a funny kind of service," she muttered.

"I didn't catch your meaning, Mrs Baines. Could you speak more clearly?"

"He it were as killed my Will'm, Sir, I'm sure of it. He tried too hard to take his place, was all my meaning."

"Your husband was engaged in unlawful trade, Mrs Baines. It is an officer's duty to prevent that and arrest such men. Smuggling is a sin, as my mentor, John Wesley, has made clear; may he rest in peace."

"You are Methody?" said Martha, forgetting herself in her amazement.

"I am a true Christian, I follow his word. As our dear departed Captain proclaimed at St Ives, and at Gwenap, many times over: bringing uncustomed goods into the country is an accursed thing, an abomination. Thus has he shown me how the Lord blesses our work. I wanted to bring this message to you, Mrs Baines, that you may find it in your heart to forgive a man for doing his duty to His Majesty and to God, even if it led to the death of your husband. I feel it would help you greatly were you to join our church, for The Reverend John Wesley understood the poor, spoke directly to them, worked for them, addressed their needs and it is up to his followers to follow him truly by spreading his wonderful words and deeds." He paused. Martha stared at him.

"And so, Mrs Baines, I invite you to attend our church to express contrition for the support you gave your husband in his abominations and enjoy our Lord's true forgiveness. You can be sure of a welcome and an uplifting service."

"But Sir, I go to church, our Church of England. The Rector has been most helpful to me, Sir, putting in a good word with Sir Oliver. I work at the manor and I have forgot the time, I need to leave at once or I s'll be late for my duties. Please excuse me, Sir, while I prepare myself."

∗∗∗

Martha felt a combination of relief and anxiety as she hurried from the hut.

"Allow me to give you a ride, Mrs Baines." He was standing with the mare at the ready.

"Oh, I couldn't, Sir, I must hurry." But he caught her arm, smiled at the terror in her face and held her firm but without hurting her.

"Now, I will help you up and you can sit in front of me. I'll have you there very shortly." He released her. "Now place your foot here." He held his cupped hands low and raised her to sit astride the mare.

As she dismounted in good time, she thanked him with real gratitude.

"I shall expect you at the new chapel next Sabbath, ten o'clock in the morning. If you are late I will give you another ride. Good day, Mrs Baines." He turned the mare and galloped away towards the village, stirring small clouds of dust behind him.

XIV

The noise of the crowd drew Richard towards the cockpit. Light from three raised braziers fell on the makeshift wooden balustrade; a far cry from the drawing rooms where invited guests had bet extravagantly in London society. The balustrade surrounded a raised platform upon which two cocks were engaged in an uneven contest. Richard walked round the pit, brushing past heavy, pipe-smoking women, woollen scarves failing to pull nit-infested locks under control. The controller was a coarse fellow in a grey wig with side curls, once extravagant, now limp and stringy. Long rows of bone buttons lined the opening of his coat, forced apart to allow a bulbous midriff to lodge itself on the balustrade. Miners waved walking sticks, clay pipes, or whatever was to hand, to cheer on their bedraggled champions.

This was not a tournament match, following weight rules, as Richard had expected, but an unofficial event put together by local petty bookkeepers, intent on taking hard-earned wages from gullible or drunken miners. He turned away, intending to seek out a backgammon session in the newly opened Assembly Rooms, when he felt someone brush against him. He raised his sleeve and shook the offending hand away.

"I am most sorry to trouble you, good Sir." A dark-haired woman, smiling flirtatiously, faced him as he turned at the voice. "But it is late to see a stranger in this part of town, especially so refined a gentleman as yourself, Sir. I was wondering if you had a place for the night, Sir, a bed so to speak. No offence, Sir, I'm sure."

"I am not so much of a stranger that I cannot find my way home, thank you, Madam." He moved away. It occurred to him that he was not sure of the way to the New Assembly Rooms. Did the new bridge and Bridge Street provide a short cut, or was it still advisable to walk up to the market square and take the old route to what was, in his younger days, a derelict daub and wattle tavern opposite the High Cross?

"Will it please you to direct me to the Assembly Rooms, Madam?" he called, aware that he had destroyed any pretence at assuming her respectability. He caught her replacing a frown with a knowing smile.

"I will better that, Sir, and accompany you there myself, so as to ensure you are not lost." As she swished up to him, he noticed her three beauty spots and smudged red-painted lips. They walked in silence for some minutes. The gravel crunched under their feet. They approached a side alley from which a strong smell of rotting sewage emerged. She paused.

"Should you need a bed, Sir, I can supply you. Rates very reasonable; reliable services provided. Gentlemen of all tastes provided for, just ask for Margaret." She indicated the alley. There must be some hovel there, he thought.

"Not for the present, Madam, the night is but a few hours old. Let us to the Assembly Rooms and a hand at the tables."

"I'll bid you good night then, Sir. Just follow your nose up yonder hill, 'tes less than a furlong." She was gone in that instant.

As he approached the High Cross, he was astonished at the brightness of the light from the upper windows of the elegant new hall. This is much more to my taste, he thought, as he was welcomed by a white-wigged flunkey.

"Mr Trewarren, Sir, you are most welcome back in Truro. I trust all is well with Sir Oliver, and his good lady wife?" A well-dressed man of early middle age proffered an outstretched hand of welcome.

"You have the advantage of me, Sir," said Richard, grasping the outstretched hand.

"Silas Galsworthy at your service: old business friend of Sir Oliver. Come and meet some local worthies. What's your fancy?"

"A brandy, if I may."

"Make it a large one," called Galsworthy as the flunkey hurried away. "Now, Trewarren, let us join the others at the table. You are here for a hand or two, I take it."

At the table the introductions were made. There was Dr Chapman, of whom his mother spoke warmly after he had attended on Emmeline and Lizzie. Now elderly, he was usually accompanied by an apprentice on his visits. Next to him, two or three mine owners or potential mine owners, who were currently surveying their lands for copper or tin.

"And now, I have the pleasure of introducing your erstwhile colonial cousin George Trewarren, on leave from His Majesty's Navy," said Silas. At this point his brandy arrived. This served as an opportunity for a break in the game whilst drinks were ordered all round. Clearly they were all eager to hear of Richard's intentions.

"I cannot believe the style and magnificence of this

building. Was it not a mere theatre pit a few years ago?" he said, suppressing his curiosity regarding his unknown cousin.

"It was reopened but a few months past, I'm told," said his cousin, "True theatre performances are forbidden here, by law I believe; for it is not a theatre royal, though by every right it should be. Look closely at the floor, cousin, where it meets the walls. Better, join me when I send a boy down to Trewarren for you. If you are theatre-minded, that is."

"Aye," muttered the old doctor, "that John Wesley saw to that, is my opinion; may the Good Lord rot his soul for the perversion of His word."

"I should enjoy that, George, it would be a chance to acquaint myself with the wider family." Richard smiled across the head of the doctor, who was used to being ignored on such occasions.

"Come, let us have another hand. I trust that it what you purposed, Richard?"

"Indeed it was, Mr Galsworthy, yet I only thought it after the disappointment at the cock pit."

"Silas, please, we don't stand on formality among the Truro gentry. Now if a cock match is your preference, I take the liberty of inviting you to my town house next month. Our select team of outstanding creatures will be matched against some upstarts from Falmouth: a fine wager in prospect. Come for dinner; bring a young companion, if I do not trespass too far in assuming you have one."

"Sadly, I do not at present, but I shall be delighted to accept the invitation on my own behalf."

"In the meantime, let us resume," said Silas, reaching for the cards. "I am sure you will join us, Richard, in a hand or two and sharpen us with your London sophistication."

At around an hour after midnight, Richard rose from his chair and took his leave.

"May I leave you my note for fifty guineas, Silas? I did not expect to wager so much. I will settle next month at the cock fight."

"Of course, dear boy, I shall look forward the more to our meeting." They all rose and nodded their farewells, except Dr Chapman whose chin rested on his chest in repose.

Outside, the night air was damp; foul-smelling water trickled down a wheel track in the road. How much was from one of the many springs and how much of human origin, he could not say, but from the scuffling in the shadows, it was clear the rats were content. Halfway down to the bridge he reached the alley, from which a middle-aged man appeared. He glanced in both directions, adjusted his wig, nodded to Richard and disappeared into the darkness towards the estuary.

Weary at the thought of the hour-long ride through the darkness, Richard turned into the alley, paused to adjust to what little light penetrated the narrow confines and edged his way along, perhaps twenty paces, before tapping on the door of a wooden hovel. A low flickering light appeared in what was now a window of sorts.

"Margaret?" he called softly. This led to scraping noises from within before the door opened to reveal Margaret in a low-cut, satin nightgown, holding a pewter pilchard-oil lamp.

"You are most welcome, Sir. We will do all in our power to meet your requirements. Pray enter, Sir." As she turned, he noticed the purple bite marks on her neck. He was in the act of turning away when she grasped his arm and drew him into the room.

XV

"Were you took poorly yesterday, Martha? I missed you at church. You do seem right as rain this morning. I took some heavy looks, I can tell you. Mrs Crabbe were on at me after the service and again this morning: she says Lady Trewarren was most concerned." Elspeth stood upright, wet scrubbing brush in hand.

"Oh I hope I haven't caused you trouble. I did intend to come, surely I did, but I were diverted. I were so nervous coming in this morning; I had hoped they would let it pass, just the once. But I fear it may happen again." Martha paused, mop resting on the floor, when she heard the tread of Mrs Crabbe.

"Not working? Do you think we want fish scales in every dish I prepare today? Sir Oliver is most particular about such."

Both maids bent to their tasks murmuring respectful assent.

"Martha Baines, I want a word with you. Come through to my desk. Elspeth I shall inspect that table presently and you will lose a farthing off your wages for every fish scale I find." Mrs Crabbe's desk was no more than a small table in the corner of the staff dining area at the far end of the kitchen.

"Am I hard of hearing, Baines, or did I hear you say you was intending to miss church again?"

"No, Mrs Crabbe, I mean yes, Mrs Crabbe." Martha stared at the floor, conscious that Elspeth could hear every word, and that Mrs Crabbe intended that she should.

"Explain yourself, girl." Martha stumbled through a garbled version of Captain Carter's insistence on her attendance at the Methodist Service, how she had tried to refuse but would do her best not to let it happen again. Still staring at the ground, she shuddered with silent sobs.

"Lady Trewarren shall hear of this, Baines. It is beyond belief that her charity towards you should be rebuffed so blatantly."

"Will I lose my position, Mrs Crabbe?" Martha looked up through her tears, but the housekeeper walked away, her head held high with distain.

***

Martha could hear the swish of Lady Elizabeth's dress approaching the dining room as she scurried out of the servants' door on her way down to the kitchen. Later, returning with clean cutlery, in answer to a summons, she was met by the steward just behind the servants' door. She turned away as Pollard re-entered.

"Mrs Crabbe tells me your protégé has deserted you, Oliver." The door closed, cutting off Lady Elizabeth's ironic tones. Martha paused, looked around and, edging back, placed her ear against the door panel.

"Indeed, my dear? She did not appear in church. A fact Francis did not fail to point out to me; as if I had not noticed on my own account." Sir Oliver's last few words were lost as he must have mopped his mouth with the slip cloth from his knee.

"She has become a Methodist, Mrs Crabbe informs me. She must be dismissed forthwith." Martha pictured in her mind one of Lady Elizabeth's haughty looks, put her hand to her mouth expecting Sir Oliver to confirm her dismissal, and hurried back to the kitchen.

Mrs Crabbe said nothing more to her that night, so Martha arrived next morning at dawn expecting dismissal. With head down, she mumbled greetings as other servants appeared. Nothing was said by Elspeth or Constance but the atmosphere was strained.

"Martha Baines, my desk." Mrs Crabbe's tone was stern and disapproving. "You are extremely fortunate, Baines. Sir Oliver has not only forgiven you, but will allow you to honour your conversion to Methodism."

"But I…"

"Is that all you can say? Heretical views have never been expressed in this house. Do you understand, never! And I will not hear them expressed in my kitchen, so be very clear. I will tolerate you, Baines, but only because I have to. I wish I had dismissed you myself. It is well within my powers." She turned away, her jowls wobbling with indignation.

"Thank you, Mrs Crabbe, thank you." Martha walked slowly back to her bowl and brush.

"Master Richard saved her," Constance whispered to Elspeth. "Pollard told me this morning. What favours did she grant or what is promised, I wonder?" She giggled.

Martha scrubbed away, head down to hide her embarrassment. Was Constance right or was she just a jealous young thing? Pollard was certainly present; she had given him the clean cutlery herself. And what if Constance was right? What price would Martha pay? If Master Richard had truly saved her position, he was not one to hold back on his demands. For all the vigour of her sweeping and scrubbing, she could not erase her fears.

XVI

"Welcome, Sister, it is good the Lord has brought you to us." A careworn face smiled at Martha, "He speaks to you through Brother Carter, so I believe?"

"He it was who introduced me, Sister." Martha was quick

to adopt the new form of address. She sat on the short wooden bench which formed part of the circle in the crowded room. Many heads were bowed in far from silent prayer. Martha lowered her own head after casting her eye across the gathering.

A powerful voice caused all to cease their private communion and look to the preacher standing before them, his back to the fireplace.

"Welcome to you all, my brothers and sisters in Christ. All are equal in His eyes, and all will be judged when they enter His kingdom. Let us welcome our new sister, Martha. Rise, my dear sister, that all may welcome you into our gathering."

There were murmurs of "Welcome, Sister," from all sides as Martha rose hesitantly to acknowledge their greeting. She wondered how many would be so welcoming had they known the price she would pay, through sin or betrayal, or both. As she sat down, and the preacher continued to expound his guidance, her encounter the previous day replayed itself in all its stark reality.

She had paused outside the dining room; there was no sign of Pollard. By mid-morning on a Saturday, it was usually safe to assume the family had broken their fast and were going about the day's business or pleasure. At the serving table she was about to gather the tureens, with their residue of flaked fat and fish bones half submerged in turgid pilchard oil, when she was conscious of someone approaching from behind. Nervous of Mrs Crabbe's constant harrying since her supposed conversion the previous Sunday, she clattered three tureens together, put the ladles in the top where they rolled noisily against each other, and turned. Richard's proximity was so unexpected that the tureens tilted forward leaving a slither of pilchard oil on his waistcoat.

"It is not the rich, but the poor that shall inherit the kingdom of heaven, for all are equal in the eyes of our Lord, He asks only that we follow His word in every aspect of our lives," intoned the preacher.

"I do beg your pardon, Sir, and your forgiveness, Sir," Martha stuttered, still disorientated by his silent proximity, and his newly stained waistcoat.

"You may well have heard, my clumsy heretic, how I pleaded for your life in spite of your betrayal?" He stood at less than an arm's length, looking down on the folds of the headscarf, from which several strands of her hair had freed themselves.

"You should be asking by what means, not to say duties, you might begin to repay my generosity. The Trewarren name is compromised by your heretical devotions, in my parents' eyes at least." The familiar dangerous smile hovered on his lips.

"Ask not for His favour, but rather ask what you can do to serve Him. That is the secret, as our great and lately departed leader reminded us, dear brothers and sisters. What can we do to spread His love to all our downtrodden and ill-used fellow men?" The preacher's question burned through her inner nightmare.

"I am sorry, Sir. I was startled by your sudden appearance. I am truly grateful, Sir." Martha raised her head to catch a glimpse of her tormentor's expression, but saw only the preacher, his unseeing smile cast benignly across the encircling worshippers.

Richard moved lightly across to the servants' entrance, looked out, then closed the door and moved towards her. Still holding the tureens, she shivered involuntarily, rattling the ladles again.

"Put the damn things down, damn you, and come here." His sudden change of mood confirmed her fears. As she approached, he grabbed her upper arms, drew her close and smiled the dangerous smile directly into her face. She dare not show her revulsion at the stale cigar smoke on his breath. "Now, Miss Methody, here is what you will do. You will ingratiate yourself with Captain Almighty Carter, use your undoubted charms." His hand slid down to the back of her thigh. "You know the charms to which I refer, no doubt?" She looked down, not daring to answer.

"You know the charms to which I refer, no doubt?" His hand squeezed her buttock so hard she cried out.

"Good. It is most important you understand the duties you are to perform. Once in his confidence, as well as his bed, you must uncover the secrets of his anti-free-trade works. What does he know? How does he know? And who does he know that threaten the free trading of goods to the benefit of Cornish towns and estates." His grip on her buttock lightened, became almost a caress.

"Give unto Caesar What is Caesar's and to God what is God's, my brothers and sisters, and therefore I ask you to honour your duty to pay the customs charges, and not to support the purchase or import of uncustomed goods, as our dearly departed leader guided us." Across the circle the brothers and sisters murmured in some confusion. Martha's eye was drawn to Captain Carter who had nodded vigorously and drowned the muttering with a timely shout.

"The Lord be praised for his wisdom."

"Amen, Amen," the brothers and sisters had intoned, with some uncertain glances. Her thoughts were dragged back again.

"When you report to me, I will test both the truth of your information, and the quality of your harlotry. It would be most unfortunate should the Methody disdain for carnal delights affect your qualities in that regard." At which Richard strode from the room.

As she left the cottage, the preacher took her hand warmly in both of his.

"The Lord be with you, Sister."

She smiled uncertainly back, and returned the friendly greetings of the brothers and sisters as she set off on the track up to the village. When would Richard demand her presence? How could she meet his demands? Why was she facing these trials?

"Sister Martha, the track is treacherous with recent

storms. Allow me to see you safely home."

"You are not riding today, Brother Carter?"

"Not on the Sabbath, Sister," said the Captain.

I need to see Molly, thought Martha; I'll walk over this afternoon.

XVII

The Galsworthy town house stood back from the road, its newly elegant front not quite concealing the more mundane architecture of the original building. Richard paused at the entrance to survey more closely a house he had passed many times in his youth. Was this the building on which, as a child, he had witnessed the stonemasons working? Silas had claimed a business friendship with his father; perhaps that had provoked the memory of a previous visit. He shook the reins and his horse walked through to the stable yard.

"Welcome, Richard, it is good to see you again. Come through and meet the other guests, cocking fanciers and gamblers all." Silas took his arm. "Though, unaccompanied as you are, I suspect you will have an interest in some hens also, what?" he chuckled.

"You know me well already, Silas." Richard glanced round the room they had now entered. Light and airy in the May sunshine, its décor confirmed that Silas's wealth and taste had outstripped the style of the original building. The buzz of animated conversation fell silent as all turned towards the newcomer.

"Richard, how good to welcome you at last to your rightful place in Truro society." George Trewarren stepped forward, smiling, and bowed lightly.

"Thank you, cousin." Richard returned the bow. "My thanks to Silas for his kindness in welcoming me to his own splendid house; it is indeed an honour." He nodded a smile towards his host as the other guests resumed their conversations. A servant approached with a tray of drinks, paused as Richard, glass in hand, nodded his acknowledgement, and moved on.

"Come cousin, let me introduce you to some of the more interesting guests." George took his arm, replacing Silas who retired to greet the next arrival. They stood for a moment, each, glass in hand, surveying the other. George looked strong and muscular beneath his cut-away jacket of deep blue velvet. His silk shirt and leg-hugging satin trousers emphasised his long legs and hard lean figure. The hair of his dark wig was tied back behind his neck, adding to his dashing appearance. A gleam of envy flashed across Richard's eyes. His smile wavered then warmed again, as George led him towards a group engaged in lively conversation.

A bell rang and a steward announced dinner, as each lady took the arm of her partner and the couples moved unhurriedly towards the dining room. Richard felt a tension in the sleeve of his jacket and saw a silk-gloved hand about to pluck the sleeve again.

"Would you be so kind, Sir?" She held an empty glass towards him.

"Certainly, Ma'mselle." He could see no ring. "If you have no escort, would you do me the honour of accepting my arm?" He placed the glass on an adjacent occasional table.

"I thank you, Sir." She took the proffered arm. "I consider we were introduced by your cousin's greeting when you made your entrance, therefore I commit no impropriety, though there are tongues here aplenty that would have it so. My name is Sophia Galsworthy, niece to Silas, with whom I see you are well acquainted."

"I am indeed, Miss Sophia. He has been a most kind friend since my return from the metropolis."

"My friends call me Sophie, Mr Trewarren. I should like that you do the same, if indeed we are to be friends." The warmth of her smile beguiled him.

"It would be a delight to be amongst those so privileged, Miss Sophie, and I hope I may prevail upon you to address me as Richard." He drew her chair from the table and held it while she sat and adjusted the long silk folds of her high-waisted dress.

Tureens were ferried in by a stream of serving maids: a thick broth, game pie, mutton shanks in stew, all lukewarm after the journey from the kitchen at the far end of the house. Exotic fruit was the only exception. No fish was served, as

Silas was above providing such common fare. Large, heavy, crystal glasses were filled and refilled from decanters of claret, as all twenty guests partook of Silas's hospitality in uninterrupted conversation. Richard was so distracted by Sophie's animation and beauty that the need to assess the likely winners of the cockfights to follow was forgotten.

"If the ladies would care to retire, the gentlemen may smoke their cigars while the room is prepared for the evening's sport." The ladies stirred in reaction to Silas's announcement. Richard rose and held Sophie's chair. She stood and smoothed the folds of her dress, dropping a glove onto the chair as she did so. They both reached down at once and their cheeks brushed momentarily.

"White Knight," she murmured as her lips passed his ear. She answered his puzzled look by moving her eyes towards a generous paunch of a man a few places down on the opposite side of the table. He watched the man light his cigar. Still perplexed he turned, but she had gone.

Stewards pushed back the table; a handler brought in a large square rush mat, placed it in the middle of the floor and ran out. Silas's cockfighting chair had been placed in the centre of the far side of the room; he took up his position.

"We have four bouts today, gentlemen; the first is between Chestnut Challenger, a young apprentice cock trained and ready for his first public bout and weighing in at three pounds on my left and Red Rooster, another three pound apprentice on my right. Handlers brought the birds to the edge of the mat, whispered to them, stroked them, and at the drop of Silas's arm, ushered them towards each other. Both birds circled warily, their bone spurs lifted ready to strike after each step. Wings raised, they charged. Challenger lost his balance, Red Rooster pounced, drawing his spur in a long curve down his opponent's thigh. Challenger flapped his wings weakly, as his opponent moved in for the kill. At that moment Challenger was scooped away by his handler. The owner conceded the fight, and saved his bird to fight again. A few small bets had been placed and notes were exchanged.

Another two bouts took place: on the latter of these Richard, feeling he had the measure of things after a conversation with his cousin, placed a modest bet of five guineas. Like many others he lost in a surprise result. Silas gave the final bout his most powerful recommendation. Both contestants weighed in at four pounds and seven ounces. The Iron Duke looked large and scarred from many battles. He had won Dr Chapman an awesome reputation as a fighting cock owner. Not that he understood the training process, but he employed a clever trainer. George recommended a heavy bet on the local favourite.

White Knight was from Falmouth. Well known there, he had not fought in Truro. In two minds, Richard glanced up at the doorway and saw Sophie catch his eye, nod and disappear from view. He walked across to the handler.

"I'll put a hundred guineas on him to win." He put a promissory note into the handler's leather pouch.

"You are well advised, Master Trewarren," said a familiar voice. He looked again, and hardly recognised the emaciated form before him.

"Surely it cannot be? Yet I truly believe it is. Is it Rawdon I speak to?" He did not wait for an answer. "My word, man, but you've changed. Have you never recovered from the kicking that feisty mare gave you? Are you no longer with the excise? Where did you learn all this, pray?"

"Too many questions, Sir, too many questions. Let us see if you place your wager wisely." He gathered White Knight in his arms, careful of its gleaming brass spurs and carried him through the bystanders to the edge of the mat.

XVIII

On the word from Silas both cocks were released. The veteran, Iron Duke, raised his wings and rushed his opponent, confident of surprising him into losing his balance. The younger White Knight rose to his full height, stretched his wings and met the charge chest on. Both claws struck out and missed. The opponents stalked each other, charged and sustained glancing blows. Iron Duke used his cunning to the full; White Knight, the speed of youth. Men crowded close so that Silas had to ask some to stand back. Roars and groans accompanied each sally. Richard, anxious for the first time that day, leaned forward just as Iron Duke stretched his neck to the full, feigning to rip his opponent's throat. As White Knight swayed to avoid the reinforced beak, the veteran struck with his great metal claw, sending the young cock sprawling.

A gasp swept round the watchers, knowing nods and murmurs as old hands acknowledged the accuracy of their predictions. So often would such a powerful blow cause the withdrawal of his opponent that Iron Duke did not follow up with the killer thrust in the brief opportunity his feint had provided. White Knight regained his balance, spread his wings, rose a full two hands off the mat and fell on Iron Duke, striking and cutting with all the fury of a hungry young warrior. Cries of amazement and dismay rose at the sudden change of fortune and, as the remorseless assault on the now defenceless veteran continued, Iron Duke lay panting and breathless, flapping his wings helplessly as blood seeped from the long curved slash on his neck. Mr Chapman signalled the handler to recover the bird to general cries of "Shame!" and angry murmurings spread among those who had lost on a certainty.

"Enough, Rawdon, you presume too much. I'll speak with you presently. Mr Galsworthy waits on me, you say?" Richard suppressed a smile.

"Indeed he does, Sir; he attends you in his study. Sorry to cause offence, Sir." Rawdon's leer reappeared as Richard made his way through the chattering guests.

"Come in, come in, my boy. Well a fine win indeed, what? I like a man prepared to take a calculated risk."

"I was well advised, Mr Galsworthy," said Richard, smiling.

"Silas, please, Richard, I thought that well established. Take a seat, take a seat, my boy, we have things to discuss."

"Rawdon suggested as much." Richard smoothed the tails of his velvet coat as he eased himself into the armchair, "I was amused to see him in such changed circumstances. Did you employ him after his unfortunate accident with the mare? A generous gesture, if I may say so, Silas."

"There was more than generosity involved, my boy, but let it rest there at present." He paused. "Richard, I congratulate you on your winnings, and in the discernment you showed in whose advice you preferred." He smiled briefly. "And, as a result, I have a proposition to which I hope you will agree." His eyes were now fixed on the young man's face, all trace of the smile gone.

"You have aroused my interest, Silas, I cannot deny it." Richard could not keep the surprise out of his voice, but controlled the temptation to smile.

"Your winnings today amount to five hundred guineas less the five lost on the earlier wager and your promissory for fifty guineas which I have kept safely here." He leaned over to his desk and picked up the carefully folded note. "I propose that you bank the four hundred and forty five guineas with me at an annual rate of five percent. I further propose that I become your personal banker, and your point of contact for any business contracts that you may consider in the future. I have performed this service for your father for many years and I am able to say that it has worked profitably for both of us over that time." He sat back.

"I am, of course, aware that Father's banking arrangements have always been sound."

"I am glad to hear it, Richard. It would make your own financial status secure in so far as your father's capital would provide substantial backing. I assume, of course, that, as the only son, you will honour the family commitment to the estate and business interests currently under your father's stewardship. A matter between you and your father, of course, but it is widely believed that you have returned from the metropolis to assume some share in the burdens of the family's rank in local society."

"It sounds almost as if my father had asked you to address me on this matter, Silas, but I take your words as both a reminder of my responsibilities and a kind offer of practical support."

"I apologise, Richard. I do not make a good sermoniser; I had not meant to give a moral lecture." Silas placed his hands on his knees and stood.

"I pray you do not apologise, Sir. Your words are a timely reminder of my true circumstances. I gladly accept your proposition." Richard stood and held out a hand. They shook hands with some vigour, then Silas took up the promissory note, held it between them and solemnly tore it through, looked straight at Richard and had an arm raised to put round his shoulder, when there was a gentle tap at the door. With no pause for a response, it opened to reveal Sophia, glowing at the sight of Richard.

"Do excuse me, Uncle, I had no idea you were so occupied." Her eyes did not leave Richard, however.

"Our business is concluded, my dear, in the most profitable manner to both parties. Now let us take a glass of port wine together to celebrate the new partnership." He took a decanter and filled three glasses.

"To the success of the Galsworthy Trewarren business enterprise. May the partnership prosper and grow as we approach the new century." He drained his glass.

"I drink to that, Silas." Richard drained his own glass.

"May our families grow ever closer." Sophie sipped her port wine, looking at Richard over her glass.

"I drink to that too," said Richard, eyes transfixed by Sophie's warmth and spirit.

"Your glass is drained already, Richard. I trust you would not mock me?" she pouted.

"We will all drink to that." Silas covered Richard's momentary embarrassment by refilling both their glasses.

"Indeed we will, Sir. I thank you. Let our families grow ever closer." They raised their glasses. "I could never bring myself to belittle or deceive such beauty and warmth as you present, Miss Sophie." He gave a slight bow and smiled.

XIX

Caesar, oblivious to the allure of Sophia's parting gaze, tossed his head in impatience at Richard's extended farewells, aware that the chill in the air would increase as the late spring evening darkened into night. Richard calmed his horse, mounted and set off at a trot. He slowed to a walk as he made his way across the bridge and up the steep climb out of the town. The tide was out; a foul stench poisoned the air from the decaying detritus that clung randomly on the steep slopes of smooth grey mud where the river narrowed. On the seaward side, an ever-widening mud flat was interspersed with narrow, fast-flowing rivulets. A primitive wooden wharf far from the low-tide waters gave many local people the opinion that Falmouth would surpass their city in importance before many years had passed. Its deep-water dock did not depend on the tide.

Once clear of the town, Richard was content to let Caesar set his own pace. Sure of his footing and more familiar than his rider with the route, he trotted steadily along. Sophia filled Richard's thoughts; in all his time in London he had not felt quite as he felt now. He let his imagination take him into her bed; he could imagine every inch of her lovely ripe body, her eager response to his caresses. He was glad of his London sophistication in such matters; they would both enjoy the benefits. Only Caesar coming to a halt jolted him back to reality. At the bottom of Trennick Lane he had to make a decision. If the tide had not turned, the quicker route would take them down to Malpas where Caesar could wade the mouth of the Tresillian comfortably enough. Within an hour of its lowest point, it would already be too deep in the dark, and Amos would not want horse and rider in his single-oared boat.

Best to take the shorter track to St Clement, cross the Tresillian where it was shallower and take the longer route through Penhale Wood and on to Merther Lane. With a pull on the rein, a touch of the stirrup and a stroke on the neck they continued on their way. Caesar trod with care and the pace had slowed. Should I take the matter further? Richard pondered. What is her reputation? Mother might well oppose further contact, let alone anything more. Yet there was clearly a business relationship with Father that Silas valued. He emerged into the village and the sky seemed lighter. A rush light in an iron holder pinned to the stone pillar of the village ale house glowed orange, brightening in a sudden eddy of air as a dark-bearded man emerged, stood, relit his clay pipe and stumbled off.

And what was Rawdon's role in Galsworthy business? How strong was the connection with the Trewarrens? Was Cousin George involved? Were they free traders? Was that the Rawdon connection? Richard smiled to himself as he recalled Rawdon's words: "too many questions, Sir, too many questions." He concentrated now on the river crossing. The water was still shallow, reaching only Caesar's knees at its deepest. The ford was marked and secured by gravel and broken rocks crushed into the river bed, but the tides could shift its course in mysterious ways, and the causeway was always covered with a layer of oozing grey mud. Once clear of the river, Richard took control of the pace. Horse and rider moved more purposefully towards the Trewarren estate.

Young Widow Baines might have some answers. Rawdon was by no means unknown to her. He smiled in the darkness as that evening with its more sordid pleasures came into his mind. It will be a most interesting enquiry: more diverting than the delicate approach needed within the family.

***

"Welcome, Martha. It must be a full three week since your last visit. I fell to thinking you had no need of your sister, now, else the reverse were true and you be so sorely troubled you can not venture so far. Sit you down and take off your bonnet. We'll have us a mug of ale. I'm glad o' the rest, truth be told."

"Molly," smiled Martha, "you know full well I my visits must fit with my duties. Besides, Josiah demands ever more of my time, so determined is he to salve and comfort my poor soul from all its wicked ways. But thank you, dear Molly." She took the proffered ale, noting the angry red wheals on her sister-in-law's fingers. "Your sisterly guidance is more to my needs than all his preaching and praying."

"Leastways you are a deal more cheerful than three weeks since. Perhaps you have found the Lord after all? It is Josiah, now, not Brother Carter; such change must signify." Molly took a deep draught of ale and smiled mischievously. "But what of that Trewarren son and heir and his threats that so preoccupied you three weeks since?" She leaned forward, resting her ale mug on her knee.

"'Tes my good fortune that he has more diversions in Truro presently. I scarcely see him now." She sipped her ale. "I did tell him that Lieutenant Carter do not do duty on the Sabbath, nor do expect such from his riders. Yet he is always quoting his mentor, God rest him, as forbidding free trade as ungodly. 'Tes little enough, it do seem to me." Martha leaned back, watching her sister-in-law's face and was rewarded with a twinkling eyed smile.

"He's surely found a Truro bitch for his doggy ways, and has forgot his threats for the diversion." Molly leaned back, laughing in her turn. "Let's drink to that." She held her mug aloft. "Long may the Truro bitch retain her heat!"

Both laughed, drank heartily, and sat in companionable silence, absorbed in their own thoughts. At length Molly rose and offered her sister-in-law more ale. Martha shook her head with a smile and watched as Molly refilled her own mug from the cask.

"So what of that scoundrel, Rawdon? His absence is noted by some as miss his influence along the trade tracks. Does Brother Carter, or must I say Josiah now?" she smiled. "Does Josiah bring his greetings or news of his recovery?"

"He'll not return to revenue riding; his wasted leg do mean he cannot make the pace. He do use his cunning in murkier ways, I suppose. I have no care if he trouble me no more," sighed Martha.

"Let you hope his nearby parts are so affected also. Yet none of this do bring poor Will'm back." Molly had lost her smile at the thought.

Martha stared into the dregs revealed by the receding foam at the base of her mug. Why I have not thought on Will'm, once today, nor for some few days when I consider. And if I did, it were to thank dear God for sparing me the beatings. She paused, and for a moment knew not whether she had spoken the words aloud or mouthed them in silence.

XX

"You sent for me, Father?"

"Come in, Richard, come in. I wanted a few words before dinner. I understand you have shown an interest in a young woman in Truro?"

"I am always interested in young women, Father, in Truro as elsewhere." Richard turned away and moved towards the window.

"Richard, show me the respect a son owes his father. I had hoped the family inheritance would be in safe hands before my dotage renders me incapable."

"I fear it is too late," he muttered.

"I beg your pardon?"

"I said, 'I hope that is not your fate', Father. Forgive me if my modern attitudes offend. I take my inheritance most seriously, I assure you." Richard moved towards his father and relaxed into a reading chair, spreading his arms on the book rest.

"Glad to hear it. Now attend to what I have to say concerning a matter I consider serious. A message came to me from Silas Galsworthy this morning. He writes that you have invested money with him and have indicated a powerful interest in his niece. I would be most interested to know the source of this money, Richard."

"It is but a trifling amount, Father; merely a token of my new maturity; the commencement of a new understanding of my responsibilities."

"Do not mock me, Richard. I am not yet in my dotage."

About to reply, Richard was distracted by a knock on the door. The butler entered and stood before Sir Oliver who nodded.

"My Lady asks if you care to join her for luncheon, Sir Oliver." With a slight bow, he moved to the open door. Sir Oliver drew his gold watch from his waistcoat pocket, noted the time, rose and straightened his jacket.

"You may tell Lady Elizabeth I shall join her presently, Bassett." He moved into the hallway and was gone. The butler glanced at Richard before continuing with his duties.

"Damn the old duffer!" Richard stared out of the window. Fluffy, grey-edged clouds scudded in from the Scillies. The lime trees lining the drive were coming into leaf, their pale green freshness fluttering in the wind. Gravel brought up from the harbour dredge renewed the surface of the drive; the dark mud no longer burst through the warm sandy look of summer.

I feel confined, boxed in, he thought, as he left the house and crossed to the stable yard. He had Caesar saddled and led out. He stroked the stallion's nose, whispered in his ear and swung himself up into the saddle. Soon he was galloping across the parkland downhill towards the tree-lined stream. He slowed to let Caesar find his footing across the rumbling stones in the fast flowing water. At Porthcurnick Beach they broke into a gallop across the hard wet sand. Caesar pulled up. Richard was astonished at the confines of this childhood wonderland. As a small boy, escaping once or twice from an elderly nanny, it had seemed to him a vast paradise.

The world is closing in, he thought: Father, Silas, business, inheritance, estate, free trade and marriage. He walked Caesar up the lane towards Rosevine: a brandy or two would salve the bruising where reality had struck. Along the cliff top the huer carried a birch broom, no doubt to clear his rock shelter as the pilchard season approached. Another constraint, thought Richard, as he approached the alehouse.

"A fine brandy you have here," he remarked to the skivvy, as she brushed the table free of cigar ash and set the half empty earthenware bottle down.

"Master do say it be one o' the greatest good things the free trade have brought us poor folk, Sir, and it surely do bring good business our way." She bent low over his table to remove a pewter plate.

"Would you share a glass with me?" He tapped the bench beside him.

"Oh Sir, I daresn't, t'd not be seemly. Master do care for the good name of his house, Sir. He do say his livelihood be gone for want of it."

"So be it." He thrust a copper coin into her hand, stood, belched and strode out to Caesar, catching a waft of stale tobacco, female body odour, ale and stale urine as he passed in front of her; repulsive, yet exciting in him his taste for the common skivvy. Martha, he thought, not so much a skivvy, but a tasty young widow unable to resist him. He urged Caesar to a steady trot.

Judging from the frequency of his patrols, it seemed to Martha, Josiah Carter must fear the free traders played fast and loose with this stretch of coast. As they returned together from the prayer meeting at Bolhothra, she rode behind him, clasping his waist, her hair flying in the chill off-sea breeze of late May. She could feel the rhythm of hard muscles in his waist as the mare trotted along the cliff top meadow. Desire stirred momentarily then faded as she remembered the pain of Rawdon's assaults, the peril of Richard's corrupt and painful threats.

Easy in each other's company after a month of prayer meetings in the Methody Cottage, they sat in the lea of the cottage in the late spring sunshine, drinking fresh water from the well.

"A fine position in good weather, Sister, your late husband must have found it most convenient. The huer cries a sighting from across the bay above Rosevine is my understanding."

"Indeed he does, Brother Carter. May I ask you, Sir, if it not be too forward, for you to use my name, by which I mean, Sir, would you call me Martha? I have but one who calls me sister, Sir and that be my Will'm's sister, Molly." She stared at the ground, moving a pebble with her boot.

"I would consider it an honour to do so, Sister, er, Martha, if you were to reciprocate."

"'Tes not a word I know, Brother Josiah, but I will surely grant your wish if only I know what it is."

"Why I merely ask you to do the same in return." A smile broke across his face. I mean you should call me Josiah is all. If you will do me that honour, I will call you Martha and thereby reciprocate." He took a deep draught of water.

"'T will not sound too forward, Josiah?" She saw his smiling nod and continued. "Then may I ask you, Josiah, what you may tell me of my late husband, that he be shot by that beast of a man, Rawdon?"

Carter's horse whinnied before he could answer. As they turned, Martha and Josiah became aware of approaching hooves. They moved together instinctively as Richard rounded the cottage and halted facing them. Caesar's nostrils dilated as he tossed his head at Carter's mare.

"A charming sight, to be sure. You indulge in love the Methody way I see, my little harlot. She is adept is she not, Sir?"

XXI

"You have the advantage of me, Sir. I do not have the doubtful pleasure of your acquaintance." Josiah rose from his stool.

"Captain Carter, Supervisor of Revenue, Lieutenant in His Majesty's Royal Navy and God fearing Methodist Christian." He bowed his head and clicked his heels. Martha looked on in amazement as Richard leaned back in the saddle, smiled down on Josiah and spoke with contempt.

"What airs and pretensions the most humble of commissions in His Majesty's Service induce in these modern times."

"I must ask you to leave, Sir, as you have conveyed your contempt for me and this good Christian widow with whom I was conversing. Since you do not deem us worthy of an introduction, I shall consider your continued presence as a formal challenge. Good day to you, Sir." Josiah turned his back on their tormentor, and resumed his seat facing Martha.

"Your impudence is even greater than your deluded pretensions. You will soon be back at sea, exploring the Antipodes, or fighting the Frenchies if they can but overcome these rebels who have overthrown their state. And as for you, my Methody love girl, there is no chance of redemption through service to your betters at Trewarren after this. You can expect a summons on your next arrival. Come Caesar, the air is foul in these parts."

Martha watched in disbelief as Richard whipped Caesar to a gallop. Neither she nor Josiah spoke until the sound of hooves had died way.

"Sister Martha," said Josiah, "I am saddened at your fearful expression. It is my earnest hope that I have not placed you in peril through my strong words. The man is a scoundrel, a disgrace to his breeding."

"Oh Brother Carter, I be so betwixt and between," said Martha, finally raising her head and looking into the distance. "I am afeard he do expose my true sinful nature to your good Christian soul."

"My good sister in Christ, you have repented of any sin. You have been weakened by widowhood, yet strengthened also. You are born again in the eyes of the Lord through your devotions as a clean and honest living Methodist. Please be reassured on this point."

"You are kindness itself, Josiah, but my means are still lost, I am without in this world. I am lost."

"Trust in our Lord, Sister, and He will provide. You have made your peace now. Trust him, I say, and pray every day. Indeed we shall pray together, though we be apart." Josiah stood, wished her farewell, mounted his horse, paused and smiled reassurance, before trotting away towards St Just.

'Though we be apart.' His words echoed through her head. He be too high bred for me, she thought, and Master Richard do prove it to him. I was foolish to think other. He speak to Master Richard as his own in breeding. We be apart truly, and I should be knowing so afore ever this all start up. I did see him as Rawdon's match but he be better bred by far.

***

Sir Oliver sat at the old oak desk. Ledgers with their neat columns of black script recorded the rises and falls of the

Trewarren fortunes. He had no intention of making any entries himself. Indeed there was no quill or ink on the desk. Yet he turned each page, ran a finger down the occasional column as if its significance might suddenly enlighten him. He reached across the desk and picked up Silas's letter, a follow-up to his earlier message. He re-read it for the seventh or eighth time since luncheon. A cloud passed across the late afternoon sun, causing him to draw the letter closer and squint a little. The library door swung open.

"Father!" Richard paused, as his father appeared transfixed in the attitude of an old man losing his mind. "Father, are you ailing?"

"I'm sorry, my boy, I was deep in thought. I have some perplexing decisions to make." Oliver's eyes followed his son, as he advanced into the room.

"Then here is an easy one, Father. Dismiss the little widow forthwith." Richard stood at the window. As the drive curved away, he could see across the parkland to the cliff top and the sea beyond, but not the cottage he had recently left.

"This is a sudden change; I had thought you approved of her role as an innocent go-between and informant for our free trade activities."

"That is no longer my view, Father. She should be dismissed forthwith."

"You have clearly taken as strongly against her, as you were so recently speaking on her behalf. Is she such a threat?"

"She has turned to harlotry, and seduced that Methody revenue captain from his calling. He is far above her in breeding and should never allow himself to dally with such a low-living creature. Yet I fear she is a turncoat, betraying our own business dealings. She is ruthless and dangerous, Father. She must be dismissed..."

"Forthwith... I am sure you will add," said his father, picking up Silas's letter. "This has nothing to do with the Galsworthy niece?"

"Sophie? No indeed, Father, how is she relevant to this? She is a young woman of fine breeding. It is unworthy to name her in the same conversation."

Oliver replaced the letter on his desk without revealing its origin or content. He rose and moved to the window to stand with his son. He placed his hand lightly on Richard's arm.

"Come, Richard, let us take a glass of port together. I will ponder your request; you may be wiser than you grasp at present on this matter."

They left the library together, his father's hand still lightly resting on Richard's arm.

XXII

"Well, Oliver, the pleasure of your company has been long delayed. I trust your affairs are in good order. No crises, no problems on the estate?" Silas Galsworthy leaned back in the leather-upholstered chair, drew on his cigar and expelled the smoke slowly, enjoying its expense to the full.

"It is always difficult to get away, Silas, always something requiring one's attention. I am no longer one for galloping off in all directions." He paused, but Silas said nothing, "I have given your proposals much thought and now feel ready to explore them more fully with you." Sir Oliver relaxed in his turn, enjoying his own cigar in a similar manner. As Silas did no more than nod his agreement, Oliver continued. "I ask you this as a friend of many years, Silas, rather than as a business partner." He noted Silas's encouraging smile. "How suited do you feel Richard and Sophia are? What is Sophia's ambition? Will she make a good wife? I have not had the pleasure of meeting her, and nor has Elizabeth. I very much fear that, should I be seen to encourage the match before my dear wife has made her own assessment, I should have to have a care not to show too great an enthusiasm."

"Perhaps it is time to reveal the whole story, Oliver. Time has passed, tongues are stilled and other scandals and horrors have replaced the scourge in people's minds. We are old friends with many interests in common, among them the understanding for discretion in such matters." He leaned forward and lowered his voice. Sir Oliver leaned forward in response. Silas related how a full ten years before, his younger sister Ruth and her family, farmers in Devon, had contracted the small pox. Sophia, lively then as now, had been the only survivor. Ruth had died first, then the two older children, and finally the father. The governess, herself very ill, sent word to Silas. The messenger, a lazy fellow, assumed they would all be dead before long, so was in no hurry. A full week later he reached Truro and appeared at the town house, the worse for drink. Silas, fearing the whole family was dead, departed next day and arrived the day after. Sophia was found, with the milkmaid, wild and unkempt.

"I hardly recognised her," said Silas, his voice hushed at the memory, "but the maid told me she'd not let the child come to harm. The child was used to the cows, indeed came frequently to the milking when she could escape in the early morning. She had a raw rash once or twice, as all the milkmaids did, but the outside air kept her away from the fetid miasma of the house."

"I had no idea, Silas. It was a wonderful thing you did. I was so preoccupied with our own dear daughters' death and its terrible impact on us all - Elizabeth has never truly recovered -that I never realised that you had suffered such a loss."

"Once the main business of burials and property were in hand, I brought Sophia home. She screamed and shouted her protests, but there was nothing else I could do." He sighed and sat back in his chair. "Nothing else I could do," he repeated.

"Richard tells me she is a fine young woman, lively and sophisticated enough for the London scene, he says."

"I allowed her more independence than is customary; a country child, who had suffered much, come to live with strangers. I am not sure that was wise, but she is devoted to me now, and that is great compensation. It is my wish to see her married to secure her future. Should Richard have genuine feelings for her, it may make a suitable match." Silas sat back. "There now you have the truth of it. I take on trust it remains a confidence between us."

"I hasten to repeat my assurances on the matter. I shall test, as well as I may, Richard's true interest and feelings in the suitability of a match."

"I shall send invitation to your family to join us for an evening of dinner and entertainment. We shall get up a select little party, and observe the young lovers discreetly."

"That is most kind, Silas, most kind."

Their conversation turned to their business interests, their hopes for a profitable pilchard season to set against the failures in the tin mines. The miners rioting in the town, driven to violence by the mine closures, were a symptom of the insecurity in the ore trade, fuelled by the buyer cartels at the auctions. Oliver did not follow in detail the ebb and flow of the process, but registered the names of the villains as Silas became more animated at the losses they caused to all but themselves. He did not explain how he, as a banker, could suffer from the process and, not wishing to challenge Silas after such a sensitive discussion, Oliver forbore to ask.

"At least the free trade prospers; with the turmoil in France there is much profitable business to be had in Brittany, I am informed by my contacts in Guernsey." Oliver rose and made his farewells. As they left the room, Oliver noticed a figure with a pronounced limp scuttle hurriedly round the end of the corridor. Silas appeared unaware of any such presence as he accompanied his guest to the front steps.

***

Every morning, Martha dreaded the sound of Mrs Crabbe's voice, summoning her to have her supposed betrayal detailed as a warning to her fellow servants followed by instant dismissal. She herself said nothing, but as a week passed in which the housekeeper remained her usual self, dour, critical and contemptuous, Martha's fear subsided. She floated in purgatory; a constant state of uncertainty left her twitchy and nervous. Elspeth, who had remained distant since she had failed to keep to her duty of ensuring Martha's church attendance, knew her better than anyone at the Manor.

"You are not yourself this past week, Martha. Be you ailing with some dropsy or such?"

"I thank thee for thy concern, Elspeth, but there is little cause for it."

"A disappointment in love perhaps?" said Elspeth.

"Truly, there is nothing that time and the Good Lord will not resolve." Martha resumed her scrubbing under the table. Elspeth shrugged, and left the kitchen to resume clearing the dining room. Constance was returning with Lady Elizabeth's breakfast tray, the food almost untouched. She caught Elspeth's expression as she passed.

"My Lady eats so little these days, 'tes wonder she does not faint away." Constance placed the tray on the table, took a mutton chop from the pewter plate and chewed her way along the bone.

"'Tes not your place to comment on the mistress and her ways, Constance. I am sure she has reason enough for what she does. 'Tes not for us to voice our ignorance."

"You speak so hoity toity of late, Martha, 'tes no wonder Elspeth is put out." A globule of congealed white mutton fat had fastened onto Constance's chin as she finished chewing at the bone and replaced it on the plate.

"Wipe your mouth before Mrs Crabbe returns."

"I 'ent said anything to be ashamed of. You really be in a contrary mood today; Elspeth did right to warn me."

"As you wish." Martha turned back to her work.

"Baines, Pawley, Dyer! A word if you please." Mrs Crabbe scuttled into the kitchen. Martha looked up, stood, and straightened her dress and apron. Elspeth hurried in with the remaining breakfast tureens. Constance put her hand to her mouth and froze.

"Never in my loyal service have I felt a higher loyalty brought me to speak of Trewarren business of which all in service should be ignorant." Mrs Crabbe had drawn herself up to her full height and spoke with all the authority she could muster. Dear Lord, thought Martha, I fear my fate is sealed.

"Some amongst us have been unable to resist the attractions of our handsome young master." She paused, as Martha stared at the floor, feeling the heat rise up her neck. "I see there is truth in that at least."

Unable to bear the suspense, Martha raised her head and looked about her. Constance was failing to strangle breathless sobs.

"I have learned that Master Richard's status may well change in the near future. It would therefore be disgraceful if such wickedness were to be presented to me." She stared at Constance, unblinking. "You, Pawley, will not leave the kitchen, scullery or ice house under any circumstances whatever, until the future is decided. Should you do so, instant dismissal!"

Constance, openly sobbing, fled into the scullery.

"Why are you two standing here? Get back to work. Should a word concerning this matter escape, you will both be dismissed instantly along with Pawley." Mrs Crabbe glared at their backs, and strode away to her command post.

XXIII

"Heva! Heva!"

Fishermen stood and turned. Clay pipes discarded, crab pots dropped, they stared up at the huer's hut.

"Heva! Heva!" came the cry on the soft inshore breeze, the trumpet distorting and lengthening the sound. Fishwives emerged from their houses and, hands on hips, stared up at the huer's hut.

"Heva! Heva!" cried the huer again, his brushes raised, pointing out towards the Lizard. White gannets circled high above the waves, each one positioning itself before diving, wings held tight, neck stretched, as it arrowed through the water, took the selected pilchard in its beak and resurfaced at a distance to enjoy its catch.

The sharp bows of the seine boat cut through the calm water. The six-man crew rowed, muscles bulging, as they pulled in well-practised rhythm. With them, a few yards to seaward, the master seiner, in the bow of the lurker boat, watched the huer's signalled directions through his eyeglass. He shouted instructions to the coxes of both boats. The follower boat with the tuck net kept pace, ready to seize the end of the freshly barked seine net and manoeuvre its vast length around the shoal.

Martha sat in the late July sunshine, sheltered from the wind, a half-empty mug of cloudy cider by her side. Josiah had left his drink untouched. He smiled across at her. Attention among the Manor servants had moved to Constance after Mrs Crabbe's dramatic statement. Still in her sixteenth year, she had found herself with child a few weeks after her secret was revealed. Sure that handsome Richard would help her discreetly, and their relationship would continue more securely, albeit in secret, she had declared her love for him and thrown herself on his mercy. Mrs Crabbe had dismissed her forthwith, leaving Martha's own position more secure.

"I was very much afeared you had returned to your old ways when you did not attend for worship." Josiah paused. "And I was not entirely wrong," he added, smiling as he held up the untouched mug of scrumpy.

"Oh, Josiah, 'tes not by free trade I have it, but 'tes made by my own hand with fruit from my sister-in-law."

"It is still the drink, Martha, the drink we good Christians forbid ourselves." He smiled again at her worried frown. "On most occasions, that is." He leaned back against the warm smooth rock and raised the mug, sipping tentatively at the frothy liquid.

"I mistook your meaning, on that wretched day when you stood up so brave to Master Richard. I was all a flummox with my shame. I d' think you purposed we should stay apart; I were too soiled to worship with such godly brothers and sisters. T'were enough you thought to pray for me at all."

Josiah's reply was lost as they heard the distant cry and rose together. Martha grabbed the hem of her skirt and ran across the scrub to the cliff edge. Josiah, caught unawares, followed with rapid strides.

"A good shoal, by looks," said Martha as he approached. "'Tes a good omen, so early in the season. Penzance seines only called last week, so Molly say."

"The Lord smiles on us." Josiah moved up to her side.

"Indeed, he does! The tide's on the ebb and the sea calm,

the sun have hours to go before he set. See the huer, Josiah, his brushes sign so clear. Young Jim Tripp have a goodun first time he be the master seiner. His father still has the ribs broke from the December storms. Pains him too much to shout."

"He taught young Jim well." Josiah sensed her excitement, and forebore to mention his suspicions. Will Tripp had not been chasing the pilchards when he broke his ribs. Did she know of his connection with the late Will Baines? It did not suit his purposes to raise the issue now.

"Proper job." Martha's excitement grew as the follower boat caught the stop end of the seine and, with the signal from the huer, began to circle in the opposite direction towards the master seiner. From their position above Rosevine, the circle of bobbing corks seemed no larger than a wagon wheel though, as the two boats drew the net ends together, it was a full quarter of a mile in circumference. Both boats now set course for Trewarren harbour, towing the great net towards the sheltered water. Young Jim, perhaps too cautious in his wish to avoid Bass Rock, called a halt and the follower boat lowered the tuck net.

On the quay, Molly joined the other women with their wicker baskets, ready to collect their share of the fish and bulk them.

"What's young Jim up to, he en't brung that seine net anywhere near enough by the looks," a heavily built woman complained.

"'Tes his first time Dorcas, give a credit, he do his best and better'n a wreck leastways."

"You be right I s'pose, Molly Bawden. I see your Thomas d' get his flat boat out afore the tide do strand him. Least he take his shovel with him. We shall be lucky to fill a basket before nightfall," Dorcas turned her head to see who else was going out to the tuck net. "Well now I d' see a right pair o' cripples." She grabbed Molly's arm and pointed.

"Well, no reward for knowing their plotting purpose." Molly was disturbed to see an older man, sitting on an upturned hull above the tide line, bent forward clutching his chest. Approaching him rapidly, though with a swaying step, almost a limp, was a man whose evil grin was known and hated in the town.

Josiah walked his horse across Porthcurnick beach, Martha behind him, arms clasping his waist. Up onto the stony track along the low cliff top, going was easier and they broke into a gentle trot.

"Molly!" cried Martha, glimpsing her sister-in-law through the mix of women, young boys and old men. "Molly, come meet Cap'n Carter."

"Cap'n Carter." Molly, bent her knee a little in an awkward attempt at respect, which made Dorcas smile as she looked on, one hand guarding Molly's basket.

"Josiah, please," said Josiah, "T'would be most unmannered if one sister addressed me more formal than the other."

"Another old friend or two be under your nose, I reckon, Cap'n Josiah, if you were to follow it towards the hulls above the tide line."

Josiah's eye followed where Molly had guided it as Rawdon joined Will Tripp on the upturned hull. The women on the quay searched for boatmen they knew and trusted and placed their tagged baskets amidships as the boats ferried out to the tuck net. The two men sat isolated and uninterested in the activity, Rawdon's smile an ominous sign as Will Tripp coughed, groaned and held his sore ribs.

XXIV

"Cock fighting! Is this one of your London pursuits?" Sir Oliver removed his pince-nez as he glanced over the letter at his son.

"I am no longer a child, Father. If you wish to engage me in a civil conversation, I would be obliged if you would acknowledge that fact." Richard drew himself up to his full, self-righteous height. There was a long pause, during which Sir Oliver held his son's eyes with a steady gaze while he organised his thoughts. Richard looked away but did not move.

"Very well, Richard, I shall read you a letter of invitation I have just received from Silas Galsworthy, and I shall read it in full." He replaced his pince-nez, held the letter up and began reading in a neutral tone.

My Dear Oliver,

I would consider it a great honour, if you, my good Sir, Lady Elizabeth, and your son Richard would care to join my niece Sophia and myself with one or two compatible guests for a weekend at our country residence at Nankilly towards the end of August.

Whilst I should be deeply indebted to you for your advice on certain issues on the estate, the opportunity would also arise for Sophia and Richard to enjoy each other's company in suitable surroundings.

Knowing of Richard's predilection for the sport of the cockpit, and his love of a wager, I have taken the liberty of arranging an event to his liking. I trust it will not offend if we follow our custom of allowing local village folk to gather behind a grille at one end of the hall to enjoy the spectacle. I assure you the sport will be conducted in the most tasteful manner, as I am sure Richard will testify.

It is my earnest hope that this invitation will lead to ever-closer family and business ties as we move towards the new century and new opportunities.

I remain, Sir,

Your most obedient servant

Silas Galsworthy

Sir Oliver placed the letter on his desk, let his pince-nez dangle on their cord, invited his son to take a seat and, turning his desk chair to face Richard, eased himself into it. The sun shone obliquely across Sir Oliver's shoulder, highlighting specks of dust floating from the disturbed chair seat.

Richard blinked from the burst of sunlight, but said nothing. His eyes followed a spiralling whirl of dust as it rose through the ray of sunlight and dispersed to rest elsewhere.

"It is clear that you impressed Silas Galsworthy, no less than his niece, and that is to the good, if indeed your intentions in that direction are honourable."

"Silas... he invited me to address him as such, Father, so there is no need for that disapproving stare. Silas is a forward-looking banker and businessman who, in my humble opinion, could profit us greatly by closer business ties. If marriage to Sophie would aid such developments, I would be content to woo her, and offer her my hand, in the certain knowledge that she would be honoured and eager to accept."

"Whilst your interest in the promise of stronger business ties is laudable, Richard, I fear you are somewhat presumptuous in supposing Sophia's eager participation in such a scheme to be an inevitable outcome."

"As in the matter of wagers in the cockpit, I suppose," Sir Oliver sighed. "Very well, I shall accept the invitation, and observe closely how such matters evolve as, you can be sure, will your mother."

***

Lady Trewarren surprised herself at the sense of anticipation she felt as she arrived at Nankilly. Sir Oliver had had some difficulty in persuading her, as she rarely emerged from Trewarren Manor. Soon after the tragic death of their second daughter, he had tried to provide distractions for her but her response had been contemptuous dismissal. Her preoccupation with grief seemed the obvious explanation to Sir Oliver. At a loss, he had turned his attention to other matters.

"It is my very great pleasure to welcome your ladyship and we are honoured by your presence." Silas himself had come out to welcome them. He had difficulty in concealing his surprise at this handsome, animated lady, presented to him by Sir Oliver.

"The pleasure is all mine, Mr Galsworthy," Lady Elizabeth replied as she accepted his arm and swept forward. A bemused Sir Oliver followed them through to meet the other guests. He was further surprised to see his nephew George holding court with tales of sea battles with the French and the American rebels. Foremost among the spellbound audience was Sophie, who seemed to hang on his every word. Richard stood behind her, impressed at the easy manner with which George held the attention of the guests, yet nervous of the obvious impact he was having on Sophie.

"Why Aunt Elizabeth! What a great pleasure to see you after all these years. Forgive me, Aunt, I was boring the guests with some trifling tales of life in the King's navy," said George.

"Thank you, George, it is a great relief and pleasure to see you safe after such hair-raising adventures." said Lady Elizabeth, as she sidled up to her son.

Silas took Sir Oliver aside for a brief moment.

"I have an exciting project to put to you, Oliver, which gives the outcome of this weekend particular importance. We need a private hour together." Moving away, Silas approached George Trewarren.

"George, it is most gallant of you to entertain our guests with tales of adventure in the King's service. I've no doubt you have undervalued your own contribution through bravery and skill, which those who know you well would readily recognise."

"Hear hear, good fellow George!" cried a number of the men present.

"The weather is clement, and I am sinfully proud of the formal garden this year. May I invite my guests to take a stroll therein? We shall reassemble to proceed into dinner when we have tired of its diversions," Silas announced, as the stewards flung open the great glass doors leading onto the terrace. A serving table offered drinks as the guests gathered round, and glasses full, dispersed throughout the gardens in twos and threes.

XXV

Silas led Sir Oliver, through to the library which, at Nankilly, had been converted from a small side reception room. In absorbing his surroundings, Sir Oliver's eye fell on an abrupt end to the frieze where it met the dark panelling of the wall behind the desk. The windows were small and set higher than he would have expected, although it was possible to observe the drive in the middle distance. A bookcase opposite held several rows of leather-bound books behind a brass grid. Gilt-framed pictures of hunting scenes and portraits hung on the corridor wall and a fanciful illustrated plan of the estate hung at an awkward height on the panelling where it joined the outside wall. Between the windows was a simple fireplace.

Silas ushered Sir Oliver into an armchair, drew two glasses from a cupboard in the desk and, with a nod from his guest, filled both with a rich, dark port.

"It is pleasing to see Elizabeth looking so well; she has been seen so little in society these last years." Silas looked across at Sir Oliver.

"I am most surprised and delighted. Your invitation seems to have drawn her out of her melancholy, at least for the present. I am most indebted to you, Silas."

"It often happens thus, I am told. Some small thing will spring a person free. Let us hope it is so with Elizabeth; she is a handsome woman of wit and intelligence; surely an asset to our enterprise."

"Speaking of which," said Sir Oliver, "I am all ears to hear your proposition, Silas."

***

Richard drew Sophie away from George, as they stood grouped on the terrace.

"Mother, allow me to introduce you to Miss Sophia Galsworthy, niece to Silas and our hostess for this weekend together."

"Welcome to Nankilly, Lady Elizabeth. It is an honour to have you as our guest."

"Thank you, my dear. I have heard reports of your outstanding beauty but they do you less than justice."

"That is most kind, my lady, but I fear you exaggerate greatly."

"My son does not think so, am I not right, Richard?"

"Indeed you are, Mother. I assure you, Sophie, Mother does not in the least exaggerate," said Richard.

"It is such a great pleasure also to see my dear nephew after so long, and looking so tall and handsome too. I do hope you will allow me to presume on your hospitality to familiarise myself with his latest exploits." Lady Elizabeth moved towards George, and guided him to walk with her down the terrace steps into the formal paths of the garden. Richard and Sophie followed, out of earshot, behind them.

"Mother is quite transformed." said Richard, "She has shunned society for so long, I never imagined she would enjoy such company again. She had her dressmaker out from Truro, and harried her over every little detail. I had thought it her protest at having to show herself in society again."

"She is handsome and determined, certainly," said Sophie. "A social asset for Uncle and your father, one might say formidable! How does she view the cockpit?"

"She knows nothing of the sport, so tends to deplore it. No doubt my cousin will explain it, though I hope he does not persuade her to wager on his choice, if his previous advice was a guide to his skill in such matters."

On their return to the house, Sophie excused herself to carry out her hostess duties.

***

"After an exploratory investigation, I am convinced we have the appropriate knowledge, skills and resources to develop a very successful business by investing in a pilchard palace," said Silas after a thoughtful pause. "I trust you are familiar with the concept." He sipped his port.

"A pilchard palace?" said Sir Oliver, taken aback. "I'm not sure I follow you, Silas. Where would such an edifice be built? What functions would it perform? What would be the return on capital? What labour would be required? What capital? What impact on the local fishing community?"

113

"Such a concept brings all the processes and skills together under one roof, economies of scale, the introduction of modern mechanisation, and stronger profits from exports. As you own much of the foreshore below Gerrans, we can improve the harbour, install a great winding capstan, and regularise the labour." Silas's enthusiasm carried him along, brushing Sir Oliver's attempted interventions aside. "My man, Rawdon, has investigated every aspect. He is very familiar with the coast, and is on excellent terms with the recently retired master seiner. I am convinced it will bring us prosperity in these uncertain times, Sir Oliver."

"Rawdon, you say? Do you trust the fellow? He is a double-sided knave if ever there was." Sir Oliver could not disguise his shock.

"No, it's not a question of trust; it is a question of pay."

"I see, you pay well for his loyalty?" It seemed a contradiction to Sir Oliver.

"He is so entangled with my interests now, each one small in itself, that to betray me in one would mean the loss of payment for all. Let me summon him. He will convince you the project is sound." Silas tugged at a cord dangling from the panelling behind him.

Rawdon entered before the cord was still. His obsequious manner did not deceive Sir Oliver, who greeted him coldly. Encouraged by Silas, Rawdon described his recent visit to Trewarren Bay: the plentiful catch, the time spent drawing in the net, his conversations with Will Tripp concerning the prosperity that might follow. With a final obsequious smile, he added, "'twill boost the prospects for a principle close to your heart, Sir Oliver, and that be the free trade in return for the exports, the which will grow prodigious to be sure."

"I resent the charge of illegal behaviour, Rawdon. Please withdraw that implication from your statement. It is not fitting in a retired Revenue man."

"I am sure I do beg your lordship's pardon, twas not my intention to offend." Rawdon bowed his head in an excess of obsequious regret.

"Thank you, Rawdon, a very full account. You may withdraw." Silas turned to Sir Oliver. Rawdon stood just inside the door, apparently unnoticed.

"I understood you to imply that the affection shown between Sophia and Richard might be encouraged to bloom in the light of such possibilities. I would value your thoughts on the matter, and how it might fit with such a scheme." Looking up, he saw Rawdon was still by the door.

"I have arranged a small test of their affections which we shall see enacted this afternoon. Whilst you digest what we have discussed this morning, we will observe the depth and maturity of their mutual affection. Rawdon, ask Mr George Trewarren to attend on us as soon as he returns to the terrace." Both men watched as Rawdon bowed and scraped his departure.

***

Sir Oliver sat deep in thought while Silas took the port and refilled their glasses. Rawdon knocked and entered, announcing George.

"Should I fetch Miss Sophia, Sir?"

A frown crossed Silas's face. "You do not fetch guests or family, Rawdon. You may tell her that I should be pleased to see her shortly."

Sir Oliver greeted George warmly and indicated a chair. Silas offered him a glass of port, which George raised to them both. He explained that he was not likely to settle back in the country, given the situation in France. War was continuing and his knowledge and experience must be dedicated to his country first and foremost. He hoped also to settle his differences with his father in New England. He was expecting a message any day to summon him to Portsmouth; meanwhile, he was enjoying the company of family and friends, and the attention of the ladies.

He had neither inclination nor wherewithal to seek a bride, but enjoyed the company of ladies, especially those as attractive as Miss Sophia. He was also pleased to see Lady Elizabeth in so lively a mood, having heard of her long melancholia after the sad loss of both daughters.

"It is a great pleasure to receive you, George, and we much admire your courage and service. Be sure we shall welcome your safe return when your duty is done. In the meantime, you could do one small favour for us which I trust will not be too burdensome." Silas smiled.

"I will do all in my power," he added hastily, "in return for your kindness."

"Miss Sophia has had a difficult early life, George, as your Uncle will acknowledge. She appears outwardly confident, if somewhat gauche at times. I believe, however, that she lacks the inner conviction of her worth. If you could show by your interest that you consider her worthy of attention, not only from her outward appearance, but also as a potential partner of substance, I am sure she, your uncle and I would be most grateful. I need not add that I am not implying any indiscreet behaviour, merely a bringing out of her true self."

Sir Oliver, watching George's reaction, was interrupted as Sophia swept into the room. Rawdon stood just inside the door. George rose gallantly, took Sophia's hand and bent low to kiss it. Silas dismissed Rawdon who shuffled out. Sir Oliver sat nonplussed, but forced a smile at Silas's conspiratorial glance.

***

Richard stood on the terrace alone, twisting a wine glass between his fingers. People were drifting back to the house in small groups. Richard entered the drawing room looking for his cousin and his mother. Hostess duties? he thought. Such duties are best carried out by summoning servants in the unlikely event that they are not ever present on such occasions. He passed into the hall. A valet appeared at his side.

"I am looking for Miss Sophia," he said.

"She is with her uncle, Sir. I am sure she will return to the guests shortly."

At that moment Rawdon emerged from Silas's study, and scuttled off down to the servants' quarters. George Trewarren emerged, clearly talking to someone over his shoulder. Sophia followed closely, laughing delightedly in response. Richard slipped unobserved back into the drawing room and made his way through other guests to a group of society wives at the centre of which was his mother. Silas and Sir Oliver entered the dining room deep in conversation, but the butler followed immediately and announced that dinner was served. Richard did not reach his mother but made his way back towards the dining room.

"I trust you will escort me in to dine?" Sophie appeared at his side.

"I trust your hostess duties will allow it," he said, offering her his arm.

"It is boorish to challenge a lady so," she said, her eyes dancing with amusement.

As they moved into dinner, Richard felt Sophie's hot breath on his ear. "Red Rooster," she whispered. Her full soft lips pecked at his earlobe. A wave of erotic pleasure passed through his body as her teeth chewed lightly at the soft flesh and her dark hair brushed against his neck. He juggled the name in his mind, 'Red Rooster,' where had he heard it before? They walked serenely towards the dining table, her hand formally resting on his arm. He held the chair for her, and with a swish of her skirts and a flirtatious smile she was seated.

XXVI

Martha sat watching as the sun set behind the Lizard in a lambent sky. Josiah had accompanied her from the meeting as was his habit and they sat together, saying little. The warm air, with scents of late summer, stirred in a gentle breeze; the sunset traced a scarlet line above the dark silhouette of the distant peninsula.

"I've not felt such peace and calm since I lost my poor Will'm," said Martha, "nor so at ease with a man as I do with you, Josiah." She turned to face him. "I hope I don't be too forward."

"I am much at ease with you too," he smiled.

She felt an irresistible power draw her towards that smile; their lips touched; her arms were round his neck; he held her waist. They went inside.

She woke as dawn light entered the hut. She lay naked and replete. God is truly great, she thought. He rewards true love with pleasures I did but dream of.

"Thank you, Lord, for bringing me the love of your true servant, Josiah. Through him you have shown me the way to paradise. May I be forgiven for past sins and continue to deserve the delights of giving and receiving love as we have shared this night. Josiah will you not join me in a prayer of thanks for the joys we have shared?" She turned and saw him standing by the window, making final adjustments to his clothing.

"Josiah? Are you on duty so early? I have a little longer as the family is away at Nankilly," she added.

"Martha, I very much regret I allowed you to tempt me to indulge my base instincts; to know you carnally, out of wedlock. Your own fall I can excuse through your lowly circumstances. I have sinned greatly; I can only pray earnestly for the Lord's forgiveness. We can no longer be together in friendship, or at meetings. There is a meeting-house in Falmouth. I shall worship there in future, if I dare to enter the Lord's presence with such a sinful stain. I bid you farewell."

"Josiah!" she called, but he was gone. She heard the horse gallop off in the cold dawn. She turned in the bed and buried her face in disbelief. It had been such a joyous revelation. Never had she experienced such overwhelming pleasure as they had enjoyed that night. In the early days of her marriage to Will'm it had been a pleasurable duty to serve his needs; he had been gentle with her in those first months, but he had never considered her own feelings, and she had not thought it possible that he should. How could such giving of each to the other be other than a hymn of praise to the good Lord above? What was troubling her beloved Josiah?

***

"Baines, I'd like a word," said Mrs Crabbe as Martha donned her apron and cap. Not now, thought Martha, please not now, I just want to work on my own.

"Baines, as you know, Constance will not be returning after her sinful behaviour with Master Richard. Look at me, Baines, when I speak to you. There is no need to stare at the floor."

"Beg pardon, Ma'm, er, Mrs Crabbe," Martha was trying not to cry.

"I have been impressed by your application since her departure, Baines, and by the common sense and household skills you have shown. Don't look so surprised," she said as Martha looked at her in amazement. "I demand high standards, and I am severe with those who do not meet them, but I encourage those who strive to do so. I have been persuaded of late that you have put your heart into your duties over the last few weeks."

"Thank you, Ma'm. I have done my best," said Martha, thinking her heart was about to break.

"The family will be returning to Trewarren Manor in a day or so, and Dyer will be with them. There will be much to do in preparation, and more again with the family in residence. Lady Trewarren has emerged from mourning, for which we should all be greatly relieved. She has resumed her place in society within and beyond the county, and this, however congenial, will put more and different pressures on staff below stairs."

"I do thank the good Lord for her recovery, Mrs Crabbe; he has smiled on her in his mercy."

"Less of that Methody talk, Baines, if I am to continue with my thoughts for your place here." Mrs Crabbe frowned.

"Yes, Ma'm. It comes so natural to me, Mrs Crabbe, Ma'm."

"Well, it must stop, Baines. Lady Trewarren will most certainly object."

***

It transpired that Constance would not be replaced. Elspeth Dyer would be Lady Trewarren's maid, and Martha would live in full time as assistant to Mrs Crabbe. For as long as the arrangement continued she would get her room and keep with no loss of her previous remuneration. Any time off duty would be at Mrs Crabbe's discretion. Before she collected the few possessions she felt least ashamed of and carried them up to her attic room next to Elspeth's, she walked over the cliffs to see Molly.

"Well, what a to-do, to be sure," said Molly. "We s'll see little of you, I suppose, now you're to be living in. You make sure you d'not fall like that poor girl. And Josiah gone an' all. Who would have thought it." She paused for breath.

"Oh Molly, I've so many questions. When shall I see you? Will Josiah come back? He's the only man I ever loved, Molly. What am I to do? I can't even go to the Methody meetings no more. Mrs Crabbe says I must go to church with her and Elspeth Dyer, sit with the servants: a household together, she says. An' that satin dress I told you of, that red dress the foul excise man Rawdon brought. Do I take it or leave it? Sir Oliver d' not like it. He said as much my first time here. And Master

Richard, can I avoid him? Can I deny him?"

"First, sister, forget all this love nonsense. 'Tes not for the likes of us. Your man treats you half decent and you give him kids is all about it. You lost your man, and he were the worse for the drink, and he beat you. If another takes you on, you be a lucky woman, if not, leastways you have a position and a home. You be better off now, sister, than you was afore all this happened. You got no kids to bring up, you could even rent out your home. You'll not be needing it now." Molly drew a dull pewter tankard of brandy from a keg behind the door. "Here," she said, "enough of my speechifying. Drink this and forget your troubles." She pushed the tankard towards Martha and filled one for herself. Martha let the brandy burn her throat; each mouthful softened her face. She let the tears come. She sat upright sipping brandy, tears streaming unchecked down her face. Henny, asleep in the corner, woke and cried out. Martha sat unaware, as Molly crossed and picked up the child.

***

She was stumbling back up to her hut. Her throat burned dry, her head seared as if an iron band tightened above her eyes, almost blinding her. The privy, she must reach the privy, her very soul should be purged. Too late, her stomach rebelled. She staggered up to a lichen-covered rock, grasped the ridge with one hand, felt the unstoppable surge in her throat, and emptied her stomach in shuddering heaves.

XXVII

The buzz of conversation around the dinner table centred on the re-emergence of Lady Elizabeth Trewarren. Behind her eyes, those who knew her well could detect a deeper sadness her animated features could not fully conceal. Yet she was good company, keen to attune to the latest gossip, and so an attentive listener. She could be relied upon to delight with her caustic wit. Servants scurried back and forth from the kitchen with great plates of mutton and pork. Silas responded with pride to the admiration of his porcelain dishes. "Cornish enterprise. St Austell is awash with Staffordshire potters and their agents. Champion has lost his monopoly; Wedgwood and Spode are after the china clay. Champion is finished by my reckoning." He leaned back as a maid took his plate, pleased to have made an impression. As his glass was refilled with finest French wine from Bordeaux, he turned to Sir Oliver, raised his glass and, in a quieter voice, asked if supplies were still coming through.

"The French are volatile by nature," said Sir Oliver, "and particularly so at the moment. Yet their love of pilchards has not diminished, indeed they compete with Genoa and Naples for salted pilchards as well as disorder. Hence our sources are secure. It is the customs men who disrupt the free trade."

"I am acquainted with a wealthy lawyer in Polperro who is highly connected. Let me know should you face any problems. He would act on our behalf should the need arise," said Silas.

"Richard mentioned such a person, when he returned from London a few months past. It is most kind of you to offer his influence should we need such a service." Oliver glanced down the table at Richard at the mention of his name. Sophie was in animated, if not flirtatious conversation with George Trewarren on her left, her lithe young body twisted towards him so that he could not but admire the effect of her low-cut dress. Richard, on her right, had enjoyed her company for the first half an hour of the meal. He had granted her the forgiveness she begged for neglecting him earlier, but would find it less easy to do so for her attentions to George. On his left was a middle-aged widow, of dull appearance and shallow intellect. He had met without enthusiasm his duty to converse with his neighbour, but he had nothing to say to the widow and was relieved when she turned to her right and engaged the occupant, an elderly clergyman, in a well-rehearsed eulogy of her deceased husband.

"There is an air of distraction about Richard, today," said his father. "Let us hope the cock fight he is so keen on rewards his enthusiasm."

"Indeed, let us hasten the servants." Silas signalled the servants to begin preparations.

Half an hour later, the tables were cleared away, the guests were seated or standing around three sides of the room and the double doors were penned off with staff and hangers-on gathering in excitement, awaiting the cockerels. Rawdon appeared, with Red Rooster under his arm. He gave the appearance of being totally preoccupied with calming the bird. Earlier he had taken a mussel shell from the folds of his cloak and brushed its razor edge, as if by accident, against the tendon low down towards the base of Red Rooster's right leg.

The cock turned, and pecked violently at Rawdon's arm as he mopped the oozing translucent fluid from the wound. He fitted the rooster's iron claw, which acted as a brace when first applied, though there was little chance it could sustain a single attack from an opponent on the fighting mat.

From his cockfighting chair, Silas announced the terms of the first contest. Red Rooster, at three pounds four ounces would have a three minute contest with Bodmin Braveheart of similar weight. Anyone wishing to wager should do so now. A few guests responded with small sums, entered in the book.

"Fifty guineas on Braveheart," said George Trewarren.

"Five hundred guineas on Red Rooster to win," called Richard, waving his arm. He did not notice Rawdon's smile as he released Red Rooster on Silas's instruction.

Bodmin Braveheart circled, wings half raised. Red Rooster moved towards him, uncertainly. Sensing his opponent's weakness, Braveheart rose with open wings and leapt on him. Red Rooster tore at his attacker's throat with his iron claw, drawing blood, but screamed as the clawed foot dangled limply, unable to take his weight as he stumbled back. Braveheart, with blood oozing from his neck, moved in for the kill. The lower classes gathered at the barrier were briefly still and silent. Red Rooster moved into a position of submission and was whisked away by Rawdon. The visitor was scooped up by his trainer to whoops of delight from those who had wagered on him. George Trewarren bowed to Sophie in delight.

"I am deeply distressed that you should favour the

unconscionable cad with your smile, Miss Sophia." Richard gave her a mock bow, and strode towards the barrier.

"Make way, you paupers, clear the way at once; a gentleman needs to pass!"

"You are no gentleman, Sir!"

Richard stood still, feeling his blood rise. He recognised his cousin's voice.

"I say you are no gentleman, Sir, unless..."

"I will defend my honour, cousin, though I fear it is your own that is sullied." Richard strode off through the local labourers and servants, who parted in amazement. He did not look back.

"Surely you will not destroy your cousin, over such a small matter?" Sophia grasped George's arm. "He spoke at the moment of greatest loss, George. I am sure he will make it up to you when he has calmed himself. He is your cousin. To spill his blood would cause a deep family rift for years to come, would it not?"

"My dear Miss Sophia, to do nothing in the face of such ungentlemanly conduct would lower the standing of both our families. Cousin Richard must learn to face the consequences of his foolish and, yes, boorish behaviour."

"Oh this is an impossible situation, I." She paused. "I admire the honour you wish to defend, but the losses will be far greater than the blood of one more Trewarren."

"Very well, Miss Sophia; in the light of your sensibilities I will give you my word that I shall not kill him. I will endeavour to wound him with pain enough to end the duel, but his life will not be at risk." George took her arm and, in looking for the way forward, noticed an animated Lady Elizabeth, directing both Silas and Sir Oliver towards the couple.

"Join me in the library if you please, Mr Trewarren," said Silas.

XXVIII

"Pollard looks so dashing, Martha. For once the starch of his clothing has not made a statue of his face." Elspeth giggled as their aprons and bonnets fluttered in the wind.

"Hush, Elspeth, they'll hear us," laughed Martha, noting how handsome the steward looked when enjoying a joke without formality. She looked along the line of waiting servants; all appeared happy at the family's impending return; all looked impeccable; and all were resisting the wind as their clothes flapped around, hands holding them in place.

"Sir Oliver's coach is approaching. Take your places, in order if you please." Gerald Bassett, the butler, was anxious to restore discipline and respect after the family's extended week–end stay at Nankilly. Martha looked across to where the drive curved round and saw the coachman's profile above the banked wall confining the deer in the parkland. Gossip ceased as the staff craned to glimpse the family. Who was returning, who going elsewhere? Martha hoped Richard would not be of the returning party. I'll soon know, she thought, as the coach rounded the bend and came to a halt in front of the House.

"Welcome home, my lady, Sir Oliver." Bassett dipped his head in a brief respectful bow as the couple passed. He followed them in, checking the staff's show of respect as he did so. Martha noted that Master Richard did not appear. She smiled her relief at Elspeth.

"Thank you, Bassett, a smart turn out." Sir Oliver nodded to the line of servants. "Are there any developments I should be aware of?"

"Within the household, minor changes have been made to cover Pawley's duties, subject to Lady Trewarren's approval. The estate manager has arranged to be near at hand for a meeting at your convenience, Sir Oliver, but may I hasten to assure you that nothing untoward has occurred during your absence." Bassett paused as Sir Oliver and his wife began to mount the staircase.

"Thank you, Bassett, that will be all. Have our trunks brought up to our rooms."

"May I enquire, Sir, how many for supper tonight? Mrs Crabbe is aiming at eight thirty this evening, if this would be convenient."

"Eight thirty is too early, too early by far. We shall not be at table before nine thirty, and there will be the two of us." Lady Elizabeth swept past her husband into the corridor and entered her dressing room without looking back.

***

Sir Oliver swirled a tot of Jamaica rum in his glass, as he sat deep in thought. What would become of Richard? How would he ever find a suitable wife? Was there any chance of business with Silas after the cock fight? Did he want a pilchard palace built on the edge of the bay? The questions were endless. He relived the interview with George in Silas's study, searching for hidden signs of hope. At least George had agreed. What were his words?

"Out of respect for Miss Sophia I would not wish to harm my cousin yet, out of respect for her, he must learn a lesson he would not forget."

Sir Oliver found it all too confusing, what would he actually do? A part of him agreed that Richard needed a lesson, yet he did not want his son hurt.

"Oliver, we must refurbish this house throughout. It has had no significant improvement since Charles II died. I would feel ashamed to invite any guests here since witnessing the elegance of Silas's residence at Nankilly."

Sir Oliver stood as his wife approached. "Can I offer you a drink before supper, my dear?" He walked to the cabinet.

"A taste of Madeira, thank you, Oliver. I shall summon a designer from Truro to discuss the matter tomorrow. You may leave the detail in my hands, but by yuletide I shall expect a transformation fit to celebrate with a gathering of society from around the county."

"Very well, my dear. Now what are we to make of young Richard? Can you see him ever pleasing a suitable bride? He has yet to outgrow his youthful pride and I have doubt that he ever will. It would perhaps be a mercy if his cousin should wound him, though I hate to see him put at risk."

"That is the very purpose of my scheme, Oliver. If he is present and approves the planned refurbishment, and I pray that will be possible, he will be seen as a man of taste. This should impress Miss Sophia. I intend to ensure our renewal matches the taste of Nankilly." Elizabeth took the proffered glass and sat upright facing her husband.

She is still a handsome woman, he thought, strikingly handsome. I hope this crisis will bring us closer again.

"You are right, of course, my dear." He risked a smile. "That is but one step of many the boy will need to take."

"Supper is served, Sir Oliver. May I take your glass, my lady?" Bassett stood by the door, a white gloved hand extended.

***

Martha stood up from adjusting the table settings, took a step back, assessed the neatness of her handiwork and moved to the side as Bassett ushered Sir Oliver and his lady into the room. At that moment Pollard moved forward to assist Lady Elizabeth to take her seat. He brushed against Martha, who was distracted by Bassett's frown at her clumsiness. There was something in the pressure of Pollard's hand against her that she felt was not solely a steadying move.

"This room is a perfect example, Oliver. It has no warmth, no lightness, no attention to fashionable entertaining. It is charmless enough to depress the most committed of suitors. Do you not agree?" Elizabeth picked at the mutton chops Martha had served her.

"It could do with a freshening up, I suppose. We so rarely entertain these days. I had not given the matter much thought." Sir Oliver drained his glass of claret and held it for Pollard to refill. "I'll ask Bassett to organise something, if it will please you."

"Which it most certainly will not, Oliver; the man will have no idea. I shall take charge of the whole matter myself. I shall go into Truro tomorrow to discover the best house decorators for such a noble property, and arrange a visit with many samples and ideas. Trewarren Manor will move into the nineteenth century as an example to the whole Duchy."

"Let us hope the son and heir lives to inherit, and to honour such devotion to his cause." Sir Oliver pushed his plate aside and stood. "Now, if you will excuse me, Elizabeth, I shall retire to the drawing room for my cigar." He smiled at her as he turned and walked away. Lady Elizabeth sat contemplating his retreating back. Was he preoccupied with Richard's fate, or too set in his ways to give much attention to her plans? No matter, she thought, I am the more determined to transform this house.

Martha had cleared what little the two diners had used. As she returned from the kitchen for a final tidy, Pollard was coming towards her. He had always seemed a remote figure, upright and correct, with no lightness of manner.

"He looks so dashing," Elspeth had said while they waited

for the family, and they had laughed as their fellow servant had lost his starchiness for once. And then that hand, she thought. Accident? Balance? Pure chance or secret message?

"Have you unfinished duties, Baines, that you return to the empty table, or do you seek some pleasurable distraction perhaps?" He stood directly in front of her.

"You offer help with the former or the latter, Pollard?" she said, surprised at herself.

"Let us commence with the latter." He turned her firmly against the corridor wall, her head resting on a sampler between two gilded frames of family hunting scenes. She felt his body press against her. As his mouth moved towards her she turned away and wriggled free. She stood two paces from him.

"I did not invite such intimacy," she said. "Allow me to pass and complete my duties."

"Choose your words with more care, Baines. Twas a clear invitation from an experienced young widow." He strode off and descended below stairs without looking back.

She had felt the strength of his shoulder as her hand had slid under his jacket in the effort to push him away. The firm hard chest as he leaned against her. A quiver ran through her as she remembered Josiah: not his parting but their night of pleasure. If only Pollard had responded more subtly, she thought, but his clumsy way had forced her to deny herself further thoughts of intimacy. She hurried into the dining hall as Lady Trewarren was passing into the drawing room. What was it they had discussed at table, a redecoration of the Manor? That would be some upheaval for them all. And Master Richard? He was in some trouble by all accounts.

XXIX

A light rustle of stiffening horse chestnut leaves preceded a rider feeling his way through unfamiliar tracks. An early morning mist lay across the River Fal as it twisted below Borlase Wood. A shiver ran through Richard's body as he halted, nervous and uncertain, at the edge of an uneven clearing. He remembered a tale his father had told, 'and, as the king walked towards the scaffold, he had been wise enough to don two shirts to prevent a shiver from the morning cold appearing to the gathered crowd to signify fear and cowardice.' His father had always stopped there, not wanting the detail of the execution to distress the lad. But Charles I knew his fate, thought Richard, whereas I shall survive my ordeal, God willing.

There being no sign of his cousin, nor yet of their seconds, he drew a small folded scrap of parchment from a pouch within his coat. Rawdon had given him a sketch of the route to the meeting place. As far as he could judge, he had arrived at the indicated clearing. He was not amused by Rawdon's sketch of a skull at the site of the duel. A note was scrawled and smeared beneath the map, partially concealed by his thumb. The church of St Michael's, across the river a mile or so as the crow flies, struck seven o'clock. A rustle of dry leaves startled him. He turned, in time to see a red squirrel dragging at some ripening beech nuts, but his movement frightened it away. He drew out his fob watch, perhaps it ran ahead of the church chimes. It too registered seven of the clock.

"Good morning, Master. I trust our punctuality has not unnerved you."

Suddenly they were there: Rawdon's voice, disingenuous as ever, and George, with his seafaring second. A young lad from the grounds at Nankilly accompanied Rawdon.

"Thank you for your concern, Rawdon. I assure you I am fully prepared to defend my honour." Richard dismounted and approached the boy from Nankilly. "You are to be my second, I take it, young fellow. I am sure you are experienced in such matters."

"Young Ned is a promising lad, Master Richard. He comes with Mr Galsworthy's blessing, ain't that right, lad?"

"He do, Mr Rawdon, Sir. He do so wish me well of it, Sir." Ned looked down in confusion.

George Trewarren and his boy surveyed the clearing. George had recognised in the lad a sound character behind the fear and had given him care and protection in the early months of pressed service. Back in commission as the French posed a renewed threat, he had ensured the boy was in his crew. At barely twelve years the lad would have given his life for his master. Now George used the opportunity to instruct him in close inspection of the lie of the land as they strolled the length of the clearing, heads close together, boy nodding repeatedly, as young Ned stared, mouth open, and Richard thought again of the martyred king's second shirt.

Rawdon had taken a small wooden table from his saddle bag and set it at the centre of the clearing. As he limped towards it with a wooden case, he called the seconds to him. He released the ornamental catch and opened the polished walnut lid. Ned's mouth opened wider. Two identical pistols, each curved into its own compartment, lay neatly in the velvet-lined box. Two stubby cow horns filled with powder and two black lead balls lay in boxes between the pistols.

"Wogdons," said Rawdon, "five years old, unused, kept dry. They are single-shot flintlocks. Choose your weapon; they are the exact same, one to the other."

George's boy leaned forward and reached for the furthest one against the hinge. He turned and felt it in his hand, balancing its weight. Ned continued gawping until further prompted when he reached awkwardly into the box, lifted the remaining pistol by the barrel, narrowly managing to avoid dropping it. Richard and George stood a little aloof, not catching each other's eye.

"Now lad, tell me, what do you notice about the barrel?"

"Smooth barrelled, Sir. Will take a good shot to hit with this, Sir." The boy held the barrel toward him and looked down it, one eye closed.

"Your'n' be the same, lad?" Rawdon watched Ned follow the boy's example.

"I do think so, Sir, I do."

"Now each take the powder horn in turn, ram the powder

down even and hard. That's it; load the balls." Rawdon watched them carefully. "Now lay them down one each side and withdraw."

"Gentlemen, approach the table if ye please." Both men approached with slow strides, heads high, avoiding each other's gaze. "I not be knowing if ye gentles be familiarised with these here Wogdons?" Neither gave any indication. "Then I do mind ye there be but one lead ball in each, but it be a mighty big'un and could take a man's arm off, if aimed aright, or should I say awrong, gentles?" His sickly smile pleased neither cousin. "I shall ask ye both to stand back to back right level with this table. I s'll count ye through ten paces. When I have spoke the tenth, ye shall turn and fire in yer own time, remembering yer weapons will add a jot of time the selves afore they discharge. Is all clear, gentles?" Both nodded.

"Very well, gentles, take your places, hold your pistols facing up and plain to see. Seconds! Stand ye clear 'til both shots be discharged. After, attend any wound in your master." The seconds retreated to the edge of the trees.

"May he whose honour be sullied be avenged. Gentles, are you set? Then let us count down the paces."

As the count reached ten both men turned. A quiver ran down Richard's arm as he saw George had already turned and aimed. He raised his pistol, the quiver setting the trigger finger in motion, so that his belated pose pretended to aim at George's heart. A small puff of smoke from George's pistol caused Richard to fall to his knees, the crack that followed sent the half inch of lead through his riding boot, gouging through the flesh and muscle of his calf and on into the scrub beyond. He screamed in pain, as his own bullet lodged in a tree away to the left of his prey at thrice the height of a man.

"Ensure his wound is cared for Rawdon. It is nought but a scratch, I fancy. Twas not my intention to harm him more. Inform Miss Sophia, if you will, Rawdon, and good day to you. Come, lad." George placed the weapon on the table, mounted his horse with the boy in front and rode off towards the port. Rawdon turned towards Richard. Ned was bent over him, struggling to remove the blood-filled boot. Richard lay on his back moaning softly. He screamed again as a sudden shaft of pain shot through his leg. Ned fell back, clutching the boot in triumph.

"I am not one of your cows, you clod!"

"Begging yer pardon, Sir, I has to get the boot off, Sir."

Rawdon turned away to conceal a smile.

"Can you use the leg at all, Sir? 'Tes likely it will stiffen, Sir, if it stop bleeding. Here boy, staunch the wound with this old saddle cloth. I thought one or other might have such need." He passed the cloth to Ned, who wrapped it around the wounded leg. Richard was helped to his feet, and placed the pistol in the box as Rawdon held it out to him. A scrap of parchment was trapped under George's pistol. He took it out. Rawdon closed the box, and limped to his mount to place the pistol box in the bags. Richard unravelled the parchment. It was identical to his sketch map, except that the spot was marked with a young woman's face.

XXX

The autumn sunshine lay across the south west front of Trewarren Manor, lightening the grey Cornish granite walls. Lady Trewarren was awaiting the arrival of her latest interior artist. She had set out on the redecoration project with enthusiasm. It is for future generations, she had told herself and any who asked. Yet it was also a means of reasserting her influence within the house and her role as a society hostess of prominence in the Duchy. A man on horseback appeared in the drive. He paused uncertainly, staring up at the manor house before walking his horse round to the tradesman's entrance.

"Mr Wainton to see you, Ma'm. By appointment, he says."

"Show him in, Martha, he is expected."

"Yes, Ma'm." Martha dropped her head respectfully and ushered the visitor into the hall. "Mr Wainton, Ma'm."

"May I offer humble greetings, Lady Trewarren? It is a great pleasure to offer my services to so highly regarded a member of society."

"Welcome, Mr Wainton. I do hope you can match my requirements where others have fallen short. Martha, we are not to be disturbed under any circumstances."

"Yes, Ma'm." Martha bobbed her head and left the hall.

***

"A new lightness, Mr Wainton, that is what I seek. You can observe the dull dreariness of this hall, magnificent in its day, no doubt, but it is a rare day when the sun penetrates the fustian atmosphere. A light, modern transformation, fitting for the dawn of the new century; that is what is required. Our son is a handsome young man of marriageable age and insists on modern décor to appeal to the modern young woman." They had strolled the length of the hall, Mr Wainton weighing up her words against the hall's reality.

"May I ask, Lady Trewarren, if you are talking of a consistent theme of elegance and modernity to include, how can I put this, furnishings more in keeping with the ambience you are aiming for? The desk and chairs for example, no doubt outstanding examples of the early Stuart style, but the slimmer, more elegant style of current furniture would increase the effect you and the young master are seeking."

"But of course, Mr Wainton, of course. Inlay work of the best of current furniture is outstanding, and its slim elegance is quite delightful." At last a craftsman who understands the true importance of my plans, thought Lady Trewarren,

"Thank you, Lady Trewarren, exactly the example I had in mind, and would you want the same theme of lightness, elegance and renewal throughout the whole manor house? Themed links between rooms can be most delightfully effective."

"But of course, Mr Wainton, that was always my intention."

"Then let us draw up a comprehensive programme for

your consideration, Lady Trewarren. We can then make adjustments to suit your wishes, and quote you a cost for works and materials."

"Exactly my own thoughts. Come, let us tour the house so that you may study the full breadth of the project." She led him through to the other public rooms one by one. He noted the windows, the direction of light and the furnishings in each.

***

Martha took a rare opportunity to rest. The Master was out, Lady Trewarren did not wish to be disturbed, and Jim Chapman had taken the visitor's horse across to the stable. It was that time of the afternoon when an occasional chance for a rest occurred. Martha sat chatting with Elspeth, mulling over the traps and attractions of various young men of their acquaintance.

"I hear naught of the free trade of late, has the master finished with the dealing? Brandy still seems there aplenty? I know you are not privy to his business, but you owes your employ to your silence, I heard." Elspeth smiled at Martha.

"That be a sudden change, Elspeth, I'm not minded to talk of it though, truth to tell, I knows nowt of the subject." Martha returned the smile.

A tapping on the outer door surprised them both. Martha rose reluctantly and approached the door. The tapping was repeated with a disturbing urgency. Martha glanced over at Elspeth, who shrugged and nodded. She opened the door and stepped back, hand over mouth.

"Well, if it ain't my little whore, Little Miss Respectable now, by all accounts."

Martha moved to slam the door on the familiar sickly smile. Rawdon moved deceptively quickly. His good leg was planted inside the jamb and his arm braced against the closing door. Martha drew back.

"I have a man who needs your help; he needs it double quick and he needs it secret. That applies to both of yous, if you grasp my meaning." Rawdon's threatening smile never left his face as he looked from one to the other. "Well?" he added sharply.

"But who is it? This man: why burden us with him?" Elspeth stood and moved forward.

"You'll know that soon enough, but betray him and you pay a high price, if you grasp my meaning." he repeated. "Now I need your muscles; come the pair of yous."

They stood together in the doorway, looking along the yard. Rawdon limped across to the servants' privy. He pushed the door half open and summoned the maids to him. They instinctively linked arms and moved forwards. He stood in the half-open space, concealing the subject of his visit. At that moment a low moan emanated from behind Rawdon. The maids stopped in their tracks.

"Hasten, you little whores, or you'll have the master to answer to," said Rawdon in a harsh low whisper. Still arm in arm, they reached the privy. As Rawdon stood aside, Martha looked down, gave a strangled cry and felt her knees about to give way. She clung firmly to Elspeth at an angle behind her.

"Master Richard," she gasped soundlessly. Elspeth, supporting her, moved up and peered over her shoulder. He groaned again.

"He be pale as death," said Elspeth. "What ails him so? I should fetch his mother at once. She'll know the best doctor. She have seen doctors aplenty these last years."

"You'll regret it bitter if you do say a word. He have a hole in his leg, 'tes all. It will heal itself in time if he can but be nursed in secret the while."

"How can we keep him secret here?" Martha was worried about the abyss opening up for them to stumble into. "And why can we not tell Sir Oliver and Lady Trewarren? Surely they will know what best to provide. They too can pay for a doctor which we cannot do."

"I do repeat Master's wishes, he be not one to cross. As I think the young widow knows well." A loud groan and movement on the privy floor cut off Rawdon's threat. "Now let you take him to his room and lay him comfortable in his bed."

***

"A yellow somewhat paler than the primrose flower, and an ivory, the shade of an elephant's tusk, would be my suggestion as the two-coloured theme; both would be light and bright, enhancing the lightness of the sunshine, and the candlelight as necessary. Candle smoke will cause darkening marks after a few months, as will cigar smoke if heavily present. If gentlemen make frequent use of the billiard room, it may require more frequent redecoration than the other rooms of the manor." Mr Wainton paused to allow Lady Trewarren to follow the sweep of his arm and of his plans for such change to centuries of fustiness.

"Excellent, Mr Wainton. When can you begin the work?"

"As agreed earlier, I shall need to map out a plan, Lady Trewarren, calculate quantities, provide a comprehensive costing, and ensure sufficient skilled workmen are available."

"I am impressed with your ideas, Mr Wainton, and impatient for the transformation to begin. Do not delay too long, I pray you. My son becomes impatient to entertain his chosen one and to impress her with the exquisite taste you have promised us."

"I shall hasten with all speed, My Lady. A detailed plan should be with you within the week."

"I shall inform my son accordingly." *If he ever makes an appearance*, she added to herself.

XXXI

Mr Wainton rode back along the track towards Truro feeling very pleased with himself. He felt he had impressed Lady Trewarren mightily with his adventurous yet tasteful ideas. He allowed himself to revel in his sense of satisfaction, knowing that the grim reality of putting the plan together in detail and costing it out would be extremely demanding. Putting the result to Lady Trewarren would require all his self-assurance and panache. Such were his thoughts when he became aware of a figure galloping towards him at speed. In full black cloak, flying scarf and black tricorn hat pulled low over the face, the figure seemed to threaten his very life. He summoned all his courage and rode on in as unconcerned a fashion as he could. The figure showed no sign of slowing down or recognising his presence.

"Good day to you, Sir," he ventured as the figure passed without acknowledgement. He followed the figure's progress briefly before continuing on his way, feeling a mixture of irritation and relief.

***

A frantic banging on the great front door at the manor caused Bassett to shake Pollard awake and follow him up to the hall. Pollard, brushing afternoon sleep from his eyes and straightening his coat, paused before further agitated hammering led Bassett to indicate his duty. As Pollard swung the great door open, he was swept aside by a sinister figure that rushed into the hall and halted in confusion by the grand staircase.

"Where is he? Is he here? Is he greatly harmed? I must see him, where is he?" The voice was high-pitched with concern.

"Excuse me, but to whom am I to offer assistance?" Bassett exuded calm superiority, while Pollard picked himself up and regained his decorum.

"I need to see Richard, Richard Trewarren. I am told he

has been wounded and has returned here to recover," said the intruder more calmly.

"I fear you have been misinformed. Master Richard has not been seen at Trewarren for several days. Pollard!" Bassett indicated that Pollard was to show the visitor out.

"Wait," cried the visitor, throwing off the cloak and removing the hat. "I am Sophia Galsworthy, niece to Mr Silas Galsworthy of Nankilly." She shook out her long fair hair which swirled above her jacket. "I should like to speak to Lady Trewarren, concerning the injury to her son. Would you be so kind as to ask her if that is convenient?"

"Of course, Miss Galsworthy." Bassett, recovering from his confusion, indicated to Pollard, who went into the drawing room.

***

Some fifteen minutes later, Bassett was summoned to the presence of Lady Trewarren. Sophia sat perched on an upright chair, hands in her lap, watching her hostess. Lady Trewarren paced the room, all thoughts of the redecoration forgotten. Surely the last of my children will not be lost, she thought, and offered up a silent prayer. Retaining her outward composure she turned as Bassett entered.

"Bassett, unlikely though it appears, I want us to ascertain the whereabouts of Master Richard by checking with every member of the household and estate staff as to any sighting they may have had. Please do so as a first step and report back to me as soon as you have any news whatever. Go now; this is a most urgent matter. He may be bleeding to death." She turned to hide her face at the thought.

"Yes, M'am, I shall see to it immediately, M'am." Bassett bowed and hurried out.

"I do hope Sir Oliver returns shortly. He may have further news." Lady Trewarren could no longer conceal her distress, and Sophia rose and moved towards her. They held each other in a comforting embrace.

When Bassett returned some time later, they had composed themselves and were sitting in comfortable silence, each in their own thoughts. They stood as he entered.

"Well, Bassett, is there news?"

"Indeed there is, my lady."

"Well, come on, man, tell us at once, a life may be at risk."

"I had almost given up hope, my Lady, as it was very unlikely that such an event could have occurred without us being aware of it. We had questioned everyone in the house at the time."

"Get on with it man; what news is there? Is there any evidence or not?"

"It was the stable lad, Ma'am. He had been attending to Mr Wainton's horse when he heard a noise in the yard. By the time he was free to look into the matter, there was no sign of anyone there but, on closer inspection, he found some blood, quite fresh, by the servant's privy, and from there a trail of bloodstains, about the size of a guinea piece, Ma'am, every few steps across the yard to the scullery entrance." Bassett's solemn expression faced them, as they stared at each other in disbelief.

***

"Pollard, what in hell and damnation gives you the boldness to come crashing into my room without so much as the courtesy of a summons, leave aside a knock."

"I do beg your forgiveness, Sir, I was sent by the butler; we did not believe it, Sir." Pollard stood, unable to control a nervous quivering.

"That wench Baines put you up to this, I'll be bound. I've noticed you've a soft spot for her, the scheming whore. Tell no one, do you hear me, tell no one." Pollard fled.

Richard lay back, exhausted with the effort of his anger. Baines would pay for this; it would be all over the house before long. He would have to suffer the ignominy of it all. Doubts circled in his head. The cock, why did it lose so badly? It had fought with such determination in the previous match. Why had Sophie been so sure it would win? Neither George nor Rawdon seemed surprised or shocked at its loss. Rawdon had vanished almost immediately. You could never trust the man. If only he could corner Rawdon; pin him down; somehow drag the truth out of him. It had all been going so well; he had obviously impressed Silas Galsworthy; Silas had picked up on his business acumen, his involvement in trade, free trade in particular, and could see the way ahead for the pilchard trade.

Not that his father could cope with all these new ideas. Far too set in his ways. Still, if Silas agreed to him marrying Sophie, and he could do a lot worse, the business opportunities were unlimited. And yet,... and yet, had he thrown it all away? He had taken a risk, that's what you did in business, that's where his father was such a burden. He would never be rich. Took too few risks and gave too much to his tenants and workers. He and Sophie would have combined to make the most of land and business capital. Sophie, Sophie,... her image floated before him as he slid into unconsciousness.

**

"Well, Pollard?" Lady Trewarren gave him no chance to voice his concerns to Bassett.

"Master Richard is in his room, Ma'am." Pollard tried to catch the eye of the butler.

"Then let us waste no time in seeing to his needs. Pollard, announce our attendance upon him at once. Come Sophia, you shall accompany me to his room. 'Twill no doubt cheer him more than somewhat to see such a pretty face express so great concern." She took Sophia's hand and led the way to the foot of the staircase. "Pollard, what are you, a tortoise? Make haste, man, there is no time to lose." She waved Pollard ahead and drew Sophia after her up the stairs.

"Master Richard appears to be asleep, Ma'am. He appears to be sleeping deeply, Ma'am." Pollard emerged from the bedroom looking anxious. Lady Trewarren opened the door and drew Sophia into the room with her. Both gasped to see only the top half of Richard's pale face, his eyes closed, blanket just below his nose in the dim light of the curtained four-poster bed.

"Richard," said Lady Trewarren softly, "Richard, are you hurt? Shall I call Dr Chapman?" She paused, but he did not stir. "Richard," she said more loudly, "look who has come to see you. Miss Sophia was very concerned for you. She has ridden all the way from Nankilly alone to see how you are."

He half opened his eyes, saw Sophie and whispered hoarsely, "I am not worthy, I do not deserve her affection, who let her see me like this? Send her away; I failed her, do not humiliate me more, I beg you." He turned away, pulled the bedding over his head, and did his best to conceal the gasp of pain from the awkward movement of his wounded leg.

"He is not himself. Bassett send for the doctor, tell him not to wait on ceremony, we need him urgently." Lady Trewarren was now at the door. Bassett hurried off to obey her command. Sophie was still at the bedside.

"Dear Richard, do not belittle yourself; you were most brave to face up to your cousin to protect my name. I would not wish you to believe I thought the less of you because of your injury. I am deep in admiration and gratitude for your courage." She leaned over the bed in a vain attempt to see his expression. He did not move.

XXXII

"Baines, a word." Pollard looked pale.

"What is it, Pollard? I do have much to do now, even if you d'not."

"Master Richard is discovered." Her hand covered her mouth. "And it be worse, Baines, much worse, for you that is."

"And why should that be? Elspeth and me did nought but help the master. We did nought but follow his wishes, and that were no easy matter, I can tell you."

"Miss Sophia arrived, all got up like a highwayman. Her demands were not for money, but to see Master Richard. They durst not refuse to seek him out. I be truly sorry, Baines, I know I have been disrespectful on occasion, but I meant you no harm, honest, I did not ..."

"Stop, Pollard! For the Lord's sake, stop. You make no sense. No sense at all." Martha raised her hands as if to fend him off. "Now slow you down, man, and make your point. I ain't ever seen you so beside yourself."

"Baines, Martha, he blames you for telling against his order. He says you will be dismissed at once and word against you spread as far as he can reach." Pollard stared at the floor.

"But when he knows the truth … "

"He ain't of a mind to consider, Martha, he be deeply riled." Pollard looked into her eyes.

"You ain't used my name afore, Pollard. What do bring this on of a sudden?"

"His threats, Martha, his threats have brought out a hidden affection in me. I d'not want you out in disgrace." He paused. "There, now I have spoke it."

"I must speak to Mr Bassett this instant, tell him truly what happened: Elspeth were witness too." Martha hurried into the corridor. Remembering Pollard, she turned and thanked him before seeking out Elspeth and Mr Bassett.

***

"I dare not bleed him more, Lady Trewarren, I do not think he has the blood to give. He is feverish; the wound is red and swollen: it feels exceeding hot. I shall return tomorrow, for he faces his crisis tonight. If he is calmer tomorrow, he will be over the worst and I can advise on further treatment. If he is restless and hot still tomorrow, I very much fear the leg will have to come off below the knee; if that be the case the sooner the better. I shall warn the barber surgeon in Truro; he's the one I favour in these matters. He is deft with knife and saw. Have some tar ready to heat for the stump. Such a wound will need to be cauterised and sealed as fast as may be if worse is to be prevented. I shall bid you good day now Lady Trewarren, and put arrangements in hand." With a brief nod, Dr Chapman strode out of the room. Elizabeth Trewarren sank into a chair, lay back and closed her eyes. It is too much, she thought, too much to happen in so short a time: Mr Wainton's enthusiasm, the disguise of Sophia, Richard's injury, and Oliver not even back from chasing around the countryside to share the burden. What was that? She opened her eyes to see Bassett hovering inside the door.

"Begging your pardon, Ma'am. May I have a word?"

"Enough for one day, Bassett, let it keep until Sir Oliver returns." She lay back and closed her eyes.

"The servants are very concerned, Ma'am, they are proposing a delegation. I forbade it Ma'am, agreeing to speak on their behalf."

"Thank you, Bassett. I ask you to tell them that Sir Oliver will be best placed to answer them. He will return shortly, no doubt." Let him shoulder some of the day's troubles, she thought, it's about time he faced up to his responsibilities.

"Very well, Ma'am." Bassett retreated below stairs.

***

"My dear Elizabeth, I am sorry to be so late. It has been nothing but delays and frustrations all day and, to cap it all, one of the horses went lame; damned badger sett."

"Oliver, your absence has been a great frustration to me, there have been ..."

"If you'll excuse me, my dear, I shall go and change for dinner, wash some of this frustration away. I am sure your news will wait a little longer. I'll join you for a drink before we eat."

"Oliver!" She raised her voice but he was gone. She sighed, leaned back and closed her eyes. He can navigate Bassett and Pollard in ignorance, she thought.

Dinner was served as usual but neither Pollard nor Martha waited to further assist. Oliver, freshened up but weary at heart, contemplated his wife across the table.

"He is restless in his sleep still, Oliver. I hope and pray he needs not to lose his leg. How could his own cousin wound him so?"

"It is the nature of a duel, Lisbet; a man once challenged must guard his honour or forever feel the shame. I fear young Richard was too hot-headed. Being shamed before Sophia, and Silas for that matter, was too much to bear. Yet I would not have wished such a fate upon him for all his youthful temper."

They lapsed into silence. Elizabeth picked at her food, eating little. Oliver ate and drank with gusto, restoring the energy lost through his endeavours and frustrations. Elizabeth retired to the drawing room, leaving Oliver to his brandy and cigar. Where the devil's Pollard? he thought, he knows damn well I like a brandy and cigar after a day out with the hunt.

"Ah Bassett, just the man! Where the devil is Pollard? I'm waiting for my brandy and cigar."

"I'll see to it personally, Sir Oliver, but might I take the liberty of a word on behalf of the staff? Bassett stood straight and correct at his side.

"I'm more likely to give 'em the answer they seek if I have a cigar and a brandy to hand, Bassett."

"I'll see to it at once, Sir Oliver." Bassett left the room with unaccustomed haste, and returned moments later.

"I trust the '75 will be satisfactory, Sir?" he said, placing glass and carafe on the table. He clipped the cigar and offered it to Sir Oliver. Once the brandy had been approved and the first cigar smoke drawn in and exhaled, Sir Oliver invited Bassett to speak his piece.

"He is a young man in distress," was his response, "and no doubt delirious also. Let us see how he is in the morning. Things will be clearer then. If necessary I'll have a word. Tell your colleagues not to fret. Meanwhile, service should continue as is customary. Make that clear."

"Yes, Sir Oliver. Thank you. I will ensure your wishes are carried out."

The foolishness of the staff is very trying at times, he thought, drawing on his cigar.

***

"And how is the patient this morning, Lady Trewarren? I trust he has enjoyed a comfortable night?"

"He is wallowing in pain, sweat and anguish, Dr Chapman; it is difficult to determine which condition dominates, though he descends into deliriums, which are cause for concern."

"And his temperature, Lady Trewarren, is he still in fever?"

"You had best examine him for yourself, doctor."

Red-faced and delirious, Richard tossed and turned restlessly. The doctor lifted the bedding away to reveal the suppurating wound.

"I think the barber surgeon should be called without delay. I have warned him of the case. He comes prepared. Have you the pitch ready to heat for cauterising the stump?" He turned to Sir Oliver, who had entered the room. Lady Trewarren's anxious face looked on from behind his shoulder.

"No!" screamed Richard from the bed, suddenly coherent. "Such ancient methods are for pirates and sea dogs. Give me brandy, brandy!" he shouted. His mother moved swiftly to the bedside and smoothed his forehead with a comforting hand. His father, still adjusting to the realities of his son's situation, turned to the doctor.

"Is there really no other way, Chapman? It's only a bullet hole, when all is said."

"It is mightily inflamed, Sir Oliver, as you can see. The enflamed blood turns to the thick green poison you see oozing into the hole. In no time the gangrene will set in and spread throughout his bones. The barber surgeon in Truro is a skilled man; near to half his patients survive the loss of a limb. Besides which, winter will soon be upon us. The blood is calm in autumn and well suited to operations. Once winter comes,

Keith McClellan

blood loses its vivacity, its life force, so to speak, with which to animate the body."

"No, Father, no! Tell him no. Give me brandy. Send me to London. There are good surgeons there, if such is necessary." Richard struggled to sit up. His mother placed pillows and cushions behind him. "Brandy!" he shouted again.

"We shall discuss this further, Dr Chapman, and will inform you of our decision, but I think you may stand your surgeon down for the moment. Thank you for your prompt attendance."

"Very well, Sir Oliver, I am at your service, but delay will not aid recovery. Winter will lessen his chances greatly. I bid you good day, my lady, Master Richard." He nodded and left the room.

"Some brandy, Father, if you can spare it. In London, I understand, they bathe a wound such as mine with brandy. It is soothing and lessens inflammation."

"Is that so? Are you sure it is not the drunken haze of consuming that brings temporary relief?"

"I am sure, Father, though I am sure also that a modest mouthful or two would further aid a lessening of pain."

"You are suddenly reanimated, Richard." The relief in his mother's voice was clear. "Your father will send for the brandy, will you not, Oliver?" At his nod Elizabeth continued, "What is all this about London? The journey would surely kill you if the surgeon does not. Ten days on those roads, in and

156

out of dubious hostelries, and where would you stay?"

Oliver had left the room and sent for the brandy. Richard seemed to have exhausted himself and lay back. "Father's schooner," he muttered. "If the sea is calm I need never leave the bunk."

"Let us see the effect of the brandy," said his mother, stroking his forehead before rising and leaving the room.

***

"Baines, no doubt Bassett has already informed staff of his instructions from Sir Oliver." Lady Trewarren paused. "However, he may not have had an opportunity to convey a personal matter. I refer to a matter which must remain confidential. As you are aware, Master Richard is quite determined that you betrayed his trust. Sir Oliver and I understand the quandary you were placed in, but if our son is to recover fully and swiftly he must be assured that you will not be in our employ when the family returns from London. You will be paid until the end of this month in the expectation that you will ensure your duties are meticulously carried out until a new housekeeper takes up the post next month."

"But Ma'am ... "

"There is no discussion to be had, Baines. Our son's health is our one concern here. Bassett has been instructed to keep the matter confidential and I am quite sure you will do the same. You may return to your duties." There was an air of excitement in the kitchen as Martha entered.

157

Keith McClellan

"London," Pollard was saying. "Why I never thought I'd ever go further than Truro, or maybe Falmouth, but London, why 'tes beyond belief, Elspeth, do you not think?"

"I am afeared of it. I have never thought on such travelling, and out to sea an' all. I can't be swimming if the boat do sink now." Elspeth looked nervous, had Martha been in a mood to observe such things. She said nothing, however, and avoided their eyes.

Jacob Winnard entered and asked for Bassett, who appeared at that moment.

"Jacob, a message needs to go to Nankilly; Sir Oliver is composing it at this minute. At high tide the coach will take the family to the mooring. The schooner sails without delay. Master Richard must reach London as soon as possible." Bassett turned to Pollard.

"Collect Sir Oliver's message whilst Mr Winnard has a horse saddled and instructs a rider."

Martha stood, uncomprehending, as the excitement at the unaccustomed bustle developed around her. Bassett seemed to be attracting her attention. She blinked herself back into consciousness and followed his indication that they would talk later.

XXXIII

Molly looked exhausted. Henny's crying rose to a roar and faded to a quiet sob.

"Molly, what ails you that you do look so pale?" Martha

picked up the bawling child who paused, stared into her face and howled again.

"Sister! What pleasure to see you, the more so for the surprise." Her smile twisted into a grimace as she turned, grasping her stomach.

"Why, Molly, what troubles you? You are not yourself at all. Are you with child again so soon?"

"I fear so, Sister, but this'un be more ockard than the last."

"But Molly you should not be pressing the oil so; 'tes work for a woman in full strength. Thomas d'not aid you?"

"'Tes woman's work, he says. 'Tes enough he do risk all to catch 'em and trade 'em. 'Twould make him the laughing stock in the taverns, he says. I would not want that for him, now would I?" She winced and grasped her stomach again.

"Come sit, woman, leave that for now. How many weeks are you gone?"

"'Tes but the third month yet. This un'll be trouble, make no mistake. Enough of me; what brings you? 'Tes not the month end."

Martha related all that had happened, noting that Molly struggled to respond, such was the pain writhing within her. She gave Henny to her mother to suckle while she cleaned and tidied the house and prepared a frugal meal for the two of them.

"Martha, you were sent by the good Lord, I do swear; I

know not what state I should suffer had you not come today."

"Still, small recompense for the comfort you gave me in my time of trouble, Sister. Where should we be if we d'not comfort each other? Family ties be all our strength in these trials the Lord sends us."

"You b'aint back to the Methody crowd, Martha?"

"What make you ask it? I haven't been near them since Josiah, nor shall neither."

"You speak with their words, my dear Sister. You speak with their words. You have troubles enough from what you say. You needs help that the rector can't give, not as he be uncle to that dog, Richard Trewarren."

Martha walked slowly down to the sea shore; should she stay with Molly and see her through her troubles? Should she call the midwife? But what of Bassett, and Pollard? No, forget Pollard, trouble enough without more heart searching. Bassett would surely understand her dilemma. She could return to the house for some days and ensure all was in order. Would she be required to guide her replacement in the ways of the household? Not least the fear that pressed upon her. By what means was she to support herself?

She stood and walked towards the track up the cliff to survey her cottage. Could she live in it now? It was some months since she had entered it.

"There's my little widow, if I'm not mistook." Recognising the voice, she could not bring herself to ignore it. She turned but said nothing.

"I hear you are cause of much distress, my pretty one." Rawdon's smile sickened her. "But all is not lost my little harlot, indeed, your saviour stands before you." He positioned himself directly in front of her, barring her way.

"Let me pass," Martha demanded.

"Come now, my pretty one. You would not scorn my help in time of need; 'twould be a foolish woman who did so; a foolish woman, alone and friendless in the world."

"You be no friend to me, Rawdon, you be the cause of all my troubles. Step aside now. I must return to my cottage."

He allowed her to pass, shouting after her, "It is but a wreck now, whore. You'll find no comfort there. I stand ready to offer such when you need it. And you will, my little whore, you will."

His words surged into her mind as she sat in her rocky refuge. No Josiah now to rescue her. Her cottage was a broken shell, emptied of all but the frame of the bed. Roof timbers cracked, door flapping in the stiff breeze, broken furniture, what little there was, dust covered. She had wept as she poked through the detritus scattered across the caked mud of the dry floor. She sat in her retreat of old. She had sat here with Will'm in their happier days, and without him to escape the violence of their later quarrels. She had first seen Josiah from here. She had witnessed Rawdon's injury through the mist from the track near-by. What did the crippled monster have in mind? What evil scheme festered in his cesspit thoughts? No, she told herself, no, have no dealings with that devil. She brushed herself down and set off briskly towards the Manor. Bassett would help her, she was sure.

PART 2

1799

I

Lady Trewarren could hold back no longer. Her face in the mirror of the new Chippendale dressing table, of which she had been so proud only a few weeks before, crumpled into uncontrollable sobs. How could he do it to them, poor dependable Oliver, oblivious to fashion, engrossed in his hunting; so committed to his estate duties and the free trade cause? How could he get himself killed? Killed! A new burst of sobbing left her gasping for breath. Hadn't she suffered enough losing her daughters? She had let it be known he had been thrown by his horse. It was a convenient explanation.

It was that white costume of Sophia's that had finally broken her resolve; had driven her up to her room with an incoherent excuse. No one could doubt its significance: a wedding delayed, a virginity prolonged. Though she had doubts about the latter. The cynical thought revived her spirits somewhat before another depressed her. Richard was now lord of the manor; he would become Sir Richard Trewarren; she was now the dowager. They had no dower house. She would be moved to a smaller room far from the centre of things. Richard would be the master. Would she face a battle with Sophia once they were married? Would she face isolation in her grief? She had few friends in whom she could confide. There was Silas, of course, but he would take Sophia's side surely? That he doted on his surrogate daughter was obvious to all.

Lady Trewarren paused at the landing rail and gazed over the crowd below. Still pale, she needed no artificial aids to take the glow from her face. Her eye was drawn to a circle of people paying admiring attention to the lively beauty of Sophia; the plain pale whiteness of her costume contrasting with the vivid animation of face and gesture.

"... so light and airy," Sophia's arm made a wide sweeping gesture, "such a contrast to one's expectations from the dark granite of earlier times: such a modern style and so unexpected in so traditional a family manor; a tribute to Sir Oliver and Lady Trewarren." Her eye caught a movement on the sweep of the staircase.

"Will you become the new Lady Trewarren, Miss Sophia?" came a voice from the circle of admirers.

"That is both indelicate and inappropriate on such a sad occasion," said Sophia.

"But your white dress, Miss Sophia? Your wedding has surely been subject to only brief delay?" insisted the voice.

"It is true that the untimely death we remember today has overwhelmed any joy we may have hoped for from the confirmation of our betrothal, but we think only of Sir Oliver's family, of Lady Trewarren and my dear Richard, both of whom have suffered grievous loss." Sophia moved forward and the circle parted as Lady Trewarren descended the stairs and moved forward to embrace her.

"Thank you, my dear, for your kind and sensitive words."

"Oh my lady; forgive me, I did not see you there. I trust you are composed?" Sophia eased herself gently from the embrace. They linked arms and moved among the guests in a show of mutual affection and friendship.

***

"Father will be sorely missed, of course, but he would not have wanted to stand in the way of our happiness." Richard had eased Silas into a corner on the periphery of the gathering.

"But my dear Richard, you must avoid undue haste. Your father was a highly respected man; an example to all in the county. If you wish to maintain the good name of the family, and it would be a costly reputation to forfeit, then it is too early to discuss detailed plans. Besides, I shall want only the happiest, brightest nuptials for my dear Sophie. Your mother, too, will need time to grieve."

"You are right, of course. My dear father's tragic end demands a respectful pause. Yet the release from his over-cautious business approach will be a blessing, as I'm sure you will agree."

Silas put his empty glass to his mouth and swallowed hard. His eyes scanned the room.

"Will you be so kind as to excuse me, Richard? I see that

Sophie is attempting to attract my attention."

"By all means, I think we understand each other." Richard watched as Silas threaded his way through the conversing groups towards the virginal white figure on the far side of the hall. His weakened leg had begun to ache; he needed a drink. As he was about to summon Pollard, the rector touched his arm.

"Uncle Francis, I was on my way to find you," said Richard. "I wanted to thank you for your very thoughtful remembrance of my poor dear father. I know my mother was deeply touched. Indeed she was extremely grateful. His tenants and the wider community shared in our grief, as the congregation's response around the Trewarren vault at the burial bore witness."

"Thank you, Richard. Your mother has been similarly generous in her opinions. But Oliver is now safe in the care of the Lord and your mother has asked me to arrange a family conference to consider the future in the light of Oliver's death. She has some concerns about the various responsibilities and duties that will fall on you. I would like also to establish in your mind what is expected of you as lord of the manor, in terms of personal qualities and responsibilities, if your father's reputation and achievements are not to be sullied."

"Such a meeting is hardly necessary, I think. I have spent twenty years observing my father, both at leisure and in the performance of his duties."

"I hardly think that ten years of childhood, and three years of profligate behaviour in London have enabled you to give serious and mature consideration to these matters, and there is no doubt that your mother is of the same opinion."

"Let us not fall out on such a day. I will discuss the matter with Mother at an opportune moment and I've no doubt she will inform you of the outcome. Ah, there is Pollard at last. Pollard, a cognac."

With a brief nod, Francis moved through the thinning crowd and drew Lady Trewarren away from Silas and his daughter.

"I fear we have cause for concern, Elizabeth," he said.

II

As Martha stirred the white lead mixture that Rawdon had told her to prepare and apply she smiled to herself, remembering how she and Elspeth had giggled over the mashing of Lady Trewarren's whitening paste. She could still see Elspeth, half exposed tongue seized between firm red lips, as she squashed the paste against the side of the bowl and watched it ooze from behind the curved back of the shallow wooden spoon.

"Lady Trewarren needs a lighter tone to her face," Elspeth had said in reply to Martha's question." She claims that the country air gives her too high a colour. It be so pleasing to see her enjoying life in society again." Elspeth had smeared a little of the paste on the back of her hand. "That should suit her ladyship."

"What is that earthy clod?" Martha was pointing at a ceramic pot next to the white lead powder jar as Elspeth took another small bowl and spooned some white lead paste into it.

"Pollard ain't around?"

"Pollard? Oh! No, not that clod." They had both burst out laughing.

"It's carmine," said Elspeth. "It adds a little rouge." She took the lump, scraped at it with the flattened spoon handle and stirred it into the white lead paste she had put aside. "Lady Trewarren says it gives a little life to her cheeks."

How much carmine did she add? Martha thought back to the reddened paste that Elspeth had been mixing. Lady Trewarren's pale face and rouged cheeks had been discreetly achieved. Rawdon would expect a bolder effect. She painted her face with the white lead paste he had supplied. She mixed in some carmine and rouged her cheeks. They looked bolder certainly. More carmine deepened the reddened paste; a misshapen rosebud blossomed below her nose. She touched a tacky finger on the tiny black satin heart that Rawdon had left.

"Place it near the side of your mouth," he had said, "like the true whore you are." Lady Trewarren had not worn one of these. Elspeth had not suggested awareness of such a thing. Martha placed it where she thought Rawdon had meant, but a glance in the mirror showed a dirty looking insect perched on a cringing rosebud. If Rawdon was not satisfied, she did not care, so long as he did not thrash her, and so far he had done no more than satisfy his lewd nature.

The men she had served in the first few days had not been in the least interested in her make-up or the gaudy red dress with its high waist and low neckline. No more than boys, eager but clumsily lacking in the ways of love, they had been far too impatient for such niceties. Rawdon had retained all their payments for rental and provision of make-up materials. He seemed to specialise in blooding young lads in the ways of love and using her as the means. He rented an upstairs room in a crumbling wooden tenement with wattle and daub walls and a thatched roof, green with mould, brown and white from the seagulls and pigeons that pecked at it and fought over it as a source for nest building. The room was divided into three: thin board covered by cheap colourless linen drapery separated the first two rooms and a further wall across the ends created a corridor to the longer room at the end. A tawdry curtain hung over each doorway.

"That's it, lad, lost it yet? Good lad, just checking my new lady be doin' her duty and makin' a man of you." Her first lad, over-eager and lacking experience, was mortified to discover Rawdon had pulled the curtain aside to observe his embarrassment.

"For your own protection, my pretty one, if a client be too drunken or violent, as they oft times are," he had smirked when she questioned the curtains. More like the meanness of a greedy skinflint, she thought, if the rest of the set-up was any guide.

The far room was occupied by an experienced woman and had space for a chair and a primitive tin washstand in addition to the bucket provided in the other rooms. Horsehair beds were provided in all three rooms, damp and itchy like the stables they came from. The stench from the buckets and the beds was overpowering like the estuary at low tide, or a piggery overdue for a clean out; Martha felt herself choking whenever she entered her room.

How had it come to this? she asked herself. Only now, after a week of this harlotry, had she even begun to accept the reality of her situation. Her mind went back to Molly. She could see her sister's twisted, suffering face; hear the breathless screaming, hoarse from day-long agony, as the dead boy was forced from her womb. The village midwife's methods were no comfort. Only when Molly's muscles weakened and relaxed through exhaustion was the dead child drawn out. The midwife tried to staunch the blood. Molly was unconscious and pale as death itself. Martha had shared her sister-in-law's agony, had nursed and comforted her, prepared meagre meals for Thomas as well as trying to entice Molly to eat. She had pressed the remaining pilchards and casked the oil. Henny had been difficult too. Martha had felt for her as her mother, recently so lively and active, was now so lethargic. Henny did not understand. She cried and shouted, and would not be consoled.

"Can't you shut that kid up?" shouted an exhausted Thomas, "fine sister you are!"

Another time, he had been drinking and cornered Martha.

"You think you do your sister's work? Well there's one job she was good for. You ain't even offered yet. Now's your chance." His lips parted in a sickly smile, a trickle of fluid ran through the rough stubble on his chin. The foul smell of ale and whisky breathed into her face as he pinned her against the stair rail. She could hear Molly protesting feebly behind him. With a supreme effort she pressed forward, and moved suddenly sideways. Off balance, he slid to the ground, reaching in vain for her leg. The thickness of the sacking apron and woollen dress acted like chain mail. His hand slid uselessly away, his head bounced against the stair base, and vomit pumped out over his woollen jacket, already suffused in stale fish and seaweed.

"Molly needs me," she had said, rushing to her side. Henny began yelling and the moment passed. Thomas had crawled to the door and retched loudly into the dusty track. Did she do right to leave the next day? Should she have left her sister-in-law? Little Henny? Were they safe with Thomas? Would she have been safe if she'd stayed? She wasn't much better placed as she was. If only Bassett had found her a position.

III

"Baines!" Rawdon pulled aside the curtain, interrupting her thoughts. "Have you painted your face yet? Oh by God's eyes, you've the beak of a parrot. Your brows are non-existent, and the head of a cockroach creeps out of your mouth. I wouldn't want you like that if I'd been cast away on a desert island for twenty years."

"What would you have me do, Mr Rawdon, Sir? I am not used to such paintin' up of my face."

"Whiten that nose some, and strengthen those eyebrows to match your mouse-coloured hair. Here!" He drew a dead mouse from a pouch on his belt, and held it up by the tail.

Martha recoiled instinctively. "We'll skin this little beauty." In her stunned silence, he left in search of Florence and a tanner's scraper.

Martha's mind went back to what might have been. She applied the white lead tentatively to her nose, and remembered that last visit to Trewarren Manor. She had entered the kitchen by the very door that Rawdon had dragged the wounded Richard through some eighteen months before. The staff had surrounded her, greeting her warmly. Pollard had been most attentive. She had seen the light of hope in his grey blue eyes, and his tentative smile. Elspeth had rushed forward and hugged her, squealing with delight. Bassett had approached with some apprehension.

"There is no chance of a return, I'm afraid, Baines. Master Richard has fully recovered, and is more than ever in the house these days, with Miss Sophia often in attendance. You know they are to be married?"

"I did not, but I wish them well," Martha had said. "But you did say, Mr Bassett, that should a maid or house servant situation come to your attention you would put in a word on my behalf. I came to ask if such had occurred." She could see from his expression that it had not.

"Nothing so far, I'm sorry to say. But I will send word if I hear of a suitable situation. Are you still with your sister-in-law?"

"I'm afraid not. I have nursed her through a time of ill health but I cannot impose upon her further. I shall return to the cottage on the hill, such as it is." As Martha turned to leave, she noted glances of consternation between Elspeth and Pollard,

"Won't you sit for a while longer and join us in a cup of tea," said Elspeth.

"Your cottage suffered much damage in the winter storms," added Pollard. "You may not find it habitable."

"I am sure it is no worse than the usual winter wear and tear. I have nowhere else so I must make do," smiled Martha. Conversation turned to local gossip, until Martha rose and said that she must reach her cottage before nightfall and the sun was already low over the Lizard.

At least she had seen out the winter, she thought, as she walked up the cliff path towards her ruined hut. The warmer spring air, the smell of the newly flowering gorse, the saxifrage bursting out, all the cowslips and primroses, clover and buttercups had her smiling in spite of her problems. She breathed in the scented spring air with deep conscious breaths, looked out to sea, deep blue in the cloud-free sunshine. Small flags, a few hundred yards apart, fluttered in the breeze, but whether they indicated a row of crabbing cages or a smuggler's crop she did not know.

The image of the damaged hut had softened in her mind over the winter, but as she approached she saw that the storms had torn further into the fabric of the ruin. She had convinced herself that she could, over time, restore a semblance of a shelter for herself, sleeping in the open over the long summer months. This dream was destroyed the moment she arrived. There were signs that nature's efforts had been assisted; she could make out axe marks on some of the beams. It was beyond repair. She poked about within the rotting beams and general detritus for a time, before she accepted the reality that faced her.

Back at the bay among the fishing boats moored by the harbour wall, she pondered whether to return to the Methodists and seek their help, or to try an approach to the rector. Sitting on a step by the harbour wall, contemplating her fate, she heard the voice again.

"I can help you, my little whore, when you are ready."

"Mr Rawdon, Sir, I fear your price would be far beyond my means."

"You can be a spiteful little bitch, but I sense desperation in your eyes."

"I sense depravity in yours, Sir. Perhaps you can correct me in that."

"Why how may I do that, my little whore?" Rawdon could not suppress his sense of triumph.

"I am in need of temporary accommodation and employment. Do you know of a household that might take me on?" There, she thought, I have lost it now.

"Indeed I do, my pretty one, indeed I do. I have a pleasant little room in Truro available this very night. Let us take the coach that leaves within the hour."

"What duties are involved in such a post? Am I to be a

maid and if so to whom? I would prefer housekeeper, as I have experience in the role."

"You will encompass all those roles, my little whore. There will be much housekeeping, and certainly you will be maid to many and will earn good pay for your services." Rawdon had smiled his sickly smile again.

"And who is to be my employer?" she had asked, when they entered the tenement.

"Florence will explain," he said

"Florence!" he shouted. "Here girl, I need you." A grotesque head and shoulders appeared round the far curtain. A pyramid of false hair was collapsing over one ear like a windblown sheaf of wheat, a huge claret rosebud gave a false pucker to the chapped lips and smallpox pits emerged from under curling black beauty spots. Neck and shoulders were bare.

"How can I 'elp you, Mr Rawdon, Sir? You're a bit previous to what you promised." Her smile distorted her rosebud into a bloody flesh wound.

"We have a new tenant, Florence. Young Martha here is to occupy the first room." He indicated the curtain on his left. "Make her welcome, Florence. Show her what's expected. You do understand me, my dear, I'm sure."

"'Course I will, Mr Rawdon. Come along, Martha, my dear; nothing to worry about. You'll get along fine with those rosy country looks. We'll have to pale you down a little bit though, dearie, and that hair, well that'll need some work and no mistake." Martha cringed from the inviting hand, but made her way hesitantly along to Florence with an impatient shove from Rawdon.

"What do the household duties involve?" she asked. Florence looked puzzled. Seeing Rawdon failing to hide his amusement, she joined him in hearty laughter but said no more.

And so it was that, less than a full week later, she was preparing herself for inspection by Florence, having only had the inexperienced young lads as visitors. A bell clanged loudly in the distance. As Florence emerged from her room and went to the window in the corridor, Martha peeped out of the doorway and joined her. Even the thumping and gasping from the middle room ceased after the crier had begun.

"What do he tell of then?" said a half-naked woman, peering from behind her own door curtain.

"Admiral Nelson, sommat. What was that? Victory? Wait, he do come nearby now."

"O yea, O yea, hear me loyal citizens, hear me. Admiral Nelson led the fleet to a great victory over the enemy last August. Napoleon is defeated at sea. The victorious fleet returns to Plymouth this day."

"Well, Mr Rawdon do owe us a drink o' rum for that I do reckon." said Florence.

IV

George Masters spread the great estate map across the library table, smoothed it with his ink-stained hands and placed paper weights on each corner. Lady Trewarren moved to the chair he had drawn up to the table. She sat upright, her shoulders back against the chair, making no attempt to study the map. Her face was pale with the merest hint of rouge; the lines around her eyes showed her age more clearly than before the loss of Oliver; her long dark hair, pulled back severely, had lost its sheen. Richard and Francis peered over her shoulders. Masters moved round to face them, viewing the map upside down.

"So where was Father killed?" asked Richard. Masters glanced warily at Lady Trewarren, who nodded.

"It was on the track above Polhendra, Sir, near the bridge. We are not sure what scared the horse," he glanced again at Lady Trewarren, "but his body was found just here." He indicated with his index finger a point on the Polhendra side of the stream. Richard moved to the side and bent over the map, tracing the route with his own finger. Masters nodded his agreement at Richard's enquiring glance.

"Forgive my curiosity, Masters; now may we move on?" He glanced at his mother, who did not meet his eye. "Mother? Uncle? Shall we move on?"

"By all means," said Francis. Elizabeth said nothing.

"The accounts are at your service, Sir, whenever you wish. Along the shore here," he traced a line where the blue of the sea met the green of the land, "are some few households, whose pilchard fishing provides a secure living. Sir Oliver has loaned them capital in the past to equip themselves for the trade. They have been able to repay the capital as well as their rent over a five-year period. Some are of assistance with free trade, but Sir Oliver never put pressure on them to do so."

"I understand therefore that, as estate manager, you are privy to all Sir Oliver's interests?" Masters acknowledged this with a nod. "It seems clear that you have revealed an area where our income may be increased, have you not?" Richard looked sideways at Francis, but his uncle was studying the map. "What do we own in the harbour area down in the village? I know we work the pilchard trade there."

"Quite true, Master Richard, Sir. Sir Oliver ensured that our tenants benefited from their work and skill with catching, pressing and salting the pilchards as well as producing the oil. As such, they were willing helpers with the free trade arrangements."

"And the boats?"

"As you know, Sir, we part-own a number of sea-going vessels. I mean those suited to trade with Guernsey, Brittany and the Middle Sea ports. The traders of Naples are very partial to our pilchards." He smiled across at them.

"Why do we part-own them? Surely, as with the schooner, we would be better to buy the other partners out and gain all the profits for ourselves. Besides, a monopoly is bound to be to our advantage."

"Richard, your father and Mr Masters worked together on this, and all their experience led them to conclude that the current arrangements best met everyone's needs," said Lady Trewarren, glancing up at Francis.

"Needs and interests are not the same thing, Mother. There is a difference, albeit one that Father failed to grasp."

"If I may, my lady? In this particular case, Sir Oliver and I were in agreement that these arrangements did best meet the estate's interests."

"Thank you, Masters. I am sure you are right. Now perhaps we can delay consideration of the farming tenants and their contribution until tomorrow. I have some letters to write." Lady Trewarren rose and waited for Richard to ease her chair back.

"Certainly, my lady, I shall be at your service whenever you wish to continue," said Masters, a note of relief in his voice.

***

"I shall ride into Truro, Mother. I wish to see Sophie and speak with her father. If I do not return tonight, I shall most certainly be back for luncheon tomorrow afternoon."

"If you must, my dear, but do be sensible of the respect your father's death demands."

"Yes, Mother, but the month end approaches. Father would not want us brooding like this. Masters, see that Chapman prepares my mount, will you?"

"Certainly, Master Richard, I'll see to it at once." Masters nodded and moved towards the door.

"Oh, and Masters?"

"Yes, Master Richard, Sir?"

"I am no longer 'Master Richard'. I am 'Sir Richard'."

"I beg your pardon, Sir Richard." He eased his way out of the room in some embarrassment and returned to the Estate Office. He is not his father's son, he thought.

Nodding his respects, Richard hurried from the room, his weaker leg causing an uneven stride, which detracted somewhat from the image of lordly dominance he had attempted to convey. He summoned Pollard to help him prepare himself for his visit to Sophie. Lady Trewarren and the rector moved into the drawing room and ordered tea.

"I must apologise for that lack of sensibility. He is not himself: I fear he feels it manly not to display his grief. But then I am so deep in grief myself that tears are never far away." Lady Trewarren wiped away a tear from her pale, drawn face.

"I quite understand, my dear, I have no desire to tax you further at present, yet I cannot forbear to say that I continue to fear for the wellbeing of our local populace should Richard not emerge from this hasty, narrow manner. He will not long be given the benefit of the affection in which Sir Oliver was held. That, after all, was based on dependability and trust. It pains me to say it, but these are not qualities with which my nephew is richly endowed." Elizabeth gave a strangled sob, reached a gloved hand to her mouth and then she was weeping, openly and freely, unable to hold back her misery.

"I am so sorry, my dear. Please forgive me; I should not have spoken so critically."

"You are right! I must face it." A fresh burst of tears drowned any further words until Pollard brought in the tea, served it and departed. Francis sipped at the sweetened liquid in the delicate Chinese cup. It was always a pleasure to drink from such refined crockery. The Chinese design, with exotic flowers in reds and blues curling around the bowl of each cup, gave the manor an air of sophistication, which must not be put at risk from the foolishness of young Richard, he thought, sipping again from his cup. Noting that Elizabeth had ignored her tea and was weeping silently, lost in her own grief-stricken reverie, he rose quietly, leaned over, patted her shoulder, and offered her solace at the rectory, or indeed in the church, should she feel so inclined.

V

Rawdon returned with two thin strips of the mouse skin.

"A good match, my pretty one, a very good match," he said, holding the strips between finger and thumb towards her face. "What good fortune they suit your hair so well." He stepped towards her, intending to press one against her eyebrow. Her arm shot up to fend him off. He lost balance and grasped at the bed-post, releasing the false eyebrow as he did so. Martha, momentarily shocked, did not anticipate the fierce slap to her head. She reeled back onto the bed, crying out in surprise and pain.

"Now, find it, you saucy whore, and apply both to your eyebrows before I punish you proper." He hobbled out and she could hear him shouting at Florence.

Martha sat up, shook her head to clear the dizziness and, holding the bedpost, stood uncertainly. After a moment, her head cleared. She grabbed a cloak and scurried down the stairs out into the afternoon sunshine. They would be serving luncheon at Trewarren, she thought, surprised by a sudden surge of heart-wrenching loss. She voiced her hatred and disgust at her fallen state, shouting as she walked, "I hate you, you disgusting man, I hate you, I hate you." Heads turned as she approached the market place. She smiled in return and felt a slight lifting of the dark clouds that threatened whenever the thunder of Rawdon's demands or the lightning of his strikes terrified her into submission.

It was but a brief release, she knew. There was little demand at this time of day, but Rawdon's invisible net would draw her back in. The consequences of attempted escape were unthinkable. Unless...., no, she must not even consider it, unless she were rescued by someone strong enough to whisk her away; someone strong enough to fend off Rawdon and all those who made up that invisible web; someone like, she dare not mouth the name, but the image in her mind was clear and bright.

Martha continued down Quay Street to the Market Square. There was no market today but a few stalls always remained at the harbour end. She could hear excited people shouting and cheering at the Falmouth Ferry quay. She walked towards the noise and found herself at the back of a fair-sized crowd. Seamen were emerging from the ferry to bursts of cheering. Martha remembered the town crier of the previous afternoon. Rawdon would be greatly cheered, she thought, at the sudden increase in demand for their services. She turned reluctantly and walked back to the grossness of her new life.

"Ah, there you are, my pretty one," Rawdon greeted her. "There be clients waiting." He followed her into her chamber. His eyes pierced her like a cobbler's gimlet and the threat in his quiet curse made her choke on her reply. "Think you can come and go, do you? Think you can please your whoring self, do you? Now you give this young lad his money's worth. Fix those eyebrows! Where do them be, whore?" He ranted on as she scrabbled through the dust at the edge of the bed. She took the water jug from the shelf by the window and moistened the dried flour paste, backed the mouse skins and attached them across her own brows. "Expect a beating if he ain't satisfied, twice as heavy as what you'll get if he is." He swept the curtain aside.

"Your pretty maid awaits you eagerly, young man, enjoy her delights to the full. I'll take your payment now." He held out his hand. Martha caught her first glimpse of a lad she guessed was about twelve years, fumbling in his purse. Red-faced, he passed a coin to Rawdon who inspected it on both sides, and felt the edge, prolonging the moment.

"Where'd you get this lad? Y'did find it in the gutter, I'll wager."

"No, Sir, it's in my pay, Sir, I did work hard for it, Sir." The lad's face puckered. He fought back the tears. Rawdon gestured impatiently and the lad pushed into Martha's chamber, still looking nervously behind him as the curtain fell back, cutting off Rawdon's glare.

"Come in, sweetheart," said Martha. "Now let's have some fun, you lovely boy." She indicated the bed for him to sit down as they heard Rawdon shuffle away.

"Thank you, madam," said the lad in blushing confusion.

"Your first time?" she said in her normal voice. He blushed again but merely nodded, "Your mates did dare you?" She acknowledged his nod. "We must give you something to impress them, I think?" She paused. "Do you have a tongue?"

"Yes ma'am."

"And can you smile?"

"Yes ma'am."

"Well show me, let me see you smile, lad." Martha was relieved to see him grin and relax a little. She took his hand in hers, feeling its gnarled hardness; the bitten down nails; the missing top joint of his little finger. Her own hands were roughened by the cleaning and washing at Trewarren, yet she felt sorry for the lad and, as she guided his hand into her low-cut bodice, she diverted him from his embarrassment by asking about his life.

He had been enlisted to fight the Frenchies, he said. There were many young lads from the countryside in the fleet.

The few who had sailed before made the recruits do all the dirtiest, toughest jobs. They ragged them mercilessly about women and drink: getting them drunk by forcing a lethal mix of rum, brandy and gin on them, all washed down by cloudy ale; daring them to do things to women they didn't understand. Mr Rawdon had been very kind.

"He seemed to understand us. He told us you would show us everything, and we were to practise with you till we were exhausted." Martha smiled ruefully. She had watched his eyes widen as she had removed all but her shift.

"Tell me some stories of your bravery: some adventures at sea, what you did, what your fellows talk of doing."

"One lad, Thomas, was a second in a duel," he said. "He helped an officer avenge his honour; I wish I could do something like that."

"Did a Frenchie insult him, or an Arab?"

"No ma'am, it was before we left, in the woods not far from here. He and his foe had quarrelled over a beautiful woman."

Martha had raised the shift towards the top of her thighs.

"Now help me, sweetheart, as I ease meself up, slide this shift under me and when I sit back raise it up over me head."

He grasped the hem awkwardly and struggled to raise the shift, embarrassed to touch her.

"'Tes not the main sail, sweetheart, no need to be so

rough," she smiled. "Come, let me show you how 'tes done for love." He gasped as Martha's hands unfastened his shirt and caressed his back and shoulders. She eased off his shirt and pushed him back onto the bed.

"Now lift that bum. I want these trousers off." She ran her hands under his buttocks, easing the trousers from him.

"You are mightily privileged, sweetheart, to have so much attention. 'Tes not normal to open my nakedness to anyone who enters here, nor to see more of them than is necessary to meet their most pressing needs," she explained as she caressed him. "But you are a handsome young lad and a kindly one by nature, and I want you to promise me that you will always act kindly to the girls you tarry with, whether they be whores or respectable young ladies."

"I will, I promise," he gasped, aroused beyond control.

"Well, if your word can truly be trusted, we will complete the act."

"Oh, yes ma'am, please ma'am."

She smiled and drew him down to enter her, although his arousal climaxed before he could experience that final pleasure.

"There, it was good, was it not?" she said.

"But I couldn't finish, I be a useless fool!"

"Shush," she said, "no one need hear of this. You are a man now, sweetheart. I would like it if you return to me before you sail. Can you raise the payment for a second visit?"

"I will try ma'am, and thank you."

"You will silence the mocking now," she said. "Be sure to tell it as I showed you. You did take your woman with energy and power. She did beg you to take her again."

He stood awkwardly, recovering his clothing. "Thank you, ma'am, you are a kind lady. I hope I do see you again."

"'Twould please me if you tell Mr Rawdon so," she said.

VI

"Master Richard Trewarren has asked to see you, Sir. He was hoping for permission to speak to Miss Sophia." Silas looked anxiously across the room at Sophie who sat at the harpsichord. The gold braid of a Naval Lieutenant's hat sparkled in the light from the chandelier.

Are you expecting a visit?" She shook her head. "Do you want to see him now?"

"I suppose we will have to; I am most surprised he should be free to visit at this time."

Very well, show him in, Povey; and, Povey, we are not to be disturbed, you understand, under any circumstances." Silas rose as the steward nodded and left the room. Sophie stood, took the hat from the top of the harpsichord and placed it on the stool. She moved forward to join her uncle.

"Richard, how are you, young man? How is your poor

mother coping with her loss?" Silas reached out his hand.

"I am well, Sir, thank you. I am champing like a hound eager for the hunt. I am as impatient for getting down to business as I am for proceeding to marriage, hence my desire to speak with my lovely bride-to-be," Richard smiled at his future wife, "and yourself, of course, Sir."

"Come, be seated; would you care for a drink, some refreshment?" Silas reached for the bell pull. Richard took the seat next to Sophie while Silas ordered drinks.

"Sophie, my dearest, I am so impatient for us to be together. The death of my father has caused an unfortunate delay in our union. It has, however, freed up some major business opportunities. I am only too aware that I have spent a profligate youth; shown poor judgement; taken foolish risks. My father's death has sobered my thoughts. I bear his memory no disrespect, but life must move on. I propose we get married within the month. We can then focus on modernising the business on the estate and in the pilchard trade."

"I am not sure …", Sophie hesitated.

"If you will permit me, my dear?" Silas glanced across at Sophie. "Not one word yet about your poor mother, Richard. It is a most grievous situation for Lady Elizabeth. She is at the centre of our thoughts. We do not feel she is ready for the celebration of such a joyous occasion as we hope and pray the wedding will be. We anticipate a delay of at least a half year, if not through the winter, until the spring of the new century. Is that not so, my dear? If I have appeared to impose too tight a rein on young love, do forgive me." He smiled at Sophie. "I do want you to enjoy the very best nuptials that the age can provide."

Sophie smoothed her satin dress across her knees, as both men looked for her response. Conscious that she was about to disappoint one of them, whatever her answer, she took time to compose herself.

"You have always been a wonderful father to me, Uncle Silas. Your guidance and love since the trauma that brought me into your care has been both kind and sound. My sensibilities have developed naturally in line with my upbringing. As a surrogate ewe rears the orphan lamb, so have you reared me. It is only natural then, that I am sensible to your feelings on this matter. I wish to enjoy my wedding and my marriage without clouds of doubt or unhappiness. I am content to wait a half year, if Lady Elizabeth will be able to throw off her mourning sufficiently in that time." Seeing Richard put his head in his hands, she leaned towards him and put a hand on his shoulder. "I'm sorry, Richard, but those are my true feelings. I would resent you ever after if I allowed you to upset your mother so, with me as the cause."

"Clearly I cannot force you, my dear, and so I must respect your wishes in the matter of the wedding, though I strain at the leash when I look upon your beauty." He smiled a rueful smile as she took her hand from his shoulder.

Povey had appeared with the drinks some minutes before. They were placed on a side table at Silas's direction. Povey's raised eyebrow had indicated surprise at not being required to serve them, but he had left as directed. Silas now poured a brandy for Richard and a Malmsey for Sophie. He passed their glasses without further comment.

"As to my mother," continued Richard, after an appreciative pause for the brandy, "it is natural for her to mourn her loss but, as my father himself found, when my two sisters died, such loss throws her into such a pit of despond, from which it can take several years for her to emerge. It was only on her visits here and to Nankilly that she was able to drag herself free. It was you, Silas, who was the true inspiration for her return to society. Of course I hope daily for her grieving to pain her less, but life must go on, opportunities must be seized, risks taken, if our generation is to profit in the years to come."

"Your impatience is understandable but the estate is in good hands, I believe; I know that Oliver had every confidence in his estate manager, Masters is it not?" Silas registered Richard's nod. "I am sure Masters will keep things running well and induct you into the details; help you get the whole thing into your bloodstream, so to speak. In six months to a year we can begin to make in depth plans for moving forward. Far more likely to get 'em right then than rushing at it now."

"Very well, but I reserve the right to act in matters of the estate independently in the meantime, should I deem it advantageous."

"That is your right, Richard; I would only ask that you think carefully before doing so."

"Our respective positions are clear. I need detain you no

longer. I shall return to Trewarren and keep you informed of any relevant activities." Richard rose and turned to Sophie. He bowed extravagantly, grasped her hand and, giving it a ceremonial kiss, said, "I only hope, my dearest, that I can contain my impatience."

Once he had left, Sophia and her uncle resumed their seats. They sat in companionable silence digesting the implications of the evening's words. A discreet tap on the door interrupted them. Povey's head appeared, looked around and then he entered.

"Are you free now, Sir?"

"What is it Povey?" but, before he could answer, the door swung open wide.

"Did I leave my hat in here? I do hope it didn't cause embarrassment." George Trewarren walked towards the harpsichord, paused uncertainly as Sophia reached the stool behind it, picked up the hat and turned to give it to him. They were far closer to each other than either had expected. Sophia broke the spell by reaching up and placing the hat on George's head at a rakish angle. She stood back and laughed as he removed the hat and chuckled with her.

VII

"Well now, little Missy Mousey, you do learn your trade fast and no mistake. I was not mistook; you are indeed well versed in the wiles of harlotry. That young cabin boy was best pleased with services rendered. These young virgin boys do value their introduction to women's ways. You have found your calling and no mistake."

"Thank you, Mr Rawdon, Sir. I try to be gentle with them."

"Gentle, eh?" he guffawed to himself, and hobbled away, muttering, "Gentle, she say! Gentle! I never did, gentle indeed!"

Martha slipped quietly out of the building, a smile on her face. Her ploy was working well so far. She needed to cleanse herself. The tide was sending wavelets up the lower reaches of the Kenway nearby. She followed the track along the bank to the wash house, crossed the washing stones, raised her skirts and stepped into the water. It was far from clean but smelt of salt and seaweed. She crouched, gasping as ice cold water coursed between her thighs. Gripping her voluminous skirts in front of her with one hand, she washed away the smell and stain of sin. Feeling cleansed, she clambered out of the river, leaving the garments beneath the dress to soak up the dampness. The sky was overcast and threatening; a sudden gust stirred the brown leaves along the bank beyond the washing stones. Leafless branches on the sycamore saplings, not yet substantial enough to burn for heat, bent under the power of the wind accompanying the tide.

A fresh gust brought a sudden flurry of hailstones, stinging her face, and the backs of her hands as she raised them instinctively. The hail attacked in waves, as the gusting wind rose and fell. Her long skirts hampered her as she hurried along the track. She crossed at the next street that met the track at right angles and stood against a high, whitewashed stone wall. Sheltered from the stinging hail, she held her skirts away from her legs, to let the melting hail stones run off. The hem dripped water. With the dampness of her cleansing, her clothing was soaked through to her skin. Her legs felt cold and chapped. She hoped fervently that there would be no more customers today.

"Are you in trouble, Miss? May I be of assistance?" A strong male voice penetrated her consciousness.

"No thank you, Sir," she said, keeping her head lowered. She could see his smart stockings and boots. I cannot take the chance he will use me, she thought. "I'll be on my way, Sir; the storm have slackened now, I'd best be moving on. Thank you kindly, Sir." She gasped involuntarily at the heavy freezing linen of her skirt pressing against her legs.

"Are you sure, Miss? You do sound troubled to me. I shall pray to the Lord to give you special care and see you safe home." He stood watching as she shuffled away.

Once back on the track along the river, she felt the force of the wind although the storm had abated. In her mind that voice had a faint note of familiarity. She turned uncertainly. He stood on the track at the end of the street she had left, looking after her. In an instant he was no longer a handsome stranger but a figure she recognised only too well. She turned and scurried along the track back to the brothel rooms, her dress, lengthened by the weight of the soaking, collected mud and dirt along the hem as it scuffed the path.

It be Josiah, to be sure, it must be him, he must be returned with the fleet. My, he did look smart an'all. I be sure it must be him. I do hope he did not know me, neither who I be nor what I be, she thought, as she stripped off the wet clothing and slid naked into the bed. She leaned back against the great pillow, pulled the blanket up to her shoulders, and the shivering soon ceased.

***

Several days later Martha emerged into the town again. Rawdon had been called away for a few days. She had washed, pressed and repaired her clothes. Her chapped thighs had healed sufficiently for her to walk in comfort. Her feet had suffered more severely. Chilblains were intermittently painful. She had persuaded Florence to excuse her from duties easily enough, accepting that with her condition she would not have been attractive to her young clients. She had been unable to drive Josiah from her mind. Had he recognised her? She thought it unlikely. Yet she half hoped he had: she both hoped and feared to see him again.

The market was busy now. Some of the fleet was restocking in Falmouth. Supply boats from Truro sailed or were rowed up and down the Fal, as the market was widely famed for its range and quality. The bulk of the fleet remained in Plymouth, but so vast were the requirements after a long campaign that the shelter of the Carrick Roads and the fine hinterland of which Truro was the hub, made an ideal supporting facility. Martha lowered her head, and walked quickly through the square. A few cat calls followed her, but other ladies made themselves available more readily.

"Martha? Martha, be that you? Ay, I thought it were, so I did."

"Why Molly! What brings you all this way to Truro? I never thought to see you looking so well; I feared I might hear you be dead or crippled."

"Well, that be a right cheerful greeting, Sister. I hope I don't disappoint."

"Of course not, Molly, love, you fair bowled me over, is all." Martha stepped the two paces between them and threw her arms round her sister-in-law.

"I do take the chance to sell some oil, and get a good price for 'em too. I can spare a few minutes for my dear sister though." Molly secured the oil kegs, drew a rope across her rickety frame on which a disused sail made a makeshift stall, and indicated another keg for Martha to sit on.

"I could have tossed a coin to choose a'tween Falmouth and Truro, but Thomas do say that Truro be best, so here I be, and pleased with sales, but the more pleased to see my sister."

"Dear Sister, are you quite recovered? I feared for you when I left you in such pain. Felt guilty for it, yet I must go for my life. Much good it did me, for all my endeavour."

"I've never felt better but it were a terrible time. After you be gone, I thought I was to die, the pain were so great. Thomas fetched the midwife."

"Molly, what happened?" Martha's hand covered her mouth in horror.

"Thomas were told to fill me with brandy to dull the pain. I lay there drunken and misty brained. She soaked her hand in oil and reached right in to me. I couldn't look at what she pulled out. I passed full away." Intent on her story, Molly barely noticed Martha's deathly pallor. "Next day the pain were moved to my head. Thomas led me to the water pump and held my head under the gush of it until I shook myself free."

"And no more pain?" asked Martha.

"I was my old self within the week and glad not to have another mouth to feed." They sat in silence for a while.

"But what of you? You look a little pale, but not quite the church mouse," said Molly.

"I be truly the fallen woman, fallen into the clutches of the devil Rawdon."

"Oh Martha! Can you not run clear way? 'Tes no life for the likes of you! I had heard rumours of such, I admit, but dismissed 'em as beer talk."

"He has a wide net, finely woven; the more you flap the more enmeshed you become. I lie still in the hope of a storm so great the net will fray and unravel. Yet where should I go? What roof, what victuals would I have?"

"Let me think on it; this oil is near gone. I go home tonight and bring more in two days. May you be free to meet here on Friday morn?"

"If the devil be not back, 'twill be easy enough. If he be, I do find some means. Yet I dare not hope you may find some device." Martha smiled, stood, gave her sister an instinctive hug, and hurried back to her cell.

VIII

Richard had every intention of riding directly back to Trewarren Manor. The darkness did not concern him. He knew the road well and he would be home soon after midnight. Anger and frustration boiled within him. Why was everyone so determined to surrender to morbid inaction? His father wouldn't have wanted it; at least if Mother didn't get to him first, he wouldn't. But Sophie, how could she do this to him? She had been so loving, so eager, had allowed herself to stray beyond the expectations of respectability, whilst holding back the ultimate pleasure until the marriage vows had been exchanged. It was all so much teasing, it seemed to him now, and his frustration boiled anew.

He slowed as he approached the track towards Boscawen; the wind was cold, it carried a dampness that chilled the very bones of a man. The Truro River lay on his right. A lantern flickered over the water. Richard slowed his horse to a walk.

"Is that you, Master Richard?" A familiar voice carried through the darkness.

"Who is it wishes to know?" Richard struggled to place the owner. The sound was distorted by the wind, but the intonation was familiar.

"Your faithful servant, Sire, with an instinct for your tastes and how they may be satisfied, Sire."

"Rawdon, by the good Lord, Rawdon, of course, I'd know

that voice anywhere. What is your business with me, you old rogue?"

"I do think you might value some business with me, Sire, being far from home on such a night." Rawdon stepped out of the dinghy, indicating to the oarsman to wait.

"What business might that be at this time of night, man? Whatever you propose will surely be unlawful; I must be on my way." Richard tightened the reins but gave his mount no command.

"Only two types of business in this place at this hour, Sire, namely that which did for your father, or that in which you are well practised at yourself, Sire. I have some very presentable young ladies of the night for your pleasure. Only a few furlongs away, Sire. Should you wish to select such a lady, I am sure she would give fullest satisfaction, Sire." Rawdon stepped forward, gave his sickly smile and stood expectantly.

"You have the insolence of a snake. You dare to speak of my father in such a manner. He has been dead barely a month. What do you know of his death that you misuse his name so?"

"Well, Sire, I am sorry to offend, I am sure. Should you choose to sample my offer to your interests, we might walk together and converse on such." Richard turned his horse without a word and began walking back along the river. Rawdon limped along beside him, having indicated to the boatman to keep pace on the water.

"Well man," said Richard at length, "be minded I make no

promise about harlotry. Now tell what you know of my father's death."

"Sir Oliver's horse bolted and threw him off," said Rawdon, swaying along to keep pace with the horse.

"If that is all, I'll leave you to your sordid ways. Such is common knowledge." Richard stopped the horse and turned it half round.

"He were returning from a visit to a smuggling partner, a free trader as we should say."

"Continue."

"I know not who or what, but it were said he drove too hard a deal, expected too much: there were shoutin' and cussin' and a group were prompted by a Guernseyman. He said he'd been robbed." He paused as they reached the first buildings of the town.

"Continue," Richard repeated, "though I must say it sounds very unlikely. My father was ever a cautious man."

"That's as maybe, Sire, but 'twere not the opinion of the traders. They claimed the price had been raised from that originally agreed: some poor beggar were commissioned to fright the horse, and earned his reward, Sire, as I heard tell."

"And who might this pauper be? It is someone not unknown to you, I'll wager."

"That be all I can tell'ee, Sire. One of my ladies will be pining for you, Sire. You'll not want to neglect the pretty wee thing now; she'll be very much to your taste, Master Richard, if I know you of old."

"Find him out, who he is, this pauper, Rawdon, yet let him not know who seeks him. If you undertake this task, I will avail myself of your service, but think you not that I still have the callowness of youth, to fall for all your scheming ways." Looking forward, Richard saw a long hovel of a building ahead, its outline a silhouette against the woods on the far bank of the river.

"Your servant as always, Sire, we are two of a kind these days in a manner of speaking. Now we be at the honeypot, Sire. Please you to dismount and prepare to meet your pleasure." Rawdon held the rein.

"I take grave exception to that remark." Richard's anger rose again. "I have nothing in common with a charlatan such as you. I am minded to depart this instant."

"That would be most inconvenient to my enquiries on your behalf, Sire, most contrary. I refer merely to our similar injuries. I would not be bold to claim above my station."

"Very well, let us proceed." Richard dismounted and cursed as his weakened leg caused him to stumble and Rawdon to conceal a smirk.

***

Martha slept fitfully. Her earlier visitors had been two contrasting cabin boys: the first shy at the start, then over-excited and eternally grateful for her gentleness; the second a great hefty lad, clumsy yet determined. She had earned an undisturbed night.

"Rawdon, you dog! You face me with the cause of all my woes. What mean you by this traitorous whore?" Richard's purple face loomed above her in the dim light as she confronted her worst nightmare. A surge of fear coursed through her chest. Her cheeks were drained of blood and were sucked in.

"'Twas my understanding, you enjoyed her to the full when you was introduced, Sire. Begging your pardon, Sire, if I have mistook, but she is a popular young gel, Sire, she is indeed." He leered as he stepped back.

"Get out, Rawdon! Get out!" Richard pulled back the blanket, pleased by Martha's scream.

***

An hour later, Richard sat on the end of the bed. He held his head in his hands, streaks of blood gleaming wetly on his shirt. He glanced at Martha's unconscious body through his spread fingers. Wet blood smears marked her belly; her face was swollen, marked with scratches and her bruised eye-sockets seemed to drown her eyes in the semi darkness. One arm dangled awkwardly down the side of the bed.

The curtain quivered and was drawn half open. There was a gasp. He looked up.

"I don't know who you be, or what you be, mister, but you have done great wrong here tonight, may the good Lord forgive you. For that be evil if ever I see it." Florence moved into the room and approached Martha's prone figure.

"You know neither who nor what I am, nor what that whore has done to me and mine, hussy." Richard reached for his trousers, stood and dressed himself for departure. As he found his way down to his horse, Florence's shout followed him. "You are no better than an animal, mister, an animal I say!" She returned to the bedside to hear Martha's weak breath bubble through the blood and fluid at the corner of her mouth.

IX

"Take care, Sophie my dear. A young woman who is promised to one man should not show too open a fondness for another," said Silas, lessening the sharpness of his rebuke with a forgiving smile.

"I do beg your pardon, Mr Galsworthy, the blame is entirely mine. Having defended Sophie's honour against her promised partner, I would not for the world impugn it now," said George.

"Don't listen to him, Uncle; George was not in the least at fault. It was a momentary lapse on my part, due to the unexpected proximity of his engaging smile."

"I'll say no more on the matter. Just ensure you avoid such unexpected proximities in the future. It could lead to much unpleasantness, especially after the unsatisfactory attitude displayed by our visitor this evening. Now, another drink before the evening quite disappears." Silas crossed to the brandy carafe and filled a glass.

"Thank you, but time moves on and I am sure you have matters to discuss with Sophie. I think perhaps I should make my way down to my lodging." George rose and presented a hand to Silas who placed the brandy glass in it. Sophie could not restrain an unladylike giggle at George's surprised expression.

"Nonsense; I am sure we can find you a bed if necessary. I want to hear your plans for the future, should you be willing to divulge them."

When all three had drinks and were settled, Silas's words took a more serious tone.

"The reason for my asking will become clear shortly, as will be the reason for my asking you to stay your departure." Sophia and George both looked across at him with surprised interest as he continued: "I have become wary of late of my earlier confidence in Richard Trewarren, both as a business partner and as a husband for Sophia. I felt initially that his brashness and headstrong manner would fade as he matured into his true role at the estate. His more flexible attitude to the links between manufacturing, farming and free trade could have been helpful in taking our interests forward in profitable ways into the next century." He paused but their eyes were now intently upon him; neither had touched their brandy. Silas himself drank from his glass. "Recent events, from the wild challenge to his cousin George here, to his unseemly rush to put aside his father's death, his disregard for his mother's distress and the guidance offered by his Uncle Francis show a lack of maturity and a lack of judgement which cause me considerable concern."

"I too was concerned by his indifference to his mother's grief," Sophia interjected, "but one can never know the full workings within such a family."

"There is one more serious issue which could confirm my gravest suspicions," said Silas, "and I am expecting clarification tonight or tomorrow. That rogue, Rawdon, is bringing a consignment of free trade goods up river from a Guernsey sloop anchored off St Mawes. It should come up on the high tide for midnight. I intend to seek the name of a witness to confirm what Rawdon intimated on a previous delivery. If what I have heard is confirmed by a third party I shall cease all contact with the man." He paused and drank from his glass.

"But, Uncle, my marriage, I am promised."

"Sophie, my dear, if what I am told is confirmed, I would not wish such a man to eye you with such desire ever again. I would rather you went to a nunnery than live with such an unfeeling rogue."

"I have no desire for such a life. I am quite revolted by the idea. I will readily admit that I have cooled somewhat in my ardour for Richard. As a result of my increased care and concern over the injury he sustained in defending my honour and the reassurance he needed that he still had my affection, I was perhaps drawn to him more than was wise. Yet spinsterhood has no attraction for me, in holy orders or not. I am intrigued nevertheless to hear of his latest lapse."

"I assure you, my dear, if Rawdon confirms his earlier account it was no mere lapse. He is later than he led me to believe. He should be here by now."

"May I ask how my future plans are relevant to what has been a fascinating and intriguing account, Mr Galsworthy?" asked George.

"That will become clearer when Rawdon has been, but perhaps you could explain your intentions with regard to a return to the American colonies. And please call me Silas. I am not one to stand on ceremony."

"The American States no longer consider themselves colonies, Silas. They have defeated the British Army, agreed a constitution and elected their first President. The Independence issue placed me in a quandary. My grandfather is a staunch supporter of the revolution, yet my father does not share his animosity to the crown, and bade me join the Royal Navy to fight the French. My grandfather says we owe the Frenchies a favour and good luck to 'em."

"Will you return to this 'New England' across the ocean then, or will you stay in England once you have served your time?" asked Sophia, leaning towards him with a serious expression.

"Oh I must return when the French are defeated. I was born an American. I love my country. There are so many restraints here, so many opportunities there, so much land, so much room for expansion, for farming, business, export; a new, young country where all men have the vote: it is a powerful temptation."

"Oh I do admire your spirit, George." She gazed across at him. "I would so love the freedom to roam the new world, see new lands, build a new life without the constraints of this narrow little town to drag me back into its narrow little ways, like an invisible chain binding me to my cell. I had hoped marriage might release me, or at least lengthen my chain, in a different cell. That seems unlikely now." She lowered her eyes at the warmth of George's understanding smile.

All three sat in silence for a while. At last following a discreet tap on the door, Povey's head appeared. Seeing them all in silence, he entered.

"Excuse me, Sir, but your expected visitor has arrived. He says he has an important message, Sir."

"Very well, Povey; wait here will you, I'll go to him at once." Silas left the room and hurried down the corridor, leaving Povey standing by the door as a chaperone.

"Constraints, constraints," muttered Sophia.

"At least we should find out what this is all about." George finished his brandy in a gulp, and held his glass for Povey to refill. Sophia walked across to the harpsichord and began to play. George paced the room, glass in hand. After the first song he approached the harpsichord and leaned on it, looking into her eyes. She smiled. Povey cleared his throat as the door opened. Silas stood there, grim-faced. They turned and stared.

"It is as serious as I feared," he said, "in every detail."

X

Martha murmured almost inaudibly as Florence wiped away the blood and tended her wounds as best as she was able. She lifted the damaged arm gently onto the bed and pulled a blanket over the semi-conscious body.

"Sleep, my pretty one, sleep," she whispered, as she took the candle and returned to her room.

Next morning, Martha awoke and immediately felt the pain. She cried out involuntarily as she tried to move. Florence pulled back the curtain and approached the bed.

"How are you, my sweet? That vicious brute should be hanged. He deserves no less for what he been doing to you." The curtain rustled again. Florence looked round. "Ah, Mr Rawdon, Sir, that gentleman did great harm to missy Martha. He should never climb these stairs again, if not be hanged for what he been doing to Martha here."

"No need to make such a row about it. I ain't best pleased to be woke at this hour. I was out on important business till the early hours, without cheap whores waking me at the break of dawn. Pull back the blanket, let me see the damage." He waved an arm and Florence gingerly lifted and pulled back the blanket over Martha's bruised body. "An ugly sight if ever I did see one. No use to man nor beast like that. You better clear out: get yourself out of that bed and out of my accommodation. You can't earn your keep in that condition."

"But Mr Rawdon, Sir, she ain't fit to get out of bed. Have pity on her, Sir, at least until she's fit to stand."

"You watch your tongue, woman, or you'll be out of your room; plenty more where you came from. Now get her out of here and clean the blood off the floor, and turn the blanket so the blood stain is at the bottom end and ain't seen by visitors." He hobbled away without looking back. Martha was shaking uncontrollably as Florence reached for the dress, lying against the wall. She lifted Martha's head and shoulders and struggled to slide the dress over her head with one hand, while supporting her against her own body and balancing her with the other arm. Martha continued to shake and moaned as the dress passed over her damaged arm. With the dress finally down to the waist, Florence rolled Martha towards her and dragged the hem of the dress under her. Exhausted, she let Martha gently down again and rested.

Martha stopped shaking. Florence lifted her legs and pulled the skirts down to her feet.

"Can you sit, Martha dear?" Florence slid an arm under Martha's shoulders and encouraged her to raise herself to a sitting position, "That's right, good girl, now swing your legs round to the floor; good girl."

"Not yet gone?" Rawdon pulled the curtain aside.

"She cannot stand as yet, Mr Rawdon, but she do try her best. I s'll have to help her; take her somewhere safe."

"Don't be long then, I want you back within the hour. The fleet will soon be gone." Rawdon softened a little when he saw Martha struggle with the pain. "He'll not trouble us no more, that gentleman won't. I am sure o' that. Martha, you should be fit for duty in a week or so. Return as soon as your appearance is sufficiently improved. Now get her out of here Florence, and mind what I said, back within the hour."

"Yes, Mr Rawdon, I'll do my best, Sir."

The cold, damp early morning air set Martha shivering after the exhausting descent of the stairs.

"Molly," she muttered, "find Molly. Market Square, selling oil," she added and collapsed into Florence's arms. Florence staggered under the sudden weight but managed to rebalance herself and pull Martha's good arm over her shoulder and across her back whilst sliding her own arm around Martha's waist. After a few struggling steps, Martha regained some strength and was able to manage her own weight but clung to Florence for balance.

Confused by the noise and bustle as people sought early morning bargains while traders were still organising their pitches, Florence was uncertain where Molly would be as they entered the market square. The cries of gulls, as they circled and swooped for the innards of freshly gutted fish, added to the shouting of traders and bargain hunters.

"Molly," mumbled Martha, "find Molly."

"I be looking for her, truly I be, but I do not know her to look at, Martha m' dear. Where do she have her pitch? Which side o' the square?"

Martha raised her head in a desperate effort to give an answer and in that instant she heard her name.

"Martha! Is that you, Sister? What ever has happened to

you, my dear Sister?" Molly rushed forward and helped Florence bring her to a stool in the shelter of the stall.

"'Twere that brute of a gentleman, so called, that Richard Trewarren. He have come to her last night, done nameless things to her, left her so bloody and bruised she can no but walk," said Florence, easing herself free.

"You sit there, Sister, I s'll send for some hot broth and add a tot or two of good strong liquor. Have you some place to stay? A body to care for you?"

"Rawdon have banned her till she do recover the look of appeal to his clients. I think she do hope for your help, missy."

"I'll see to her, don't you fret. What sister wouldn't?"

"I must away back or I s'll suffer likewise; Rawdon being the unforgiving rogue that he is. Farewell, dear Martha, and may you soon be recovered. A curse on that brute Trewarren, may he rot in hell." Florence gathered her skirts and hurried away.

"Did I hear the name of Richard Trewarren spoken in anger?" Molly turned to see a tall naval officer standing at the front of the stall. As they stood back Martha's condition was revealed.

"Martha! Is it truly you? Oh my poor, dear friend. Who could do such violence to so gentle a person?"

XI

While Povey filled Silas's glass, Sophie and George moved back to their seats.

"Thank you, Povey."

"Thank you, Sir." Povey nodded and left the room.

"Well, Uncle, please divulge the bad news. We are all ears."

"Rawdon had with him another of doubtful character whom he claimed was his boatman and who had witnessed the scene at the cave where Trewarren's betrayal took place."

"Do you mean Sir Oliver, or Richard?" asked Sophia. George said nothing.

"In a sense, both. But I would say that Oliver was drawn into the situation in true ignorance of how it had arisen. However, to resume: as Rawdon's boat was approaching the Truro wharf, about three furlongs out, he said, they chanced upon Richard on horseback leaving the town, along the road by the river."

"On his way home from here." Sophia could not contain herself.

"Quite. To continue: the boatman recognised him without hesitation and confirmed it to me a few moments ago. They were delayed as Rawdon reluctantly agreed to escort Richard to a house of ill repute before rejoining the boatman at the wharf."

"I thought he was riding home. How could that be true?"

"Rawdon had hailed him from the boat, so that his man could have a view of his face, the better to identify him. Richard told Rawdon he had been frustrated in his quest and begged Rawdon's assistance. It became clear to Rawdon that to deny his pressing demands would simply delay matters further. He was anxious not to inconvenience me more than was already unavoidable. Now if I ... "

"But that is such an insult. To suggest he views our future together as providing the services of a whore. I never want to be in his presence again. Never!"

"It is a grave insinuation, an unbearable insult to Sophie. He has clearly learned nothing from my challenge. I shall not be so generous again." George rose and stood behind Sophia, resting a comforting arm on the satin-covered shoulder. She turned and smiled her gratitude up at him.

"It has most certainly strengthened my growing distaste for the more sordid side of his nature. But we now have hard evidence of his short-sighted greed and corrupt ways in business. Such was the cause of his own father's death."

"So there **was** more to it than a frightened horse," said George.

"There most certainly was, very much more. According to Rawdon, Sir Oliver had agreed with his contacts that the usual price would be paid for the consignment due the week before. At the same time he had explained that he was introducing his son to the business and now that the price was agreed his son would take over the detail. He would still be available should they have any concerns and they could contact him through the usual channels. When Oliver set out the situation for Richard and explained the procedure, Richard quibbled at the price. Oliver told him it had already been agreed, they had paid the same price for some years and both parties had been happy. Richard must have been dissatisfied for when he had the goods checked out and presented payment it had been reduced by ten percent."

"Was a figure mentioned between Sir Oliver and the traders?" asked George.

"There was no need, both parties understood the terms. Trust had been built up over many years. Trust that Richard destroyed, along with his father's life, in one act of greed and betrayal." Silas paused, expecting another interruption, but both his listeners were intent on grasping the enormity of the deed. "When the payment was short of the agreed sum, a message was sent to Oliver who asked Richard if the payment had been delivered as agreed. Was there perhaps a shortage in the agreed supplies, he asked, but Richard claimed that all was as agreed. Oliver rode over to assure the traders of that fact, whereupon they grew very angry. Henry, the boatman, was moored by the entrance to the cave, swabbing the decks of his boat. He heard angry voices. Oliver appeared and rode off on his horse. The customary handshakes and farewells were not seen. Almost immediately, a swarthy figure, cloaked and masked, left at a gallop. By the time Henry had emptied his swab bucket and stowed his mop, the rider had returned and shortly after the whole lot of them slunk off down to the beach, uncovered their dinghies and disappeared from the

213

cove." Silas sat back in his chair and took a draught of whisky. There was a thoughtful silence.

George resumed his seat, but edged nearer to Sophie. They glanced at each other.

"Does Richard acknowledge his evil act?" said Sophie.

"Does that coward admit his crime?" said George.

"When you both speak at once it is difficult to fathom your meaning, but I venture to suppose you ask if he accepts responsibility. I am not privy to his private thoughts but I know Elizabeth has her suspicions, as does Francis. Clearly he has not confessed the detail to either of them."

"But, I still don't understand..."

"Sophie, my dear, I am too exhausted to think any more on the matter. I shall retire to my room and I suggest you both do the same, since I can hardly leave you alone together at this time of night." He stood, ran his hands down his coat, shook George's hand, nodded to Sophia and held the door for them to precede him.

XII

Molly was at a loss. How was she to get Martha home when she had only her handcart to transport the tapped barrels of pilchard oil? Could she store them safely and take Martha in the cart? But of course not: she needed to refill the empties for her next market day. It was almost every day now. She could not afford to miss the opportunity while the fleet was restocking. She would think on for the rest of the morning, maybe an idea would come to her. Other customers came and went, keeping her busy so that she forgot poor Martha's presence for much of the time.

Martha lay back in the chair, semi-conscious; her mind floating in a dreamlike world. She thought she had heard Josiah return to her. She had not seen him again since his rushed departure from her bed. Her face attempted a smile as pictures of that most memorable night in her whole life drifted into her head, only to be chased out by the harsh accusations that led to his departure. She involuntarily screwed her face in the pain of reliving the moment, as she had so often over the last two years.

Molly's voice penetrated her thoughts as she sought to offer sustenance. Her mouth was very painful, but she was able to take in a little water.

"How do we get you home?" Molly wondered aloud. "Can you walk at all? No, I can see that you cannot. Leastways, you'll not make the five mile. What are we to do?" She moved to serve another customer and, as he paid her and took his flagon away, a figure appeared riding a donkey. His feet were almost dragging on the ground but the donkey kept a steady pace. As he approached, Molly recognised the man who had spoken to Martha when she had first been brought to the stall.

"Greetings again, Madam oil-seller. Seeing Martha brought here this morning has preyed on my mind. I did her a grave disservice some years past. I thought to make amends to her. I observe that you travel back and forth on foot, dragging that handcart. Is that indeed so?"

"It is, Sir. I need to take her home to Trewarren Bay to settle her there to recover, yet she cannot walk in her current state and I fear I have neither room in the cart nor strength to draw it along with the weight of her, skin and bone though she is. I am truly at a loss."

"I feared such was the case, hence I have borrowed this ass from a good friend in the Lord, who has seen fit to help me without charge, though I must return the beast to him tonight." He dismounted and held the ass by the halter.

The steady pace of the donkey rocked Martha into a reverie through which Josiah's words floated. The rumble of Molly's handcart varied in volume depending on her distance and the surface of the track. Through the mists of her brain, thickening and clearing as they travelled, she became aware of Josiah's impassioned voice.

"I have learned much on my travels," he said. "I knew the navy was home and shelter to many and varied men and boys: many calm under fire, others inclined to panic; some distraught by loss of eye or limb, others philosophic, yet others brave and determined. Likewise, in port, many will carouse and fornicate and such pleasuring is surely tempting to the most faithful of men after months of abstinence and the harsh threat of the yard arm or the keel haul. Strangely Martha, this has led me to view our brief fall into sin as less of a sin than ..."

"Cap'n Carter, Sir, the cart have a broken wheel. Can ye halt a moment and help me see to it?"

"Why surely; whoa there!"

Martha slumped forward and seemed about to slide off. Josiah steadied her; she lay forward with her head resting between the animal's ears. Smiling at her position, Josiah walked back some thirty yards to the stricken cart. Molly was stacking the kegs at the side of the track. They upended the cart between them; two wooden spokes had broken. This had caused the wooden wheel to crack within its metal tyre which had formed a flattened section about a third of its length. Josiah found a sapling of similar girth and measured off two spoke lengths. With his naval dagger he worked at shaping them to replace the broken ones.

Josiah glanced back at the donkey from time to time but Martha appeared to be sleeping. Neither she nor the ass had moved. As he looked, the animal bent its head to graze and he ran to save Martha from sliding off. Molly helped him ease her on to the side of the track. They propped her against a tree and tied the donkey loosely so that it could feed. Martha was in a stupor. Josiah wondered how much she had heard or understood of what he had said.

With a great effort, they refitted the temporary spokes and righted the cart.

"Thank you greatly, Cap'n, I don't know how I should go on if I do not have your help." said Molly, as she reloaded the kegs.

"It is but a temporary measure; 'twill need the attention of a wheelwright before you venture again, but it should get us the last few furlongs. Now I s'll require your assistance with Martha here."

***

With Martha settled on her bed, Molly set out to distribute the empty kegs and the proceeds from selling the oil. She collected Henny from the fishwife who cared for her while Molly took her wares to market. Josiah sat with Martha, offering her water to sip as needed.

"I know not what you heard or minded from our journey, Martha my dear, but I have little time before returning the beast so I will cut my ponderings short and say that experience has taught me our intimate encounter was far from selfish carnality on either side. Had we been but married, it would have been a delight and a celebration of our love." He looked at Martha whose eyes were upon him. Did she comprehend? He could not tell. "Therefore, I would humbly beg your forgiveness for tarnishing a moment in which we expressed our growing love for each other and it is my wish that, in good time, when you are fully recovered from this dreadful ordeal, we may resume progress, chastely I assure you, towards a possible marriage. I will leave the thought with you' Martha my dear, and hope you are soon fully recovered." He touched her hand and stood. She was still staring at him without a word. At the base of the stairs he fancied he heard a muffled sob.

XIII

"There were trouble brewing at the tavern yester evening, Mr Masters. The tenants is up in arms at the new rents." Nat Hoblyn stood, arms at his sides, before the estate manager. "People can't believe you could treat them so harsh. Maybe them Frenchies was driven so 'ard, some are sayin'. I was hoping to bring our worries to ye afore the violence flares up. If last night be any sort of sign, it won't be long afore they do march on the manor house. They won't take no account of poor Lady Trewarren in her widow's weeds. A month or three has passed since the untimely death and ain't we all suffering? I ask ye, Mr Masters. It ain't like yerself to bring in these charges in hard times."

"Enough, Hoblyn, enough. You've made your point. You'd be wise to return to your work now."

"But Mr Masters, have you heard me, what I'm saying? It bain't just for meself and mine I be speaking. If nothing be done, there be violence afoot. Hotheads is already stirring the pot. The rabble ain't easily roused, but they be nearer than I seen in all Sir Oliver's time."

"Sir Oliver's time has passed, God rest his soul, and Sir Richard is determined to modernise the management of the estate. I've heard your complaint, Hoblyn. Get back to your land if you truly value it." Masters opened a leather-bound ledger, took up a quill and began to work his way down a column of figures. He did not look up again. Nat Hoblyn stood for a full minute before abruptly turning and striding out of the office. Trouble is certainly brewing, thought Masters, but 'tes best not to mention names to Sir Richard. The difficulty is how to persuade him to moderate his demands. His father's name do enrage him and he do single out any tenant who protest as a trouble maker and evict him. I should warn him of the stirring in the tavern, leastways then I s'll have done right by both sides. With these thoughts, he resumed his calculations.

***

Richard sat astride Caesar, watching the workmen break up the remains of the hovel. The wind off the sea tugged at his tricorn hat as fluffy white clouds scudded across from the south west. The sweet, coconut-like scent of gorse was strong, but would soon be lost as the men stuffed wood shavings and tinder under and between the beams and planks they had piled high for burning. He was determined to wipe out all traces of the little whore he blamed for all his misfortunes. The fire was slow to take hold, but within half an hour the flames roared high and fierce in the April air.

"Well done, men, what are your names?"

"I be Cornwallis, Sir, and this be young Doe. We likes to do a proper job, Sir."

"Cornwallis and Doe; I'll remember your good work as long as nothing but ash remains. Stay to ensure the very last splinter is devoured in the flames. Do you understand me?" He edged his mount towards them.

"Oh yes indeed, Sir Richard, we s'll see to it; have no fear to that." Both men busied themselves collecting stubs of burnt wood on the periphery of the fire and tossing them into the white hot centre.

Satisfied, Richard turned and rode along the cliff top, following the curve round towards the bay. Perhaps now, with the only remaining trace a pile of ash to be scattered by the wind, he could finally free himself from her curse. Baines, you thought to compromise and betray me, yet you are now expunged from my life. You are debased and destroyed, Baines. There is a lesson for you to share with your kind. Do not denigrate your betters; do not soil their lives with your sordid presence. He smiled as he pictured her blood-besmirched body in Rawdon's brothel. It had been worth the price and worth the wait. His thoughts trailed on.

A great constraint was lifted from his mind, a curse removed. Sophie will be mine, Silas open to business: wealth and success beckoned, he could feel it in his bones. Better to wait a month or so before renewing his courtship: use the time to regularise the new contracts, rents and wages on the estate. He must find another free trade partner too. The mad Guernsey man had milked his father for too long and turned violent when caught out. He had thought to give chase to the murdering pirate but the means were not to hand. It wouldn't have been fair to his mother to risk his own life with his father's already lost; and the cruel truth was that the death did have advantages. It was very sad and regrettable, of course, particularly for Mama, but sadly poor Father was lost in the past. Outdated attitudes were no way to maximise profits and bring the estate up to modern business standards.

Such thoughts brought him back to the Manor. The stable lad appeared from the outbuildings and took the bridle while his master dismounted. Richard set off towards the house without a backward glance. He needed to wash the smell of smoke and the wind-blown dust from his face; he needed a drink.

"Excuse me, Sir Richard." Bassett caught him as he was about to ascend the staircase. "Mr Masters would like a word,

Sir; said it was quite urgent, Sir."

"Not now, Bassett, I'll see him later. I'm sure it can wait until I've washed off the dust from my ride. Bring me a large brandy up to my room. I'm in need of a drink."

"Very good, Sir Richard, Shall I tell Mr Masters you will see him when you come down?"

"Then or in the morning, Bassett. I'll decide in due course."

"Very good, Sir Richard."

"Don't forget the brandy, Bassett." He called as he approached the first landing.

***

Lady Elizabeth stood in the drawing room, her black mourning wear a stark contrast to the fresh lightness of the décor, which was enhanced by the late afternoon spring sunshine angling its sparkle across to the glass-fronted cabinet against the white wall beyond the fireplace. At least the delay in the wedding has left me the lady of the house, she thought. Though, for all his fusty ways, I would a thousand times prefer that Oliver were still alive. Richard is running out of control, there is no containing him. She moved across to the chaise longue. I never thought I would miss the smell of Oliver's cigars, for all the continuing lightness of the walls and windows. I was counting too much on Silas's good will: such a man for society, and dear Sophia too, but I fear a distance grows between our families.

Richard entered the room.

"Be of good cheer, Mama, things are in hand to improve the income from many of our interests, nay all of them to be exact."

"Oh Richard, can you not greet even your mother without puffing out your chest with such boasts before some small show of respect for good manners?"

"Why Mama, I am merely trying to cheer you with news of our progress. The time is past for the endless rounds of politesse. Look to France for what happens when standing on ceremony takes the whole day." Richard smiled and walked forward to face his mother. "Would you like a drink before dinner, Mama: an aperitif perhaps?" He bent low in a mock bow of respect.

She smiled. He could be amusing at times, she thought, in spite of his infuriating ways. "I'll take a glass of port," she said.

At Richard's summons, Pollard appeared, served Elizabeth with the port and indicated to Richard that Mr Masters was anxious to speak with him.

"I am well aware of his wishes, Pollard. I will see him tomorrow morning. I do not wish to be interrupted further this evening. I would be most grateful if you would convey that message to Masters on my behalf."

"Certainly, Sir Richard." Pollard hurried away.

XIV

In the Nankilly garden the daffodils were in full bloom. They swayed in the April sunshine.

"These grow wild on the edge of the woods." Sophia bent and plucked one. "The woods by the estuary. Have you seen them?" She held it up to examine it. George smiled as she eyed him with mischievous innocence over the delicate yellow trumpet.

He in turn bent and plucked a stem. He too examined it, before facing her and pinning it on her shawl with her ruby-studded brooch. As he pulled away to admire his handiwork, she drew him forward to attach her daffodil to the buttonhole of his coat. He came towards her slightly off balance. She raised her face to his in some confusion. His mouth hovered above hers; she could not deny the sudden rush of desire and allowed his lips to brush her own. Inevitably, the embrace released the desire they had both repressed.

She pulled away with difficulty.

"Sophie," he said, "please forgive me. I gave way to a long-held temptation. I do apologise. I fear we must cut short our walk and return to the house."

"But it was my fault. I was most clumsy. Pray let us continue. Tell me of life in New England: is it freer or more constrained than here? Are there grand manors or merely wooden shacks to live in? And what of the natives? One hears such terrifying tales of these semi-naked heathens."

"New England is only part of the newest nation on earth," said George, happily distracted. "It is the most beautiful country, with much still to be explored. There are houses, churches and colleges now, and many wise and educated men. Not so much attention is given to one's place in society, certainly not to the class one is born into. People prosper or not on their true merits."

"I should fail miserably then," she smiled.

"Nonsense; your beauty and warmth would charm everyone, as it does here."

They approached an ornate metal bench placed under an ancient oak tree. Sophie paused momentarily and sat; George joined her.

"Will you return there?" she asked, turning to look at him.

"I cannot say. On the one hand they are in league with the French, on the other, should anything happen to my father I should not forgive myself were we not to have made our peace."

"Yet you risk your life defending your old country every day you are at sea."

"I feel it my duty but, more than that, I spent my earliest years in Cornwall, without the suffering and challenges my father and mother faced from the constant rioting of the miners. I was too young to grasp the threat they felt to their lives. I thought it exaggerated, though my father allows that I was too young to understand, just in order to remain on terms with me.   My coming to England has sorely tested his affections."

"Then it seems to me you will return once this war is won."   Sophia stood, smoothed her dress and, feeling the sudden gust of cold wind, pulled her shawl around her shoulders. George moved to her side.

"If my father lives, I shall feel under an obligation to make my peace with him. Yet whether such a return would be for the rest of my life I cannot know." He smiled and they strolled back in the direction of the house.

***

Early the same evening, Silas arrived from Truro to spend a few days at Nankilly. He had ridden in to town early that morning to sign a contract he had been angling for over the past months.   Now the details were settled he was in expansive mood. George entered the library just as Silas was pouring himself his first port of the evening.

"I pray you Mr Galsworthy, Sir, to excuse me, but if it is not inconvenient I would crave a word in confidence."

"Why George, my boy, come in, come in, Care to join me with a port? Here let me pour it, save calling Povey. Take a seat, take a seat." He indicated an armchair.

"Now, my, boy what is it?"

"I am placed in a difficult situation, Sir, on a number of counts. I am seeking your understanding and guidance, as I have come to hold a strong affection for you as well as a respect and trust in your judgements. Yet I have no wish to burden you with my problems."

"Come, come man, if, as I suspect, Sophie is part of your concerns, then we can hardly avoid discussing them." He sipped his port and gave George a look of encouragement.

"Sophie is at the very heart of my concerns, Sir."

"Silas please, George, there is no need for such formality. I shall feel far more comfortable with informality if we are to discuss personal matters," he smiled.

George smiled in return and was visibly more relaxed.

"I have formed a very strong affection for Sophie and I sense that she returns this affection, although we have not confided such feelings to one another in any formal sense. There is, firstly, the issue of Cousin Richard. I know that there was a strong connection between them and that the promised marriage was more than simply a union. I have no knowledge of the details, but I understood from certain of Richard's comments that a business partnership to both families' advantage was to be facilitated by the match." George paused to gather his thoughts.

"That was indeed the case but you will readily understand that, after Rawdon's revelations, neither Sophie nor I have any desire to proceed. His unfeeling impatience after Oliver's death could have been put aside in due course, but the betrayal of trust at the heart of the murder has banished him from all thought of the marriage or the business."

George went on to raise the issue of his continued naval service, and his need ultimately to return to New England. The strongly held views of his father would pose a further complication.

"I am torn, Silas. If Sophie is truly free from her commitment to Richard, I would dearly like to seek her hand. I detect signs that she might accept a proposal, yet these other commitments are indefinable in length. I have no wish to raise the thought with her until I can be sure to honour such a commitment, yet to delay may mean I would lose her. All this depends, of course, on your permission to court her at all." George sighed as he looked down in confusion, his port untouched.

There was a long, thoughtful silence. Finally Silas spoke.

"It is most honourable of you to state the circumstances so openly. I thank you for that. I am supposing that what you might bring to such a marriage, by way of security and a state of comfort to which she has become accustomed, is unclear through the very circumstances you describe?"

George could only nod, cursing himself for not expressing such a fundamental issue.

"I shall give these issues very careful thought, George. However, I will say this: were the circumstances straightforward, I would have no hesitation in permitting you to court Sophie, should she share your affection. Now drink up that port and let me put the matter aside until I have had the opportunity to give it the attention it warrants."

XV

Martha smiled as Henny toddled up to her. She sat on the makeshift couch and wrapped her good arm round her niece, hugging the little girl to her. Henny, whose run was more of a totter, could only burble her pleasure at a friendly adult who could give her so much attention. Times were better for Molly now, thought Martha. Her sister was free of pain and the oil was fetching a good price. Thomas too seemed more contented. Perhaps because crabbing and fishing were more profitable, or perhaps Molly was more of a wife to him now that she was her old self again.

Martha was regaining her strength. Her broken arm was less painful. She eyed the skilfully bandaged splint and wondered again at the appearance from nowhere of the surgeon. From Falmouth, Molly had said, and he would take no payment. Already met, he'd said. She could still taste that strange herbal drink he gave her, she ran her tongue over the roof of her mouth, to deaden the pain he had said. Yet she had never felt such agony as his straightening the arm. Two bones, he said, must line 'em up so they rejoin; then the cut in the arm while he squeezed all that green poison out. She'd screamed then, couldn't stop herself. He poured the brandy over it and bound it up. Said if it still hurt unbearably after two days he'd have to cut it off. Watch the inside of your arm, he said, look in your armpit. If you get a red line spreading up there it means poison. I'll come back and cut it off for you. But it hasn't, she thought, holding the arm away from her and looking at the healthy blue line of the vein. It does not feel uncommon hot as he said it should if it meant to cause more trouble.

229

Holding Henny's hand with her good arm, she asked the little girl to help her to the door. She smiled as Henny took on the task. At the doorway she let go of the child and opened the door. There was a stiff breeze; white clouds scudded across a blue sky. Warm bursts of sunshine were interspersed with colder, darker moments spread by the changing shapes of the clouds. Martha took great pleasure from the child's company. Henny was a delight in herself, but also as a means by which she could repay Molly who had sacrificed so much to rescue and provide for her. She thought back to the rescue, the nightmare journey on the donkey. Josiah was there, difficult to believe that now, but Molly had confirmed it. It was like a dream she thought, that half-recognised voice, fading and strengthening like the waves of the sea. What had he said? Why was he there? Would she ever know? The great sense of relief when she was laid on the makeshift bed at last; his voice then, an impassioned prayer, perhaps, as the pain took control and she drifted into unconsciousness. Molly could add little except to confirm his kindness and concern. She knew of course about the repair to the cart, but that added nothing to his purpose in being there.

As she regained her strength, she felt a renewed determination to find out more concerning his reappearance in her life. No less strong was her determination to have no more contact or dealings with Rawdon or Sir Richard. The latter was unexpectedly reinforced when Thomas came home. The three sat together for a meal in the evening.

"There do be a right old riot at the Trewarren Arms last night, so I be told." Thomas washed down bread and oil with a great gulp of ale. "Tenants objecting to new rents, I do hear.

Young Sir Richard ain't like his father. Right vicious landlord by what they been saying; won't listen to reason neither. Anyways, I ain't doing what your Will'm did for 'em, no ways; whatever he offer. Don't trust the devil; father was all right but that young Richard, well he be a devil and no mistake."

"What did my Will'm do for them? He was no more than a fisherman and a carrier when needed."

"He did more than that, Martha dear, or why do that Rawdon shoot him dead?" said Molly.

"Bain't normal to shoot the carriers; arrest 'em aye, and drag 'em off to Bodmin Gaol and forget 'em for a year or two, magistrate conniving, But Will'm weren't armed. Reckoned he could defend himself 'gainst all as come at him, me included," Thomas added ruefully.

"'Twere Rawdon as shot my Will'm?"

"Aye, Old Tripp himself did tell me. Rawdon told him as how Will'm knew too much for his own good. Saw both sides of Rawdon's dealings. Thought he should have a share of the takings bein' as how he said nothing about Rawdon's playing the Excise man when it suited." Thomas took another swig of ale and sat back in his chair, more relaxed than Martha ever remembered him. He's enjoying himself, she thought.

"Did his cap'n not discipline him? He should be hanged for murder where all could spit on him, or made to rot his life away in Bodmin Gaol." Molly had said nothing until now but a sudden burst of anger boiled within her.

"Well, Rawdon had his accident and were replaced by that Methody fellow as cap'n, your admirer himself, Martha, Cap'n Carter ain't it? A Methody known to be against the free trade. Things began to tighten up. Rawdon looked elsewhere for his evil ways and many a bootlegger went begging while Carter patrolled the Roseland." Thomas paused and went to the keg for more ale.

"I have never heard this so plain; so many whisperings; so many sideways looks. Is this why Sir Richard be so hard on me? For sure he is bound up in this somewhere." Martha felt more alert than for many months.

"He needed Rawdon's knowledge for more than the free trade, and when you knew nothing of such and showed a fancy for his great enemy, Cap'n Carter, you was finished." Molly was calmer now as she made connections with all the incidents with which she was familiar.

"I've heard none of this afore today, yet it none do surprise me. I only wish my Josiah would return to me and like me for what I am. Not hate me for what I have done."

"You may be surprised there. From what I did glean before and after that dreadful journey, he rued his sudden departure from your life."

"I hardly dare credit that but I must needs get back my strength the soonest I'm able. Yet am I not weakness itself against Master Richard and that devil, Rawdon? I have no means; I know not of Josiah's intentions. He cannot tarry long though he might wish so. He must rejoin his ship and return to battle. He may even be killed." She slumped in her chair as quickly as she had blossomed a few moments before.

XVI

Carriers sat on their carts, wrapped against the wind in the weak April sunshine. The auction at Wynn's Hotel promised good business. They formed an unofficial guild. There was little disputing, but much calling to likely customers and banter among themselves. The earliest arrivals were in prime positions, hoping for a promissory from buyers without their own conveyances. The wind brought the smell of the sea up from the Fal estuary and funnelled it through the narrow street between the warehouses and tenements along the harbour as buyers, drawn by the tempting list of prizes captured from various French vessels off the French and Spanish coasts, began to arrive. Some came by coach, others on horseback.

Inside the Assembly Rooms, the bold décor was still visible below the wide arches that spanned the podium on which the musicians ensured that the fortnightly balls had a lively reputation. The auctioneer's bench now stood where the bandleader usually held sway. Screens protected the lower level of the walls and further staging displayed the trophies of His Majesty's Navy's prowess. George and Silas eyed the goods critically.

"Almost seven hundred hogsheads of good quality wine. There must be something there for us," said George.

"Indeed it appears their finest export out of Bordeaux. There will be some keen interest there, I fancy. I wonder the deck hands did not take such for themselves."

"They would not have gone empty handed. How many ships were taken? The names appear on the wall there; *Le Benjamin*, *La Thane*, *La Nancy*; there are near a dozen listed and their entire cargoes taken, aye, and their very anchors too," said George.

"A very large crane, all complete, capable of lifting the greatest weights," read Silas. "I might use that at Nankilly."

"More likely a mine owner will pay highly for that. His need will be greater than you'd need on the farm, would it not?"

"I have mining interests of my own. It would not have to remain at Nankilly. It could be hired out for rent I don't doubt."

They pushed through the increasing crowd to view the hogsheads and casks. At the barrels of beef and salt pork Silas recognised a coat ahead in the crowd.

"Sir Richard, I fancy, with his estate manager, Masters, is it?" he said.

"Why so it is," George grabbed Silas's arm to hold him back. "But look. Who approaches with such determination?" Both stood still, not wishing to be seen as the newcomer reached his prey.

"Trewarren, Sir, a word if I may."

"No you may not, Sir," replied Richard, turning back to the food barrels. George and Silas looked at each other with questioning eyes. Masters had excused himself and retreated to the staves and hoops on a low table in the far corner. The newcomer stepped forward and tapped Richard on the shoulder.

"A word in private, Sir; the concern I have is best spoken of in private. Please be so kind as to join me outside to discuss a matter in confidence."

"I have nothing to discuss with you, Carter. Now respect my will and leave the building at once. If you do not I shall call the constable. I take it you are too much of a coward to challenge me?"

"So that's who he is! There was something familiar about him." Seeing George's puzzled look, Silas continued: "he was the Revenue man before rejoining the navy: one of these Methodists if I remember aright."

Before George could respond with more than a nod they saw Josiah tap Richard firmly on the shoulder. Richard turned in fury to find Josiah's face was only inches from his own.

"I had no desire to make public your violent and abusive beating of that young woman. Your intransigence forces me to confront you, Sir Richard Trewarren, before all these good people and seek a statement of remorse and an offer of compensation."

By now, a circle of buyers and traders had formed around the pair. Silas and George slipped back and watched between the tricorn hats of those in front.

"The fate of a harlot who has done all in her power to

haunt and destroy me is of no further interest or concern. If you find her charms so alluring that you would risk expulsion from those anti-free-trade Methodists, I warn you she is a whore with all the wiles such creatures employ. I wish to go about my business here and I suggest you do the same." As he turned away Josiah grabbed his arm. Unable to contain his fury, Richard lashed out and caught Josiah a glancing blow on the shoulder. As Josiah faced him squarely with arms down, Richard punched again. Josiah had opened his mouth to speak. The blow caught his lip and forced it against his teeth, drawing blood.

George freed himself from Silas's restraining arm, forced his way through the murmuring crowd, and placed himself between the two protagonists.

"Come Sirs, this is no place for violence. If you have unresolved issues between you, I suggest you allow me to escort you from the sale room to a quiet place where we may resolve, if not the issue at the heart of this quarrel, at least an immediate means of restoring calm to this celebration and sale that so many have awaited with enthusiasm."

"Why, Cousin George! How fortunate that you were in attendance here. I thought you away at sea some days since. Let us dismiss this mad Methody and return to the sale," said Richard, ignoring the invitation to leave the saleroom.

"I am gladdened that you take our previous disagreement so lightly, cousin, but I feel we must allow your current challenger to confirm his acceptance of such a move or we shall be plagued by his concerns for evermore."

"If I may voice my grave concerns, Sir?" said Josiah. "I do not have the honour of knowing who you are, though it is clear you have a family connection with my adversary. I do hope you are free of his more deplorable traits."

"I beg your forgiveness, Sir, I am George Trewarren, cousin to Sir Richard, and lately returned from the Americas to fight for the King. I return to the fleet within the week. And you, Sir? I have not had the pleasure …"

"Josiah Carter, purser, former officer of His Majesty's Revenue Service, also returned to the fleet, Sir. I simply wish to state that Sir Richard has assaulted a widow and former servant of his father's household, left her badly wounded and barely conscious and, since it is nigh impossible to prosecute a landowner of his status, it is only right that he should offer some compensation, if only to ease his conscience."

"I feel no compunction in beating a whore who has spent the last three years doing her utmost to destroy my social standing within my family and the wider community and, most recently, even my life. She'll gain no compensation from me. My advice to you, Sir, is to leave well alone. Further involvement will bring only trouble."

"I do not believe she is a harlot, Sirs, but I see Sir Richard is not to be moved on the matter at present. Rest assured I shall continue to seek justice on her behalf. I thank you for your calming actions, Mr Trewarren; you have saved me from disgracing myself. I shall leave you now to enjoy the sale." Josiah bowed to George, glanced at Richard who avoided his eyes, and strode out through the sale room into the street. As he left them Richard shouted after him, "Ask Rawdon if she is not a harlot. She whores for him by the river in Truro."

George looked at his cousin sharply, but said nothing as they resumed their interest in the sale.

XVII

Josiah strode from the Assembly Rooms, ignoring the carriers chatting by the entrance. He felt both angry and ashamed. Fortunate that the cousin was there, he thought. Not all the Trewarren family are heartless and dishonest, however much he detested Richard. Sir Richard indeed, he was not worthy of the title. He walked briskly down to the harbour and then out along the track towards the headland. The old castle of Pendennis stood on the rock with its cannon facing across the estuary towards St Mawes. I should not have lost control of my temper, he thought, it was shameful to do so in such a place. He walked on at a vigorous pace, oblivious to the coming and going of fishing boats in the waters below or the gulls following noisily in their wake.

The sun strengthened and the wind slackened to a breeze as midday approached. Josiah felt the sweat around his neck and chest but did not slow his pace. A harlot for Rawdon? Surely not his beloved Martha? Trewarren must have been baiting him like some basking shark. He reached the end of the headland and rested on a rock below the Castle. The cliff-top saxifrage and thrift were in bud, the scent of the sea was strong. The surface broke to reveal the head of a seal, its enquiring face seeming to establish its bearings before, oily black and sleek, it looped over into a dive only to surface a few moments later in the quiet bay beyond. Was that all he was ashamed of? That temper loss? He could not dismiss those words of Trewarren, Rawdon's whore. Why had he felt so foolish when Trewarren had laughed at his angry disbelief? The thought would not go away. He stood and began the walk back. He would have to find the truth. If there were truth in the story, he would be filled with self-disgust at his blindness to her true nature. Yet if it were a lie, he would feel shame at doubting her.

He walked up from the shore to the Methodist Chapel, entered and prayed for guidance. When he emerged he knew he had to go back to Truro. Back at the quay, a cart drew away as his clerk was checking the list of provisions. Josiah exchanged a few words and went aboard to check on progress. It was mid afternoon. He could take a ferry if the tide was right. If it turned before he reached Malpas, he would be better travelling by road. The tide times did not appear favourable so he walked across to Wynn's Hotel to take the coach.

It was dark when the coach came to a halt in the Market Square. Josiah hurried down to the quay, crossed the bridge over the creek, and saw immediately the decaying framework of Rawdon's brothel on the Malpas road. A rush light flared in the doorway; lighting could be seen at the upstairs windows.

"Welcome, Sir. Your last chance for a dalliance before you sail, Sir, if I may so presume?" Rawdon did not recognise Josiah in the dim light.

"You may not, Sir. I wish to enquire after a certain

239

Martha Baines.   Is she in your employ in this shameful establishment?"

"And who wants to know?" asked Rawdon, his ingratiating tone discarded.

"I found this woman brutally assaulted some days since. I offered her protection, and am led to understand that she served here as a whore?"

"And what is your purpose? Why is it of any concern to a gentleman such as yourself? If you want an attractive young whore for a dalliance I can provide for your needs. I do not supply such information as you require without charge and without guarantees."

"Mr Rawdon, I would remind you that I am Josiah Carter, current purser to the rear admiral of the Mediterranean fleet. I am also a former captain of the Roseland Excise Men. I do have knowledge of your felonious dealings under the former captain which, had we not both left the service, albeit for very different reasons, I would have had lain before the justice. You would have been rotting away behind the bars of Bodmin Gaol." Josiah's eyes pierced the dim light.

"Captain Carter, Sir! Why of course, didn't recognise you, Sir, not the sort of gentleman we expect to entertain, though, of course, you'd always be sure of our finest young ladies."

"Enough, Rawdon. Martha Baines, did she whore for you or no?"

"Well the truth is, Cap'n, I took pity on the poor lass.

Thrown out of the household, she was, by the new lord of Trewarren. Shouldn't speak ill of the gentry, I know, Cap'n, but young Sir Richard, well he ain't like his father now. That's a certainty."

"So she is a whore?"

"As I say, Cap'n, I took pity on the poor lass and she lived here for free and she coached the young lads in the ways of the world so to speak. Loved her they did, she were that kindly with 'em."

"Was she truly here of her own free will? How is it she was so dreadfully assaulted?"

"She had nowhere to live, Cap'n. No livelihood, nor no chance of one. She were truly grateful to take up my offer. As for the assault, you had best ask Sir Richard. He came here desperate for an assignation. Demanded the freshest young delight I could offer, as any gentleman of his standing has a right to expect. Would not be diverted, Cap'n. Brushed her curtain aside and set on her. She were ill-prepared for such is all I can say."

"So you threw her out?"

"She left, Cap'n. Left of her own accord. She knew she were no attraction for gentlemen in that state, Cap'n. No attraction at all."

Josiah descended the stairs in the flickering light without another word. He continued along the Malpas road, reaching the village after half an hour. The inn was quieter there. He took a room and ordered supper. He could take a ferry back to Falmouth at dawn.

The serving wench placed the mutton stew and dumplings in front of him and offered a choice of wines or a flagon of ale or porter. Josiah asked for spring water. She eyed him suspiciously.

"You bain't from the Excise?"

"The drink poisons the body, mind and soul; the Good Lord's temple is thus defiled."

"Spring water then." She disappeared, muttering quietly. Returning with a flagon of water and a pewter tankard, she placed them on the table and hurried away without a word.

From what he knew of Rawdon, though mostly based on the anecdotes of others, he could not imagine the old rogue acting out of pity. His story would be told to protect himself. Yet the picture he painted of Sir Richard tallied with Martha's account. It was clear that she had lived in the whorehouse. With Rawdon she would have had to earn her keep. She must have been whoring for Rawdon; that seemed clear. He went up to his room. He slept fitfully. The warmth of his body drew the bed bugs to him. Who was the true Martha? Could he believe Rawdon? How far was Richard's grotesque account his protective imagination? What of Martha's own story? Surely he should believe her description of events before all others? But he had never asked her if she was a whore. The impossibility of doing so led him to wrestle with the issues between fitful dozes. He was relieved to see the dawn.

XVIII

"You have a bargain there," said Richard as Silas stood by the carrier's cart. Silas had purchased fifty hogsheads of the quality wine but had decided against the crane. Richard's affability had grated on George, who had excused himself to return to his ship.

"I certainly hope so. You can never be entirely sure, but it's unlike the French to carry inferior wine," said Silas.

"Indeed not." He paused but, mindful of the near completion of the loading process, felt he had to seize the opportunity. "If I may be so bold?" Silas's face turned sharply to face him, "I wonder if I may renew my acquaintanceship with Sophie. I would like to put the disruptions and misunderstandings of the past months out of mind and restore our strong understanding. Perhaps we might sample your purchase of today, should such a meeting turn out as I hope and expect." Richard smiled.

"I will certainly ask Sophie if she has an interest in such a meeting. I am sure she will want to give the matter some thought. I will endeavour to pen a reply to you at Trewarren during the next ten days."

"Surely that is more time than she needs?" He paused. "Of course, it is entirely at her pleasure. I cannot conceal my eagerness to enjoy her company again. I shall exercise patience as well as I can, but please assure her of my deep and abiding affection for her."

"Certainly." Silas turned to his coachman. "Are we loaded?" At the driver's nod he entered the coach, leaned from the window, and gave Richard a wave of farewell.

Richard watched the coach trundle down towards the quay with the carrier's cart following on behind. Should he stay in Falmouth for the evening, go up to Truro or cross to St Mawes and take a boat round to Trewarren Bay? The fleet would be sailing on tomorrow's ebb tide, the brothels would be full and the cockfights would be even more raucous than usual. Cock fighting no longer attracted him as it used to.

"Excuse me, Sir Richard." George Masters stood by his shoulder. "The wagon is loaded; I am about to move down to the quay to catch the ebb tide."

"Very good, Masters. I will return in due time. A good day's work was it not?"

"Yes indeed, Sir. If there is nothing further?" At Richard's nod he waved the wagon on and followed.

***

Richard sat in the Pandora at Mylor Bridge, and cast his eye over the serving wenches. The tavern was throbbing with life; fishermen and inshore boatmen had enjoyed the presence of the fleet and the sale of booty down at Falmouth. One young man grasped the skirts of a passing wench only to receive the flagon of cider over his head, to the uproarious amusement of the men drinking with him.

"Sweetly done, my beauty," said Richard as she passed.

"Why thank you, Sir. 'Twould be a privilege to serve you the same," she said as she swirled past.

"I would value your service, my beauty, though I fancy I could redirect your enthusiasm. How say you?"

"I do return, Sir, when I have served my waiting custom," she smiled as she swung away to another rowdy table where she reached down between bushy beards and protruding clay pipes billowing smoke to refill pewter tankards.

"Give us a song, Nancy; add a sweet sound to our shanty, gel." A great hulk of a man had risen and, grasping her waist, held her firm. At his signal, another man drew up a fiddle and plucked at the strings before drawing the bow and striking up a well-known sea shanty. They all cheered and simultaneously sang a chorus:

Oh Falmouth is a fine town with ships in the bay

And I wish from my heart it's there I was today;

I wish from my heart I was far away from here.

Sitting in my parlour and talking to my dear.

For it's home, dearie, home, it's home I want to be.

Our topsails are hoisted and we'll away to sea.

They prompted the wench to sing a verse. The fiddler marked time until she gave in and it became clear why they had asked her. Her voice was sweet and true, as she sang each verse of the sad ballad. For it was more a ballad than a shanty, Richard realised.

As she passed on the way back to the kitchen, he stopped her.

"I do be with you directly, Sir." She moved to pass him.

"I wonder if you might serve me in the comfort of my own room, my beauty, where I might congratulate you away from the mocking eyes of these drunken peasants."

"'Tes my living, Sir. Besides they mean no harm and I likes to sing with 'em, when time allows."

"Nevertheless my beauty, you will earn a month's wages for such a service and you can sing every other night of the week." He paused. She said nothing. "So, a bottle of best brandy and two glasses to my room, Nancy, as soon as you can."

"Very good, Sir." She slipped past him.

***

As with the singing, she put up spirited resistance to his seductive demands but, by the time the brandy was half empty, his desire was almost beyond control. As she surrendered, he realised that she was as adept at satisfying his needs as she had been at singing earlier.

When he awoke next morning she was nowhere to be seen. He took a hearty breakfast and set off for the King Harry ferry. Falmouth quay would be teeming with sailors and pressed men; pursers checking supplies; midshipmen checking crews on board; and bo'suns preparing ships to sail on the next ebb tide. On the hill beyond, towards Glendurgan, he passed a train of donkeys, endless it seemed, all roped together with their panniers of tin ore heading for the streaming pump at Devoran. He was soon over the ferry and on the road home. He approached his own lands around midday.

"Lord Skinflint, 'isself, if I b'aint mistook," shouted a bearded old man sitting leaning against the tavern wall. A mob the worse for the cheapest gin fought with each other to get through the tavern door and jeer as he rode through the village. He whipped Caesar into a gallop and the jeering faded. I'll have the lot of them evicted, he thought, drunken wasters. I'll have Masters see to it directly. Father was too soft with them, and that's the result. No respect for their betters.

XIX

"Hitch the border loop over that hook. Is your arm strong enough? That's the way. Now unwind her along to the next hook." Molly drew more of the seine net from the folded heap as Martha pulled, stretched and hooked it, section by section, along the barking house wall and out to the stakes spaced along the yard. After half an hour the net was hung: Martha was exhausted.

"Come now, we'm ready to start. Watch me check her for breaks or loose threads. Like this, see? Any weak link, tie a strip of hemp so we can see 'un. Start at the other end, work to me." Molly resumed tugging and twisting at the net. She worked along with a reel of hemp hanging from her shoulder.

Martha walked to the far end and began the same process, hesitantly at first, but after finding two or three weak or broken links she felt more confident. She had felt fully recovered and determined to give her sister all the help she could. I've lived off her kindness for half the year, she thought, I must help her all I am able. After struggling with the net, she realised it was many months since she had done hard physical work. She tired far too easily; she would not give way.

"She ain't too bad, considering last season's catches. I think we can mend her up and soak her in the coal tar," said Molly, when they had checked the whole net. The iron pot, its rim encrusted with years of dried tar, hung on a chain from the rafter over a smouldering wood fire. The fresh coal tar gave off noxious fumes through the plopping of large slowly developing bubbles. Henny, dozing in a wicket basket, coughed herself awake as the fumes drifted towards the air vent in the wall. She began to cry.

"Shush, Baby, Mam's here," said Molly, glancing briefly across at the basket.

"Want drink," said Henny. "Mam, drink," she shouted, and coughed again.

"In the cask, Martha, will you see to her?" She pointed at the sacking she had brought with them. Martha moved to the bag, took out a stone cask and poured some weak ale into a wooden tankard.

"Here you are, treasure, sit up and Auntie will pass you the cup." Henny grabbed the tankard in both hands and drank noisily. She gasped for breath as she passed the tankard back.

They worked all day on the net, taking only a short break for some bread and ale. Henny found some wooden pegs and some rusty iron bars which she marshalled into sailors and fishermen who struggled through storms and giant sea creatures. By early evening the net was strung out to dry, with repairs and new coal tar coating completed. Henny was asleep in her basket again.

"Time to go home," said Molly, lifting Henny on to her hip. They left the barking house and walked along the quay. Out to sea a flotilla of sails was silhouetted against the early evening sunset. Come back safe, Josiah, Martha thought to herself. Henny pointed over her mother's shoulder. "Boats, lots o' boats, Mam, look Mam, sailing away. Where they going, Mam?"

"Our brave sailors are going to get old Boney and beat the Frenchies," said Molly. "Ain't that right, Auntie Martha?"

"That's right, sure enough. Let's hope they come back safe," said Martha, thinking of one particular sailor. A cold gust whipped a drift of sand along the beach beyond the quay as stars appeared in the clear April sky.

"I'll heat up some broth," said Molly. "We've earned it today."

***

Josiah sat in the officers' day room with his inventories. He needed to recheck the gun deck and the armament stores before they rejoined the Rear Admiral at Spithead. He knew the ships would turn under cover of darkness and tack their way up the south coast. His mind drifted back to his chance encounter with George Trewarren while the fleet waited for the tide to turn. He'd been standing on deck checking in the final supplies when an officer on the quay had addressed him. He hadn't recognised him at first.

"Did you get satisfaction, man?" said the officer, smiling up at his bewilderment.

"I ask your pardon, Sir, to what do you refer?" said Josiah. Sudden recognition lit his face.

"I see you recall me now; do you have a moment?"

"Certainly, Sir; I'll disembark at once. We await the tide turn to sail. We have an hour or two by my reckoning."

They shook hands and retired to a quayside tavern. George ordered a glass of Malmsey but to George's amusement Josiah refused his offer of the same in favour of a dandelion and burdock.

"You appeared to have an unresolved issue with my cousin."

"I do indeed. He attacked and seriously injured a woman after having his way with her in a filthy brothel by the river in Truro. A woman, moreover, forced into prostitution against her very nature by his unjust treatment of her whilst in his father's employ."

"You make a very serious allegation, Sir. You should exercise extreme care. Yet I sense you have not revealed your true interest in the matter."

"The truth is, I feel some guilt or, if not guilt, responsibility. Sir Richard's animosity originates from the occasion he came across the widow taking refreshment with me outside her house. I had accompanied her home from our weekly worship."

"You suggest he did not expect her to have company?" asked George.

"A former Excise man, Rawdon by name, had led him to believe that Martha, the woman in question, recently widowed, would not resist his advances. She had gained employment at the Manor at her husband's death. He regarded her as his property. He saw me as her act of defiance."

"Rawdon, the scoundrel, I might have expected his involvement."

"It was my opinion that the honourable reaction for Sir Richard, once the anger cooled, would be an apology and a payment of compensation. This was evidently beyond his comprehension," concluded Josiah.

"When did this assault take place? Can you recall the occasion?"

"Very soon after Sir Oliver's death; a day or so after Admiral Nelson's great victory off the coast of Egypt was announced."

"Well, thank you, Carter. Very interesting, very interesting indeed. Rest assured it will do you no harm to have revealed this to me." George rose to his feet and put out his hand, "Good day to you, Carter. Have a safe voyage, and bag a few Frenchmen." He strode off along the quay.

Josiah turned back to his inventories. He had recalled the meeting word for word, but felt unsure of the implications. Was Martha safer or more at risk? Should he have confessed his true feelings of guilt: the way he had abandoned her; left her open to such a life. He would not have wished it on her or any woman for that matter. He fell on his knees and prayed long and earnestly for the Lord's guidance.

PART 3

Six months later

I

"Cheats, the lot of you; nothing but cheating rascals; not fit company for a respectable gentleman to engage with." Richard belched, threw down his cards and pushed back his chair. He steadied himself and attempted to walk sedately away, his drunken stagger emphasised by his weak leg. Navigating the three steps with exaggerated care, he unbuttoned his trousers and relieved himself into the flow of stinking liquid flushing along the cobbled gutter. He scrambled onto Caesar's back and made his way to Rawdon's brothel where he climbed the stairs with difficulty, pulled back a curtain and found a couple fully engaged in their business.

"Florence," he called, "Florence, find me a whore."

Florence appeared, panic in her face. "All busy, Sir Richard; all occupied." She stood irresolute. He leaned on the wall to steady himself. He had no intention of leaving.

"I suppose you may wait in my room. I'll call you when one's free."

Richard flopped down on her bed. She sat in a chair in the doorway ready to call him. A few minutes later he had fallen asleep, signalling the loss of urgency by the loud regular rhythm of his snoring.

As he rode home next morning, self-disgust welled up like physical vomit. He blamed Silas. They could have achieved so much if only he could have married Sophia. A new business empire awaited, but Silas chose to turn his back. Well, he'd pay the price. Sophia was promised, whatever they said now. Sophia had changed her mind, had she? She'd destroyed the whole ambitious project with one feminine flounce, and Silas had fallen for it. Rawdon had much to answer for as well. That rascal betrayed trust within hours of his promise. All his exaggerations were pure evil. And where had it all led? Tenants rebelling, refusing rent rises, inspired by French revolutionaries, no doubt; free-trading partners deserted, and no capital for new projects. Who could blame him for trying to build capital through gambling? It was all he had left and now, thanks to those scoundrels at the Assembly Rooms, he'd been cheated out of even that resource.

There was still one certain means of getting enough to pay off debts and rebuild a business of sorts. He would sue Sophia through Silas for breach of promise. He was certain to win. He blamed himself for not doing so before, but he had thought if he could just get back on his feet, start to turn the estate around, she might change her mind. Silas might have made her see sense. Six months was long enough. Clearly it was not to be. They'd had their chance. He'd write to his lawyer as soon as he got back to Trewarren.

"Lady Trewarren would like a word with you, Sir. The Reverend Francis Trewarren is with her." Bassett had positioned himself to guide Richard into the drawing room.

Richard paused. He was tempted to refuse and tell Bassett to stand aside but allowed himself to be ushered into their presence. The midday autumn sunshine showed Elizabeth's transformation of the decor at its best. There was a light airy feel to the room which ill suited Richard's mood. "Richard, I feel it is time we had a serious talk about the conduct of your affairs and the business of the estate and Francis agrees with me. In short, things cannot go on as they are or the estate will be bankrupt and we will be the centre of a revolt like the French aristocracy have suffered."

"Good morning, Mother, Francis. I trust you are well. It is unlike you to ignore the common courtesies, Mother. Is there some impending threat I am unaware of?"

"Your mother's increasing concerns could be contained no longer. She invited me to advise her. We sought and obtained from Masters a full report of the estate's condition and prospects and were most alarmed to find things are worse than we could ever have imagined," said Francis.

"To say nothing of your falling out with Silas Galsworthy and losing all hope of that favourable marriage," added his mother.

"Shall we sit down and discuss this calmly?" said Richard, struggling to stay calm himself. He indicated the sofa, waited for them to be seated and took his place in an armchair opposite. "Putting aside the fact that Masters far exceeded his duties in revealing such details, I have developed a plan to recover our position of which he is unaware."

"Richard, it requires a complete change of attitude toward those you are responsible for. I have poor parishioners begging me to help them. The new rents are way beyond their means. Those already evicted and those threatened are in a desperate condition. You will soon have no farm labour available. The fishermen contribute nothing now that you have sold the business on to that free-trade proponent of a lawyer in Polperro and, incidentally, where is the capital from that transaction? I will not raise the free trade issue except to say that, since Oliver's death, contacts have ceased." Francis glanced at Elizabeth. "I'm sorry, I did not intend to embark on a list of problems."

"An interesting list to be sure," said Richard. "But we have to pay our way, and my dear father was too soft on these people."

"Masters doesn't think so," interjected his mother, "and he has been running the estate under your father's direction since you were a child."

"Masters is stuck in the past. He has no appreciation of modern business. Besides, this is all irrelevant, Mother. I have a means of raising the money that will clear all these problems away."

"More gambling?"

"Certainly not; I shall sue Sophia through Silas for breach of promise. With his wealth I am sure to be awarded a large sum with costs and damages. I was about to write to our lawyers when you had me dragged in here."

"But Richard ... " Elizabeth looked at Francis in disbelief. "You have forfeited every right to such a payment by your appalling conduct. Instead of doing your utmost to convince her of your loyalty and patience, you ... ."

"Yes, yes Mother, I don't think we need to cover these matters yet again. The fact is I am still pleased to marry her and she has broken her promise to me." He stood, nodded to them both and left the room.

II

"Mam, a man have come. He at the door. Mam, the man have come." Henny rolled to the cellar stairs in her walking frame.

"Stay, Henny, I be there directly," called Molly, wiping the fish innards and salt from her chapped hands. "Who would that be?" she said to Martha. "Thomas ain't back yet, I'm sure o' that. If he were home so soon he be down the tavern, that be one thing I'm sure on." She climbed the steps, still holding the towel, twisted Henny's walking frame and pushed her to one side, smiling at her as she did so.

"Molly? Lieutenant Carter, Josiah. Good day to you. I am hoping you will be kind enough to inform me of the whereabouts of Martha Baines. You may remember I assisted you in conveying her here after the assault she suffered some months ago."

"Why Cap'n Carter, come in, come in. We are ever in

your debt. Martha is here and fully recovered." Molly stood back to allow Josiah entry. The smell of pressed and salted pilchards sharpened. "Martha, 'tes Cap'n Carter to see you. Come you up so he do see you are strong and in good health again."

Martha laid the gutted pilchard she was holding on the bed of salt, its head against the tail of Molly's last fish. Her head swam. Josiah? Why? How? What did he want from her? Did she dare hope? She reached for the cloth to wipe her hands.

"Martha! Leave them now; they'll not come to harm for a half hour." Molly called down again.

Martha approached from the cellar steps uncertainly. She gasped as Josiah rose to greet her. His uniform, crumpled from the recent journey, gave him a distinguished air, she thought.

"Martha," he stepped forward, offering his hand. "How are you? Fully recovered, I hope. You most certainly look as attractive as ever."

She looked down at her feet. The compliment had confused her further. She drew breath and looked up. I am a strong woman now, she reminded herself.

"Josiah." She took his hand lightly. "I am well thank you and grateful for your assistance at the time of my trouble."

"Please, let us sit." He indicated the chairs, and accepted a glass from Molly, who returned to the cellar but ensured she could hear all that was said.

"The first part of my concern is already answered, and very happily. You are clearly well and actively employed with your sister-in-law; a tower of strength to you without doubt."

"That she is. I am so very fortunate in her."

"Do I understand aright, that neither that rogue Rawdon nor Trewarren have given trouble during my absence?" he asked. "I understood Trewarren owned the seining rights hereabouts.

"He sold them to a lawyer in Polperro. Thomas, that is Molly's man, tells that when Sir Oliver died Sir Richard tried to break the part-ownership of the seiners' boats which they d'not want him to do. He offered no money for to buy the men's shares. They say they will burn the boats. He say they were no better than a gang o'frenchies and he waste no time with the likes o' them. He sold his share to this lawyer who came to talk to the men and agreed to keep the arrangement. So far he keep his word."

Josiah nodded at the satisfaction in her voice. They sat in silence for a while.

"Has the fleet returned to Falmouth?" asked Martha.

"We are in Portsmouth to revictual for one week. I have taken the schooner to Plymouth and the coach from there. I must take the return in two days at the latest. The master's clerk has my list. I shall check it for price and quality on return. Had I not taken the opportunity to visit, I know not when I would have been able to do so."

"I be deeply touched you should feel such concern for my recovery," said Martha, "but I sense you have further concerns."

"I have dreaded this moment but I have prayed to the good Lord every day of the voyage for guidance and it is clear I must ask you directly. Trewarren and Rawdon both dismissed you as a harlot and a whore. I did not believe them, yet the visit I made in Truro suggested the likelihood of some truth in their sordid remarks." He paused and looked at her pale face. She said nothing, forcing him to continue. "The last time I saw you, after the assault, I told you as you lay there, do you remember?" She shook her head. "Well I said that I regretted the way I broke off our earlier closeness, bitterly regretted it. I had come to realise that it was not of the low carnality I witnessed all too often amongst the able seamen around me. There was a lack of any mutual affection in their lustful doings. That was not so with us, I am convinced. Is it not so, Martha? I felt it was an expression of a warmth that could have led us to, well, was it not?" The appeal in his eyes brought a tear to hers.

"Oh Josiah, if only, but yes, it was the strongest affection I had ever felt for a man that led me to give so much of myself."

"But do you not see, if you are truly a harlot, a common whore, then that whole image is a false picture embedded in my brain through my own weakness. I have to know. That is why I came, and that is the truth of it." He leaned back in his chair and closed his eyes. Martha said nothing. She could hear Molly working in the cellar. She was chatting quietly to Henny. Martha realised her sister must have come up and lifted her daughter from the walking frame without Martha noticing. The stillness in the room continued.

III

"Why, this is outrageous. Has the man no pride, no concern for his reputation?" The paper quivered in Silas's hand as his indignation increased. Sophia had watched him take the letter from the tray that Povey offered and break the seal. Most unusually, he had stood and read it instead of taking it through to the library.

"What is it? Not business surely?"

"I think it is the most outrageous demand I have ever received. I recognised a lawyer's seal. I was curious, but this is not what I expected; not from someone claiming to be a gentleman."

"What is it? I have never seen you so angry."

"Listen to this: 'I have been instructed by my client, Sir Richard Trewarren, to sue Miss Sophia Galsworthy, through Silas Galsworthy Esquire, guardian of said Sophia, for breach of promise in that a formal proposal of marriage had been accepted and confirmed and has since been repudiated by said Sophia, notwithstanding my client's continued commitment to such a marriage." He dropped the letter to his side, removed his pince-nez and looked across at his niece.

Sophia sat down, pale with shock. "Does this mean I must marry him after all? I can't bear the thought of him now."

"And you will not have to, my dearest. You will not have

to. However we settle this, I am not prepared to sacrifice your happiness to this scoundrel's threat."

"He has a point, though, we cannot deny it. We were engaged and I did break it off."

"And your reasons were sound. I fully approved. We'll see what's behind this. I'll make further enquiries. I'll write to Lady Trewarren and ask discreetly what her son would require to settle this matter." Silas went immediately to the library to compose his request.

In the evening, when the missive had been dispatched, a visitor was heard knocking on the door. Sophia was in the drawing room where Silas was about to join her. He stood in the door-way, pausing at the sound.

"It couldn't be him, surely? My letter is barely out of town. Do you think you should retire briefly to your room until our impatient visitor's identity is established?"

"That is not necessary," Sophie smiled. "Povey will attend to it and ask whether we will receive a visitor."

They heard the door open and, after a few moments, Povey appeared. "Mr Trewarren to see you, Sir, and Miss Sophia if you will permit."

"Mr George Trewarren, not Sir Richard?" asked Silas. Povey looked slightly offended.

"I am sorry if I was not clear, Sir. It was *Mr* Trewarren I referred to."

George was shown in without more ceremony and apologised for his dishevelled state. "I am in possession of information I feel you should be aware of, Silas, but I have only another three days to return to my ship at Portsmouth." George still seemed out of breath.

"Come, take a seat, some refreshment?" Silas indicated a chair. Sophia stood across the room, staring in disbelief. George, regaining his composure, looked across at her. The warmth of his smile gave the reassurance she had hoped for. Povey was instructed to bring refreshments and they settled to hear George's news.

"No doubt you remember the fellow who accosted Richard at the sale in Falmouth?" said George. Silas nodded.

"I had not known it, but he is purser on another ship of the fleet. We met briefly on the quay before sailing from Falmouth. I raised the issue with him. His accosting of Richard, I refer to. He told me that not only did Richard go straight from here to a whorehouse, as Rawdon has already said, but that he beat the whore most cruelly when he had had his way with her. This man, Carter by name, assisted in conveying her to a house of safety with her sister-in-law. The woman had fallen on bad times, by all accounts." George looked at their shocked faces, "I was most anxious that Sophie did not reconsider in my prolonged absence, or feel honour bound to keep to her solemn commitment to wed him without knowing of his violent nature."

"Excuse me for a moment," said Silas. He walked through to the library, retrieved the letter, returned and gave it to

George without a word.   George read it through, before looking across at both of them in disbelief.

"But this is damnable, begging your pardon, Sophie, I am speechless," he said.

"I have written to Lady Trewarren this afternoon, and set unofficial enquiries in train as to his business and financial circumstances," said Silas.   "I shall await the outcome with interest.   In the meantime, it is important to keep any friendship between Sophie and yourself as entirely informal and above suspicion, whatever your true feelings."

"Of course, I agree we must provide no evidence that could be used to support his claim.   As it is, I shall depart tomorrow to return to the fleet.   I wished to pass on the information and to reassure Sophie of my continued affection. I shall find a bed in an inn in the town and begin my return journey on the first available coach.   At least I have been able to enjoy a short time with Sophie and will keep a picture of her in my mind until I can return."

"When will you return?   Will you be able to stay longer next time?" said Sophie.   "It is torture to glimpse you thus and let you go."   She stood and stepped towards him.   He took her hand, raised it to his lips and, with one last look deep into her eyes, thanked Silas and left.

"How strange," said Sophia, as her uncle returned from the hall.

"Strange?   I am not sure I understand."

"Well, the information he gave was appalling, and it was a delight to see him again, but in all the circumstances it is merely a confirmation of the faults in Richard's character. It seems disproportionate to exhaust himself in travelling the breadth of the country and back with such a short period in which to do so."

"Do you not think he had other concerns?" smiled her uncle.

"But he spoke of nothing else."

"He didn't have to. He has not set eyes on you for six months, nor had any meaningful conversation with you. Did you not see that lovelorn expression? Did you not see that he feasted his eyes on you? That in itself was reason enough."

"You are suggesting that the tale of Richard's violence was no more than an excuse for coming here?" asked Sophia.

"Not exactly; he clearly thought it was important, but he must have feared you might return to Richard. After all, he knows you almost married him. Six months at sea can arouse such fears in the best of men."

"It is true there is no formal arrangement between us."

"And there cannot be until this matter with Richard is resolved. In the meantime, if you are seriously intent on marriage to George, you need to consider the implications of emigration. I would feel such a loss very deeply, my dear Sophie, should it come to that," said Silas.

IV

"I cannot lie to you," said Martha at last. "But I was forced by my own ignorance and despair to degrade myself in that way. It has been an unbearable period in my life."

"I feared as much, but at least you are honest," said Josiah. "It is a great pity, yet in my heart I feared it was true."

"Let me tell how I was placed; you will see I had no choice." Without waiting for his agreement, Martha embarked on a detailed account from the death of Will'm, shot by Rawdon, as she had recently discovered, through Richard's vindictiveness and Rawdon's trickery to the beating from which Molly and he had rescued her. "But I am stronger now," she concluded, "and they will never force such degrading ways on me again."

"It is a truly distressing tale," said Josiah, visibly moved. "No woman should have to suffer so. Yet we cannot escape or deny the fact that you are defiled. It is to be bitterly regretted but cannot be ignored."

"What are you saying? That we have no future together?" said Martha, anxiety rising within her.

"For me, it has raised grave doubts. I have spent months wrestling with my conscience, reading the scriptures, praying to Almighty God for guidance. I have finally convinced myself that our carnal act together was truly an act borne out of a deepening affection for each other. It was not carnality for its own sake, as I have seen so often from sailors landing in port after months at sea. Your words have thrown the truth and wisdom of this into doubt. Did I persuade myself out of my own weakness? Were you destined for damnation and drawing me with you? I fear it may be so."

Martha stood with hands on hips and looked directly into his eyes. "You would condemn me to eternal damnation? I do think you are less forgiving than the good Lord himself. Do you not know how I longed for your forgiveness in all those days and nights, weeks and months since we celebrated the truth of our love? How I thanked the good Lord for the expression of his mercy through your help to Molly and the surgeon you engaged on my behalf? How I have prayed for your safe return, that I may be protected from the power of the devil brought through Rawdon and Sir Richard? There, I have never spoke so much all in one breath." She continued looking at him as her hands dropped to her sides.

"'Tes well spoken and 'tes the truth, Cap'n Carter. She is a good un and she's got a bit o' sap now. You take care afore you cast her into hell. The good Lord ain't given up on her yet, you mark my words." Molly had emerged from the cellar steps to stand with Martha. The two women looked down on Josiah, who was still seated. Henny cried out from the cellar and broke the tension. Molly went down and brought her back up. She stood holding her.

"This is Cap'n Carter, Henny. Say how d'ye do."

"No," she said, burying her face in Molly's shoulder.

Josiah stood up and held out a hand to Henny. "Hello, little one; don't be afraid."

Henny half turned her head. "Say hello," said Molly. "He ain't damned you to hell yet."

"Hello," said Henny, immediately burying her face in her mother's shoulder.

Josiah moved towards the door. "I must return to the ship, I have much to think about."

Martha stepped close to him, slid her arms round his waist and rested her face against his chest. She could feel the rhythm of his breathing, the firmness beneath his shirt. He rested his hands on her hips in an automatic gesture but there was no give in his body.

"I had begun to dare to dream of a life together, secure in care and affection for each other. I understand now that I do not warrant it. Yet I do dream," she said.

"I will struggle mightily to come to terms with what I have learned today. I will read and pray between duties. Now I must leave you." He moved her away from him.

"You can save me, Josiah, if you should wish to. Keep that in your thoughts if you will." She watched as he set off back towards his ship.

"I do not understand that man, truly I do not," said Molly, still holding Henny in her arms.

"Do we have more fish to baulk, while there is still some light?" asked Martha.

"One layer, I should think. The salt is already set. I am

right proud o' you; right proud. You spoke up like you would never do before. Must be true love as does it," she smiled. Martha said nothing but went down into the cellar, took up the knife and resumed gutting and baulking the pilchards.

V

"Francis, welcome and thank you for coming so promptly. I resisted the temptation to berate Richard on receipt of this letter from Silas Galsworthy. He is as yet unaware that I have received it. I would appreciate your advice on how to respond." Lady Trewarren handed Francis Silas's letter. A blustery wind was sending dark clouds scudding across the sky. Francis sat near the drawing room window and held the letter up to the light. It was a brief message, unambiguous in its meaning. Francis lowered it and looked across at his sister-in-law.

"What should I do? Should I tell Richard of this? Give Silas the information without mentioning it to him? Or agree a response with him? My instinct is to arrange a meeting with Silas, to explore the whole issue before committing myself or involving Richard. Yet much could go awry if I do so. What are your thoughts?"

"One never likes broken promises of course, but it is clear there is no future in this relationship. That being so, we should avoid a court case if it is possible. Richard will not be satisfied without a generous settlement; he has large debts with no other means of meeting them, as far as we know. Yet it seems insufficient simply to supply Silas with a list of assets and debts," said Francis.

"That is my feeling but, if I invite Silas here, Richard would discover it: worse, he may actually come crashing in on us unawares. If, on the other hand, I arrange to go into Truro to see him, Richard will ask why the carriage is being prepared and so on. He cannot avoid seeing it depart or return."

"If you have no objection to my presence, I would be happy to arrange a meeting at the rectory. In that way you would be visiting me, would not need your carriage and, if Silas were also there, you would have chanced upon us. I would be present or not at your discretion. What do you think?"

"I do think that may be the answer. I would certainly be pleased to have you present, as such an interview could provoke moments of intense discomfort. Would you be kind enough to write to Silas, on behalf of both of us, inviting him to such a meeting? We can take the summary given us by Masters as the basis of fact." Elizabeth was visibly relieved by Francis's suggestion.

"Very well, I shall return to the rectory and write to him immediately." Francis rose from his chair and held both her hands in his. "God bless you, my dear. I will inform you as soon as I have an answer."

***

Rawdon was pleased to be digging into the details of Richard's life amongst the lower sort. He visited the Assembly Rooms to gather details of his gambling debts, travelled down to Trewarren Bay to talk to old Tripp on the matter of the pilchard fishing sale and even crossed to Falmouth, mentioning the name with a smile in every low-life tavern in the town. At the Pandora, on the way back to Truro, Rawdon had a very interesting chat with the barmaid, concerning Sir Richard's visit earlier in the year. He did not approach Masters on the estate, but sat in the Trewarren Arms and bought a flagon of ale to share with anyone who cared to relate their stories of Sir Richard. In this way, he was able to provide a detailed view from those whose lives had been damaged by the new lord of the manor; a task he interpreted with his own colourful distortions for Silas Galsworthy's benefit.

**

"I am very grateful to you both for your invitation," said Silas as the three of them sat together in the rectory drawing room a few days later. "I hope most sincerely that we can settle the matter without going to court. Besides the unnecessary expense, I would not want to pain you with the revelations in public that would have to be presented in Sophia's defence in order to defend her honour."

"Then we are of like mind. We have here a current list of debits and credits on the estate from Masters, the estate manager," said Francis.

"Richard does not yet know of this meeting, as far as we are aware," added Lady Trewarren, "as we want to be fully acquainted with all the facts and the proposed solution to the problem before advising him. He seems unable to understand the reality of his situation."

"That was my reading also," said Silas, "so let us work towards a proposal for a settlement figure, with a clear understanding of the case to be raised against him should the proposal not be accepted. I should perhaps state at the outset that Sophia and I accept that a betrothal was agreed; and that Sophia is no longer prepared to enter into a marriage with Richard; and that therefore there is legally a breach of promise. However, we both also believe that Sophia has very good grounds for not honouring the betrothal. I can rehearse those grounds now, if you wish, or we could follow my suggestion and look first at assessing a reasonable settlement figure."

"We have here the accounts of the estate, as I mentioned before, but we have little idea of his personal finances, except to say that we are aware that he has been betting at the card tables in recent months and appears not to have made the gains he anticipated. So, ignoring that for the moment, the estate now brings in a reduced amount; there is almost no free-trade income and the pilchard seining has been sold on. In order to meet the immediate shortfall on the estate, I estimate two hundred guineas would see us through to the year end in March." Francis looked at Elizabeth and was gratified by her warm smile of agreement.

"Two hundred guineas would see him to the year end, and this would give him time to pull the estate round to cover its costs in the following year?" asked Silas.

"Always supposing there was no repeat of the pilchard situation, where a similar amount was debited as personal expenses."

"An interesting point, as I have some information as to those gambling debts. I am reliably informed that he has issued promissory notes to the value of two hundred and fifty guineas. In addition, I am told that he has made vague promises in the tavern and elsewhere of settlements in due course but has left no note as to the amounts. From what I hear, these would amount to somewhere between ten and twelve guineas. Thus a sum of five hundred guineas would resolve the issue and, were he to accept, there would be no further action or discussion on the matter," said Silas.

"I take that as a very handsome offer in the circumstances. What say you, Elizabeth?"

"I agree. That is most generous of you, Silas. I am sure we can persuade him of that."

"Should he not accept, I feel, with some reluctance, that the consequences should be spelled out to him. I refer, not to his continuing debt, but to the grounds for Sophia's change of heart. Such detail would, in all honesty, have to be presented in her defence," said Silas.

"We quite understand that, don't we, Francis?"

"Of course we do, my dear."

"I am afraid it is a sorry and, in parts, a sordid tale of wantonness and frustration," said Silas, and proceeded to recount the whoring and seductions, the violence and the breakdown of trust with tenants and free traders. "There is one particularly sensitive issue, which may distress you deeply, Lady Trewarren, and it concerns the death of your late husband."

"I know he showed little respect in the period after poor Oliver's death, and there were signs that it was not quite such a straightforward accident as it appeared. Was there more to it?" asked Lady Trewarren.

"My understanding, from an independent witness, is that there was. Are you sure you want me to give the details?" said Silas.

"He was my husband; I must know every detail, however harrowing." She looked across at Francis, who nodded.

When Silas had explained Richard's part in the death, all three sat in silence. Elizabeth felt her head spin and she sank into a faint. Francis went out and returned with smelling salts. How can I ever face him again? she thought, as she struggled to recover from her dizziness.

VI

Richard had lost himself in the raucous crowd at the cockpit. He had no wish to be identified. He had little ready cash but was no longer welcome at the card tables in the Assembly Rooms, or at social events at the houses of any well-to-do people. It was here in the press of the crowd that Rawdon surprised him. His coat and hat were filthy, as was his shirt collar, but the quality of the cloth was unmistakeable.

"Well, if I didn't know better, I would be thinking I'd found a brazen thief. That coat would have honoured Sir William Lemon himself when 'twas in its rightful condition."

"Rawdon, you have birds fighting here? If so, I shall avoid

them like the smallpox itself," said Richard.

"Oh aye, Richard, I have a few likely winners, if I can be of service."

"You are too familiar man. That is no way to address me."

"I do humbly beg your pardon, Sir Richard Trewarren, I thought you had no wish to be identified as a member of the gentry, given what hard times have brought you down to," said Rawdon, raising his voice so that those immediately around could not conceal their curiosity.

"Enough, Sir. Now go and disturb me no more," said Richard. Wry smiles were exchanged among the bystanders.

"I thought I might assist you, Sir. I can advise on some small wagers that might build some gains for a big killing later on." Rawdon had lowered his voice and spoke in his old seductive tone.

"I wouldn't trust your assistance in such matters if you suggested I wager on a sparrow hawk against a finch. Now leave me to decide my own wagers."

"I am very sorry you feel that, Sir, very sorry indeed. If it's proof of my good offices you need, then I will give you the names of the next three winners. Should you not trust me, leave the first and observe. If it win you may trust the next two. You will see, Sir, I do not jest." Rawdon made a show of whispering three names in Richard's ear.

The first cock, Hotspur, destroyed his opponent after a brief skirmish. *Perhaps Rawdon is honest here. He must* respect my standing, though he's never one to show it, thought Richard. I will place a guinea on Digger; he looks a likely bet at three to one. Having collected his winnings from Digger's success, he placed two guineas on Truro Boy who retuned him ten guineas. Rawdon appeared from behind his left shoulder as he returned to his place against the wall. Those around him showed amused interest as Rawdon mouthed the name of the final wager, worth a heavy sum. To the smiles and whispers of those around, Richard totalled all his ready cash at twenty-five guineas and placed it on Caesar. He was convinced he was a winner. It must be an omen: his very own horse, his beloved Caesar who had stayed loyal through all the desertions and betrayals of those around him. The shared name could not belong to a loser. Rawdon had been true to his word with the previous three, surely it was a near certainty.

He watched the preparations in keen anticipation. The cocks were introduced and circled round each other. Both were top weight and experienced fighters. Caesar was a large, dark brown bird with a white starred chest. His deep pink crest stood proudly firm and upright on his head. His opponent, Hannibal, was a dusty, black-feathered rooster. His crest was torn and flopped to one side. He looked a rugged fighter. Past his best, thought Richard, as Caesar put his head down and charged. He raised his head, tried to rise and strike with his iron claw, but Hannibal was too fast. He moved sideways and reared up, and the pair faced off as they scraped their claws down each other's chests; thin spots of blood on each. The crowd roared as one at the evenly matched pair. Each marked the other without a defining wound. Richard felt a creeping anxiety. Doubt crept in about his chance of a hundred-guinea gain. Caesar held his own for several minutes. He did not lack aggression or determination, yet Hannibal was gaining the upper claw. Caesar was tiring rapidly; his responses were slower by the minute. Finally Hannibal retreated and, as Caesar advanced, Hannibal turned, rose with opened wings and fell on the neck of his exhausted opponent.

A great roar arose from the crowd as they raised their arms and cheered. Richard felt his chest tighten. A hundred guineas there for the taking, lost in a fleeting moment. He took a last look at the pit, and was astonished to see Rawdon holding Hannibal under his arm. The bookkeeper was counting coins into Rawdon's awkwardly held purse as Hannibal began pecking at the draw cord. Caesar was being carried away, head trailing, feet tied together.

Richard thrust his way forward through the crowd but met increasing resistance. People he pushed turned to punch or push him away. He was buffeted back and forth, caught by sticks, hot clay pipes and flagons being emptied down throats in celebration or commiseration. Rawdon had long gone from the position he had last seen him. Reluctantly, he made his way back to the tavern where Caesar, the loyal one he told himself, was stabled for the day. He set off for Trewarren Manor, blaming Rawdon for all his misfortunes. After all, he told himself, it was Rawdon who originally introduced him to that whore, Baines. In a sense he was responsible for the way she had undermined him at every turn. Why, now he came to think, it was Rawdon who had tempted him into that harlot's room, when all he had wanted was to pleasure himself on a common whore. At least he'd finally taught her a lesson; she

277

wouldn't trouble him again, he was sure of that.

Then there was the previous cock fight, the one that had led to the duel.   Richard was convinced Rawdon had had something to do with that unexpected result. Much as he now resented Sophie for her disloyalty, he was sure she had been as shocked as he was at the loss of that fight. After all, she had ridden over hotfoot when he was injured in the duel. How could he have let that villain best him today? No doubt he would claim innocent miscalculation. He could hear him now. "A bet is a gamble, Sir, there are no certainties, as you know from previous experience, Sir. I guided you well at first, but you can never be sure, Sir, you can never be sure." I can be damned sure of one thing, he thought, that's it for Rawdon. I won't rest until he is in his grave, however long it takes.

VII

Martha felt stronger as winter approached. She had worked hard carrying the great baskets of pilchards, gutting and salting down the fish and pressing for the first draining of oil. All this had built up her strength again, and now they were filling the hogsheads, forcing the fish from the baulks firmly down with the lever press, until a full three thousand were safely stamped in. Further oil was pressed out in the process. They kept some back for the chill lamps, took some to the church as part of the tithe, and sold the rest at Truro market. The new senior partner in Sir Oliver's seine sent his agent to collect the takings and distribute the share to each, according to his percentage of the catch.

The new owner, a Mr Hardwick from Polperro, no longer

used Rawdon as guide or assistant to the agent. The agent kept accurate records of every catch, and could calculate measures of oil and number of hogsheads as the agreed totals. It was on this figure that fishermen's shares were calculated. Whether the final income was more or less, these were the figures for payment. Now Rawdon was not involved, everyone noticed a small but significant increase in income.

Martha's contribution eased the life of Molly's family, and the extra income from a good season untroubled by Rawdon enabled them to manage the extra person to feed and support. It pleased her that someone had been strong enough to dispense with his interference.

As the winter days shortened and chilled, the three of them and little Henny spent more time together. Thomas did frequent the tavern but was at home for longer than in the summer.

"What am I to do about Josiah?" Martha asked her sister-in-law. "I like him as much as any man I ever have, more so to be honest. We could make a good marriage, I know we could. Yet he ponders all these questions in his head that turn me dizzy. I am minded to tell him, when he next comes calling, that he must take his chance. The longer he wait the more chance I s'll find another worthy man."

"That's right, my gal. You could waste all your child-bearing years a lovelorn lass before you find he don't want the likes of you. Yet 'tes my feeling he is really struck. Just his finicky Methody ways as holds him back."

"That rogue, Rawdon, he's the cause of all my troubles. I

am twenty-four years old, been married three years, widowed almost two and turned into a harlot for three months. I've no child yet and no chance of one, the way things is going. He shot my poor Will'm, took advantage of me in my grief, forced that dreadful Trewarren on me, so I could never return to my position at the manor. He forced me into becoming a whore and deliberately incited the dreaded Trewarren to beat me within an inch of my life. I'd have that bastard in the pillory, I would. I'd hire stagecoaches of ragamuffins to come and pelt him with rocks. Or I'd lock him up with the Frenchies in that prison in Plymouth. If it wasn't for his hobbledy leg, I'd get him pressed into the navy; lure him down to Falmouth and let the gangs press him."

"Did I hear the word pillory?" said Thomas, who had shown no interest in their conversation.

"We want Rawdon locked in it, leastways Martha does; either that or in the Frenchie prison in Plymouth."

"Be well liked by the fishermen if he was, I do know that. But pillory ain't been used for years, nor even the stocks. Bodmin Gaol's a good'un. We might get him in there," said Thomas.

"He's slippery as a sea snake. I doubt he'll fall for any charges. 'Tes a pleasing thought though," said Martha.

"If you are going to win Cap'n Carter, you need to beauty up some," said Thomas. "I don't care how strict a Methody he be, he'll like a gal as looks summat special to him."

"Come, Tom, Martha's a lovely lass. I suppose we could

do more with her hair; maybe spruce up her dress some. We shall wash and press that dress you was wearing at Rawdon's place. Remake it a little to look pretty but modest. What do you say, Martha?"

"I don't know. I suppose I've not thought of my looks lately, just pleased to get away from all that rouge and those mouse-skin eyebrows. Perhaps if you help me, but I do impose on you quite enough already, especially cost wise."

"You are a great worker, isn't she Tom? Tom, wake up!" said Molly, as Tom slumped in his chair.

"What? What? Did you say something?"

"I said Martha's a great worker, ain't she?"

"She works hard like we all do; no more'n you'd expect from a strapping young wench." He closed his eyes and turned away.

"Take no notice of him. We'll beauty you up, lovey. He won't be able to resist you." Molly's face broke into a smile and she looked at her sister-in-law with deep affection. Martha smiled back, feeling more secure than she could remember in her adult life.

VIII

Richard sat at his father's desk. His distended stomach pressed against the rim as he reached for his brandy. His reddened cheeks bulged a little through the side whiskers he had affected since assuming the lordship of the manor. Outside, by mid afternoon, darkness was already closing in.

The room itself, with its dark oak shelving and furniture, had benefitted least from the redecoration that Lady Trewarren had overseen in happier times. The candles were already lit.

"I cannot imagine what purpose will be served by discussing this matter here. My lawyer will deal directly with Silas or his lawyer to resolve the case. However, if you insist on discussing it, I can spare a few minutes to do so." Richard leaned back expansively, placing both hands on the edge of the desk.

"We have met with Silas at his request," said Francis.

"Going behind my back, was he? Well, it will count against him when I report to the court."

"Please, Richard, take this seriously. Silas is a good man. He will make a generous offer of compensation on certain conditions. Please let Francis explain," said his mother.

"This business should all be conducted through lawyers, and the court if that becomes necessary. However, to please you, Mother, I will hear what you both have to say."

The worry lines eased on Lady Trewarren's face as Francis cleared his throat and began. "Silas and Sophia accept that there has been a breach of promise. They accept that you should receive a payment in recompense. Silas sought our guidance in calculating the amount that would be appropriate, and made clear there were certain conditions, and that grave consequences would be inevitable should the offer be challenged."

"You have me intrigued, I admit. If the offer is generous enough, doubtful though that may be, I suppose it would save the expense and delay of the courts." Richard still felt in command of the situation, but his expression of indulgent superiority had been replaced by one of engagement.

"With the help and advice of those who know something of your financial situation, Silas came to the conclusion that a sum of five hundred guineas would enable you to pay off current debts and set the estate on a sound footing for the future. He therefore proposes to offer that sum when he is given an assurance that his conditions will be met." Francis and Elizabeth studied Richard's face as he registered the impact of the offer.

"I am bemused. Who would be in a position to provide such information and, furthermore, to do so without consulting me? I would not know if this represented an accurate figure. Does it include compensation for the insult to my honour, let alone my broken heart?"

"Come now, do not jest," smiled Francis. "The estimate comes from figures your mother and I gathered, from various sources, to ensure that you were compensated to a level where all your financial problems could be solved. I recall this was your own answer to the pit you found yourself in. Silas interpreted them generously in his final offer."

"Please accept, my son. Let us put all this behind us, get the estate back to good health, settle down; find yourself a suitable wife so that the Trewarren line may be continued." Lady Trewarren could not keep the pleading note from her voice.

They sat in silence for some minutes, the flickering of the candles the only movement as darkness closed in outside the windows.

I knew this would work, thought Richard. Right is on my side in this and five hundred guineas is a tidy sum. New outfits, all the women I want, buy back Father's seine on my own terms and hold my head up in the Assembly Rooms in Truro again. What a cunning businessman I am. He smiled to himself. There are conditions, it seems. They can be overcome or evaded, no doubt, but I might need a wrangle, I might still need the lawyer, and did Francis say something of dire consequences? Mother went quiet at that. Good old Mama, she still loves her son - or needs to stay in favour. He looked across at their anxious faces and smiled.

"It seems a reasonable offer. I shall have to give it some thought and do some calculations of my own before finally accepting. Oh, and did you mention meeting some conditions? It would be useful to know what they are before embarking on a detailed study of my debts and assets."

Lady Trewarren rose with a kerchief to her face. She sensed the arrogance and lack of remorse conveyed by Richard's tone and his expression: such a contrast with the self-pitying whine of previous weeks. "If you will excuse me, Francis, you are more competent than I to discuss the legal details. I shall retire to my room. I find this business tires me to the point of exhaustion." She nodded lightly in Richard's direction and hurried from their presence. Richard raised an eyebrow at her back and turned to Francis.

"The conditions are not unduly onerous," said Francis. "You or your lawyer must give a signed statement acknowledging that your claim for breach of promise has been settled in full. Accordingly, you will not raise the issue again, nor will you trouble Miss Sophia in any way, nor will you pass insulting or disparaging comments or rumours about her."

"The latter would be difficult to prove," said Richard. "The truth sometimes sounds insulting."

"My strong advice would be to think not just of yourself but of the future of the family; its continuity, reputation and prosperity. You will be remembered far more favourably if you restore and promote its fortunes."

"Noble thoughts, worthy of a rector, I'm sure. I'll try to remember to say my prayers every night at bedtime as well."

"There is no need for such insolence. I see it as my duty to support your mother in her time of need. If that means dealing more harshly with you, have no doubt I shall do so," said Francis, his voice hardening.

"Oh dear. I will go and examine the books and see you tomorrow, if I may, to confirm the settlement." Richard sat up in the chair as if to rise.

"Just be aware, Richard, that, if you do not, the consequences would bring shame and more on you, and drag the name of Trewarren through an open sewer; and not without reason."

"I have no notion of your meaning but as it is likely I shall accept, it may well be an irrelevance." Richard stood and indicated the door. "After you, Uncle."

Francis stood and straightened his jacket. He moved towards the door. He turned and looked directly at Richard. "Your mother was greatly distressed to hear of the deception you played on your father that led to his death. Were that to be detailed in the public record in court – well, I will leave it to your imagination." And he was gone.

"But, Uncle – wait!"

IX

Sophia walked Ailla along the ridge above the Trevella Stream. She loved the steep-sided valley with the fast-flowing water far below, and the opposite ridge only the distance a fit man could throw a small rock. They had had a fine gallop across from Nankilly and up the ridge. Now she brought Ailla to a halt and absorbed the richness of her surroundings. Would New England hold anything so beautiful, so rugged and yet so full of seasonal colour? Would George's father accept her? Would there be others to whom she could relate, with whom she had interests in common? How hard a life would it be? What dangers awaited her? She was so grateful to Silas for the generous settlement he had offered to Richard. How could she now abandon him to grow old here alone? Would she ever see him again? Would it break his heart? The questions ran through her mind every day but she was no nearer answers. If only George would return, some at least might be resolved. Meanwhile she hoped Richard would not make more trouble. His poor mother. She had felt much sympathy for Lady Trewarren: losing two daughters was heartbreaking but to lose your husband through the greed and deception of your one remaining child must be unbearable. Enough of such pondering, she thought. Patting Ailla on the neck, she turned her and galloped across the open ground at an angle to the ridge and on to the track back to Nankilly.

Over dinner that night, Silas, who had returned unexpectedly from Truro, showed her the signed document from Richard's lawyer. "The matter is finally settled. You are now free to respond to George's advances if you wish, my dear."

"Thank you, Uncle, thank you so much. I shall be forever in your debt for this. Yet I feel constrained to deepen my attachment to George. It seems the height of selfishness to repay you for all you have done for me by crossing the ocean to an unknown country without you."

"My dear girl, your happiness is all I have ever wanted for you. If I can contribute to that in any way it is my determination to do so. If you truly love George and feel that your happiness requires you to follow him to America, then I cannot bear the thought of depriving you of that future."

"I am truly grateful, for everything. But nothing is decided yet. I wish George would return. Our feelings may have changed in his absence." The meal continued in a comfortable silence. At length Silas excused himself and retired to his study.

***

Richard had to admit to himself that the conversation had surprised him. Although he was reluctant to concede that Silas had been generous, the offer had been more than he had imagined in all his fantasies of new-found wealth, yet he was intrigued by a number of points that had been put to him. By the time he had retired for the night he had determined to have a final meeting with Silas. He would sign the agreement and ensure it was delivered. After a week or so he would seek a private meeting with Silas at his town house. Over the week his mind considered and dismissed a number of approaches, but as the day grew nearer a clear path shaped itself in his thoughts.

***

"Sir Richard Trewarren asks if he may speak with you, Sir." The manservant's face was expressionless. Before Silas could conceal his confusion, Richard stepped forward.

"I am sorry to descend upon you without warning, Silas but, as I was in town I wanted to take the opportunity to satisfy myself that you had received my signature to the agreement, and to thank you for your ready acceptance of culpability. It was most gentlemanly of you. Please also convey my thanks to Miss Sophia and my best wishes for her future happiness."

"Why, thank you, Richard. Won't you come through to the office for a moment?" There is more to this than a thank you, I am certain, thought Silas, as he ushered Richard into the office at the heart of his business activities.

"How is your dear mother? Is she still overburdened with

grief?" Silas continued when they were seated.

"She is as well as can be expected. Uncle Francis has been a great support. It would be foolish to deny that a pall of misery hangs over the manor. I spend as little time there as possible. It is time to move on, and your settlement has given me the opportunity."

"I fervently hope that you have learned from these dreadful times. If you are to succeed in business, it is very short-sighted to concentrate on every last farthing of profit. One must look to the future, to the industries that will develop and expand: china clay, tin, iron and their uses. Look at Trevithick, for example, using the new mining opportunities to develop steam and transport. Move beyond the county: Bristol, the Severn, Manchester and Liverpool will soon be buzzing with industry. They will all need finance and they will all need trust. Above all, there must be trust, Richard. That's the one quality your father had and no one questioned. He may have been slow to take on new ideas but no one questioned his trust; not until his final day, that is." Silas paused. He watched Richard take in his full meaning. After a long silence, Richard began to reply several times but could not articulate a sentence.

"Finance and trust go together, and combined with good judgement they make for successful business. All three are required for success. It should be the practice to ask oneself if all three are in place before a commitment is made." Silas sat back and smiled. "Sermon over," he said, and added as an afterthought, "with the settlement, Richard, you have the chance to start again, resolve your current problems and introduce judgement and trust with the remaining finance to establish business enterprises to be proud of." Silas stood to indicate the end of the meeting and surprised himself by adding, "if, after six months, you have demonstrated these qualities in your use of the money, there may well be a future for joint business ventures together. We face exciting times in the new century and we shall need new ideas. Thank you for calling by, Richard, it has been reassuring."

It was only as he was riding away that Richard realised he had asked none of the questions he had intended.

X

George's ship was part of a small flotilla patrolling the Channel and the Western Approaches. Napoleon, by now First Consul, was concentrating his attention on Austria, and his main fleet was consolidating in the Mediterranean Sea. George's flotilla was picking off French coastal and Atlantic merchantmen for their spoils and harassing their trade with the Peninsula. As the turn of the year approached, the seas in the Bay of Biscay were wild and stormy. The order was given to return to Portsmouth for restocking and repairs. Thus, both George and Josiah stood off the south coast as the new century dawned. The winds were so strong that the rear admiral judged that the chances of running aground on the Godwins were not worth the risk. The flotilla tacked down to the shelter of Plymouth. With at least two weeks before repairs could be completed, crews were instructed to report back in mid January. George and Josiah both took the stage-coach to Bodmin, and then on to Truro.

For much of the journey, Josiah rested his head against the bulge at the top of the seat. His eyes were closed. He either dozed or pretended to doze. George looked out at the bare trees silhouetted against the darkening sky. He glanced across at his fellow passengers from time to time: two more mariners and two women; mother and daughter? He was not sure. The coach stopped at the Royal coaching inn on the main street in the small town of Bodmin. The passengers descended and went their separate ways; George entered the hotel and sought a room for the night. Josiah sought the hire of a horse. His small baggage would fit easily into saddle bags; he could be at his lodgings in Truro in under two hours and as yet it was only a little after seven of the evening.

Next morning there was a heavy frost. Josiah's horse breathed out a fine mist as he trotted down through the town. The cobbles were slippery. Josiah slowed to a walk. Dark cart tracks were clear in the white frost, as it began to melt. Pools of water were frozen beside the track and in the wheel ruts as his horse picked its way towards Trewarren Bay. What would he say to her? He must forgive her, he had decided; that was the Lord's will, the answer he had felt through his prayers. On a more earthly level, could the warmth of the time of innocence be recreated? Would the strong attraction still be there? He longed to see her, yet he also dreaded the meeting. The matter must be resolved, he had decided. He lifted the horse's head and broke into a trot.

***

George took the Truro stage mid morning and arrived at midday. He walked to the town house.

"Mr Galsworthy and Miss Sophia are resting at Nankilly, Sir, but I am sure they would be delighted to see you. Were they expecting you, if I may ask?" said the under butler.

"I did not expect to be here myself, so my arrival will no doubt surprise them."

"The stable lad will harness up a light trap for you, Sir, if you would like to come inside and rest until it is ready"

"That is most kind. Thank you." George entered and accepted some refreshment.

***

Sophia looked down from the frozen ridge. Up here, the frost still clung to the scrub and hardened the ground. A hazy sun was too weak to melt the freezing soil on the northern face of the hill. She walked Ailla along the ridge, enjoying the sense of space and freedom. As the sun dipped towards the horizon, she turned Ailla onto the track that descended from the ridge and noticed, in the valley far below, the silhouette of a horse and trap trotting towards Nankilly House. Her uncle had made no mention of visitors. Had he been out, perhaps, whilst she herself had been enjoying her freedom? He had made no mention of doing so. As she reached the stable yard, the lad was throwing a blanket over the visitor's horse. She noticed the trap being backed into the coach house. It was her uncle's, she could see that now. So he had been out. She gave Ailla an affectionate pat and returned to the house.

***

Josiah approached the Bawden house with a warm glow in his heart. He was about to commit a truly Christian act of forgiveness which he knew would clear all doubts from his conscience. He could already sense the lightness he would feel in the glow of her deep gratitude. He gave the door a firm knock and stood back.

"Oh, Cap'n Carter! It be Martha you wants, if I am not mistook," said Molly.

"It is indeed, Mrs Bawden. I have a momentous message for her. May I speak with her?"

"She ain't here at the minute, Cap'n. She and Thomas be building an oven. She'll be baking bread afore long; expanding the family business like."

"Ah yes, very commendable. Where will I find her? Where will this oven be?"

"They be out gathering stone. They have made a good start. Look round the side of the house where the chimney is so they can let the oven smoke in through that wall. I can't hear 'em at the moment but they'll soon be back. Come, I'll show you." Molly led him round the side of the cottage. A construction was well under way. The firing area was complete and the oven lacked only some form of closure. What remained was a flue connecting to the original cottage chimney. Shards of stone and dust lay around the base, with a tidier pile of rough hewn, grey limestone bricks ready for use. As Josiah inspected the handiwork, Molly's old cart trundled up to them pulled by Thomas, with Martha walking behind and watching for rocks bouncing off on the uneven track.

"Cap'n Carter to see you, Martha," said Molly with a knowing smile.

"Josiah!" said Martha. "I was not expecting you. I am not dressed for visitors."

"I am anxious to speak to you, Martha; may we have a conversation in private?"

"We must unload the cart. Thomas can then shape some bricks. You can help if you wish."

"Of course," said Josiah, a little taken aback by her apparent air of confidence. He could see the value of what they were doing and was soon heaving rocks off the cart with the two of them. In only a few minutes there was nothing but a layer of dust in the cart and Thomas was sizing up his choice for hewing into shape.

"Thank you, Josiah. Now come inside for some refreshment. We can each tell of progress since your last visit."

XI

"The Frenchies didn't sink you then. I be pleased at that," said Martha, handing him a pewter mug of weak ale.

"No indeed, we had some rewarding successes but we sustained some damage from the Biscay storms and the French cannon; hence our return to port for some serious repairs. However, I did not come to report on our campaign but to discuss the future." An air of frustration had crept into his voice.

"I do beg your pardon, Sire," said Martha with a disarming smile.

"My dear Martha, from the time of our last meeting I have been praying for guidance from the good Lord above. He has answered my prayers and lightened my heart. It has become clear to me that I must forgive you without reservation for past carnal sins. I refer not to our own fall from grace, where I accept shared responsibility, but your subsequent plunge into licentious squalor from which, with the aid of your sister-in-law, I was able to recover you. I feel a deep sense of forgiveness. I feel we can think of the future with no weight of guilt and remorse hanging over us. What say you, my dearest Martha?" Josiah sat back and smiled benignly across at her.

"You forgive me? Me? A poor widow who be beaten and abused with not the strength to resist? Me, dragged into slavery for no fault of mine? It is most kind of the good Lord, most kind. And you forgive that monster, Rawdon, also, and the noble Sir Richard, for their violent assaults, their lies, their depravity? Is the good Lord as generous to them? For, if he is, I fail as a Christian; for I cannot forgive them. Nay I would be revenged if I could but see the way." She looked across at him, her chin raised and eyes piercing in defiance. He was clearly taken aback. He raised the tankard, sensed the ale and replaced it untouched.

"I cannot say if the evils they perpetrated would be forgiven. I sought merely to remove the doubts I brought to you at our last meeting. I can truly say that those doubts have fled. That I would hope to court you as my future wife, and to do so as ardently as my service to our country will allow," he said, looking down.

Her anger defused. She looked across at his saddened face. He was, after all, the kindest and most caring man she knew. He was genuine in his words in a way that few men were. Not only that but he offered her security, and she still felt drawn to him as she had from the time she had held herself against him on those rides to the Methodist services.

"That last attack has changed me, Josiah. I am determined to take charge of my own life. I am working towards providing an oven here for wives to bake their bread on certain days. Molly and Thomas will add to the income from the pilchards. In that way I can stay here without shame."

"That pleases me greatly," said Josiah, smiling across at her with renewed hope.

"You are the kindest man I have ever known. I would be foolish to spurn your attentions. But I am a different person. It would be wrong to commit to a courtship before you get to know me again."

"I have two weeks before I must return to Plymouth, although I should return with a few days to spare to carry out my duties. May I help with the construction of the oven? This would help you complete it more speedily and I would get to know this new Martha a little."

"Josiah, that would be wonderful!" Martha could not conceal her amazement. "I must tell Thomas at once." She rose, gave him a winning smile, and moved towards the door.

"Good, then I shall go and seek lodgings." He followed her out of the room.

***

A week later all four of them, with Henny sat in the crook of her mother's arm, watched as Thomas lit the first oven fire. Josiah had ridden up to the ruins of Martha's old cottage and brought back a few pieces of iron buried beneath the wood-ash and clay. He had taken them to the local forge and instructed the blacksmith in the dimensions required. The result was a flat iron base above the fire, a grille for the fire ash to fall through and some firm oven doors. Thomas had obtained a pig's bladder, which they had converted into a small bellows. This proved effective and smoke soon billowed from the chimney. Molly and Martha had kneaded some dough and left it overnight, protected from rats. They now placed it in the oven. Neighbours gathered round in wonder and celebration. Ale was brought out; the first loaves eagerly anticipated.

With the celebrations at their height, Josiah took Martha aside.

"I have learned much this week," he said happily, "but I fear I must return to my duty. I ask you humbly to wait for me. I promise I will return as soon as duty allows."

"Your help has been wonderful. I thank you from the bottom of my heart. I hope that the doubts you had have vanished as fully as my own," she said.

"Truly they have. It pains me to leave at this joyous moment. I shall return, never fear." He held out his hand. She took his hand in hers and moved close to him.

"I shall struggle to contain my impatience. Please take great care of yourself."

He put an arm round her waist and, still holding her hand, drew her tightly to him. Then he released her, turned away and strode off into the night.

XII

"George! How lovely to see you. Does Uncle know you are here?" asked Sophia, coming into the drawing room.

"Sophie! My dearest girl! Your high colour suits you. Have you been out riding?"

"My favourite ride, along the ridge. It is perfect in winter, as in the spring: in fact I love it all year round. You must join me; you would love it. But does Uncle know you are here? Have you heard the good news?"

"The servant has gone to tell him. What good news?" said George.

"I should perhaps let him tell you himself. We have reached a settlement with Richard. He no longer has any call on me."

Silas caught her final phrase as he entered the room.

"What a pleasant surprise. How are you, George?" They

shook hands.

"I am delighted to be here, thank you, and eager to hear your news," said George.

Silas related the story of how the settlement had been reached, and summarised his advice to Richard. Sophia chipped in once or twice to add detail.

"I can only say that I think you have been most generous. It is clear that Sophia also appreciates your generosity. Trust that old rogue Rawdon to come up with useful information. I hope Richard has the sense to take your advice with regard to a new start and a deeper understanding of business," said George.

"I have my doubts on that," said Sophia.

"Well, the offer is there if he shows the maturity to take it," said Silas, "but it does leave Sophie free to respond as she wishes to any advances that may be made to her from now on," he smiled.

"Perhaps I may ride out with you tomorrow, Sophie? You say that you favour the ride along a nearby ridge. I would be pleased to see if we share the same taste in such matters. I have almost two weeks before I need to return to Plymouth."

"You are to be our guest for as long as you need," said Silas.

***

Next morning, after a leisurely breakfast, George and Sophia had their horses saddled up and set out at a trot. The sky was heavy with snow, but none had fallen. The groom had warned of a likely storm, but Sophia was determined to show George the delights of the ridge, including a shallow dell, sheltered from the prevailing wind, where she liked to dismount and sit, absorbing the changes through the seasons across the woods and hills to the sea some twelve miles to the south. She spread a blanket on the broad flat rock she always used in the dell. There was still a dampness from the frost, although the sun was beginning to steam the moisture away.

"Have you used one of these?" asked George, taking a telescope from a pocket inside his top coat.

"What is it? A telescope? How does it work?"

"I'll show you," he said, moving round behind her, "Now hold it like this, up to the eye – that's right. Now twist it like this to focus it. Is the picture all blurred?"

She nodded. He took the telescope from her, focussed it and gave it back to her, an arm each side of her head. "Try it now. You may have to adjust it a little but it should be more or less in focus. What can you see?"

"This is wonderful; I can see several inshore boats along the coast. Crabbers or pilot boats I should suppose. Beyond them the dark thunder clouds are billowing up. I can't believe it is all so far away." She turned her head suddenly in the excitement of the moment. Her face brushed his as he failed to withdraw his head in time. "I'm sorry," she said, giggling, "I didn't realise you were so close."

"Perhaps we had better return," he said.

"Wait, George. Here, take this," she said, handing him the telescope. "I wonder why you are here? Are we to evade the issue every time it arises? I am no longer promised to Richard. What are your intentions?"

"You refer to our possible future? Together?"

"At last! Now what are your thoughts?"

"I have not seen you for some months; circumstances have changed. Silas presented them very bluntly last night. I wanted to spend time with you. When I am at sea I spend many hours going through things in my mind."

"To what conclusion?" She looked at him intently.

"Supposing you were to accept me. Would you leave your uncle and come to New England? How would you settle in such a different way of life? There is no refined society; no lords and ladies. How could I forgive myself if you were not happy? How would my father react to you? There would be no turning back." George stared out over the sea as the storm clouds neared.

"Oh George!" She resisted the urge to put her arms around him but instead placed her hand on his. He turned to look at her. His face expressed such a mix of anguish and desire that she slid her arms around him and kissed him full on the mouth. In response he held her to him, sliding his hand up between her shoulder blades. They pulled apart. She smiled at his shocked expression.

"I have discussed these matters with Uncle Silas," she said, after a moment. "It is clear that you had raised these matters with him before you returned to your ship at the end of the summer. He has made it clear that he puts my happiness before all else. You have been in my thoughts through all these months."

"And you in mine," said George. "It is because I care for you so deeply that I have been so hesitant in expressing my intentions."

"I suggest we ride back and speak to Uncle together. You may then think it appropriate to make a formal proposal. If not ..."

"Very well," he smiled. "Let us do so at once."

XIII

Richard was dining alone. Elizabeth rarely joined him these days. She had what little she ate sent up to her room. He indicated to Pollard to refill his brandy glass and clip him a cigar. His head was still aglow from his business acumen. He had turned a disaster into a spectacular success. He had wheedled a small fortune out of Silas and few could claim that. It irritated him slightly that Silas had relied on Masters for the calculations. He'd also heard that rogue Rawdon had provided information on his more dubious expenses. Only the good Lord knew what devious lies that scoundrel had told.

Silas's sermonising had been well intentioned, he could see that. There was also his intriguing offer of joint projects in the future. That had been a complete surprise, Richard admitted to himself. It must mean that Silas had an underlying admiration for his gift for business, in spite of everything. Tomorrow he'd go into Truro and clear his bills at the card tables. Perhaps have a small flutter to make up a bit of that loss. After that he would need to consider. He took a final tot of brandy, stubbed out the cigar and went up to his room.

***

"Good morning, Sir. I trust you slept well," said Bassett next morning. "Mr Masters would like a word, Sir, at your earliest convenience. He sounded rather agitated if I may say so."

"Thank you, Bassett. I shall be going to Truro this morning. I'll speak to him later."

"Very well, Sir. It did sound rather urgent, Sir."

Richard was about to brush the comment aside when the conversation with Silas flitted across his mind.

"I'll speak to him after breakfast," he said.

"I'll inform him at once, Sir. Thank you, Sir," added Bassett, the relief clear in his face.

Masters dealt with most issues on the estate calmly enough. He had a deep knowledge and understanding of every aspect of the annual round of estate life; what made a good year, and what made a bad; what the tenants could manage and what drove them to desperation. Under Sir Oliver his judgement had rarely been questioned. They would discuss together the plan for the year ahead, hammering out the details and Sir Oliver had taken a deep interest in the progress of the plans and the wellbeing of the tenants. Sir Richard seemed to regard this as an old fashioned and unbusinesslike approach.

"Good morning, Masters, I understand there is an urgent matter you wish to discuss. I have delayed my departure for Truro, so I do hope it is truly urgent."

"Good morning, Sir Richard. A number of our tenants are in great difficulty this winter. They have little food or access to it and no resources to fall back on. If we demand rents at the higher levels recently introduced, or even the old rates at the moment, they will be destitute and unable to pay."

"It is unfortunate, but I am afraid we are not a charity, Masters. We can perhaps offer a week's extension but no more. They must organise their lives to live within their means or take the consequences." Richard moved as if to leave.

"We will gain nothing if we do that, Sir. There are no solvent farm workers waiting for a tenancy. There will be little ploughing and sowing in the spring. May I ask if a solution was reached to the problem Lady Trewarren and the rector were investigating?"

"What do you know of that?" said Richard, taken aback by the question.

"Nothing, Sir. They said it was for the resolution of a legal matter, Sir. They were not at liberty to reveal the detail. I understood some compensation might be payable and so I included every possible cost, but nothing that could not be verified."

"That was most loyal of you, Masters." Richard was momentarily touched. "But why do you have an interest in the matter? It is a private family concern."

"Forgive me, Sir. I thought perhaps a large payment may be a means of investment in a creative project that would alleviate the poverty by meaningful profitable work," said Masters.

"I'll give it some thought Masters; meanwhile hold fire on any evictions. Now I must bid you good day."

"Thank you, Sir, they will be most grateful," said Masters to Richard's retreating back.

As Richard rode into town, his mind dwelt on that ride back from Falmouth; he'd certainly enjoyed the night at the Pandora Inn, but next morning he had ridden past the string of donkeys, carrying tin ore to Devoran for sieving. A common enough sight, but it had stuck in his mind. There must be money in tin; Silas had shares in tin mines. Was there any trace of tin on the estate, he wondered . If so it could be the promised joint project. He was sure Silas would be persuaded if he could see poverty on the estate alleviated. He'd raise it with Masters on his return.

He entered Truro, crossed the market square and secured Caesar outside the Assembly Rooms. The card players were not there at this time but he hoped a clerk may be able to resolve the issue of his promissory notes.

"I am sorry, Sir Richard, clients generally prefer these matters to remain discreet, not to say confidential. Clients would be deeply upset if such matters were disclosed to a servant."

"Oh come man, it is my own debts I speak of and I am anxious to clear them to the satisfaction of all concerned."

"I do understand, Sir Richard, but rules is rules. An exception would lead to all sorts of unfortunate consequences. If you was to return in an hour or two, Sir, I've no doubt you will get satisfaction."

"I see there is no shifting you at present, but you are giving insult to the gentry by this cussedness. I shall see you regret it in due course." Richard turned on his heel and, doing his best to disguise his limp, walked across to the Trelawney Arms on the far side of the square.

XIV

"Airy-mouse, airy-mouse, fly over my head,

And you shall have a crust of my bread,

And when I brew, or when I bake,

You shall have a piece of my wedding cake."

Martha sang.

"It is good to see you smiling and singing so. Times change, I must say. I suspect 'tes the prospect of Josiah's return. He cannot be long delayed," said Molly, as they kneaded dough together.

"Well, he must be returning soon and he did promise me marriage," smiled Martha.

"I was so proud of you. I always hoped you would really be yourself. A lesser man would have upped and left but he ... Well, a worthy and well deserved man after all your troubles."

"And a great help with building the oven," said Martha.

"That too," laughed Molly.

The oven had meant a steady new income to the household. Many of the fishing community brought their loaves to be baked. Martha and Molly charged fair prices. They also baked their own bread and pasties for Thomas. 'Tes true, thought Martha, I am happier than I ever was. I am more me, more the Martha I want to be. And 'tes true Josiah saw and accepted. I only hope these three months with his fellow sailors do not give him cause to doubt.

***

The Martha he had encountered when he had finally found it in himself to return had been a quite different person from his expectations. He recognised that he would have to adjust in many ways if he were to go ahead with the marriage. At times he was full of admiration. He was impatient to see if she maintained this unlikely air of independence; if it had developed or been lost in the day to day of life with her sister-in-law's family. At other times he felt wary. He envisaged years of giving way to a woman's dominance. How would he retain respect beyond the home? He would assuredly be mocked at chapel and among the Excise riders, if such he resumed.

Three months later he had further leave for restocking and repairs to winter damage. They had continued patrolling the Channel and islands and the western approaches down to Gibraltar. Storms had hit them in Biscay and some cannon shot near the waterline had needed caulking. He saw to the arrangements and costs for repairs and issued lists for replenishing the stores before taking his leave. He was now in his Truro lodgings preparing his mind for a meeting with Martha. Was she the right wife for him? In fairness to both of them, he must decide in this remaining week of leave. He took the coach to Trewarren Bay and walked back along the harbour round to the Bawden cottage. A short queue waited there to collect their freshly baked bread. Martha was serving the women, smiling and chatting cheerily with all who waited. Josiah felt moved by this sign of mundane village life unfolding. Martha was clearly contented now. The question rose again within him. Leave her to her current world, a world where she was happy and secure, or ask her ... ask her what exactly?

With the last customer gone, Martha looked up and saw him.

"Josiah!" she said. "You're back!"

"I am." He smiled and moved towards her. He could smell flour and new baked bread on her apron. She made a small cloud of flour dust as she rubbed her hands together.

She smiled up at him, a broad open smile of undisguised pleasure.

"Come in, come and have some refreshment," she said, as he took hold of both her hands and squeezed them lightly. He held her gaze. He could not stop himself smiling. All his doubts faded as he followed her into the house.

"Sit," she said, indicating a chair. Ignoring his abstention from alcohol, as she had on his previous visit, she filled a tankard with cool weak ale and passed it to him.

They exchanged pleasantries. He took a tentative sip.

"A few mouthfuls will not turn you into a drunkard," she said, smiling at his expression. He smiled in return and took a mouthful. The journey had left his mouth dry with dust from the coach.

She told of the success of the oven, and the pleasure in being able to contribute in return for Molly and her family's help. He told of his time at sea and the shortness of his remaining leave. This prompted him to more personal issues.

"On my last visit we spoke of a more permanent relationship," he said.

"I took you to mean a courtship and marriage. I am happy to anticipate such an outcome." She smiled at his reaction to her frankness. "Your leave is but a few days;

I have thought much on this in your absence. I am a simple woman. I see no gain in fine words if your intentions are clear and your heart true."

"You are right, of course. I must get used to such plain speaking. It is much like my shipmates – without the cursing and blaspheming, of course," he said.

"I am used to cussing, among the fishing folk. Not that I cuss meself, 'cept in extremes."

"I thought to marry with the Methodists, and I have lodgings in Truro. They have sufficed whilst I am a bachelor serving at sea. You might like to visit and see for yourself."

"I'll not be in Truro on my own; not with that monster Rawdon there. My work is here and my family. If I get with child, which so far I ain't, I s'll need Molly with me. The Methodists is good for the marriage. I go regular as I can. I need to live here, though; leastways hereabouts."

"Can we walk together a little? It will be easier to consider these matters so," said Josiah.

She removed her apron and took a cloak from behind the door and they strolled down by the harbour and along the shore. By the time they returned they had agreed to marry on his next leave. He would speak with the Methodist minister and she would enquire after a cottage to rent once they were married. She asked him to consider resigning his commission and leaving the Navy but he was reluctant to do so. The country is still under threat, he had said, and his duty was clear.

XV

Richard sipped at his brandy. He felt good about himself as he gazed round the bar of the Trelawney Arms. A few lonely old men sat steadily drinking their way to oblivion. One or two conducted business over a brandy, but there was little of interest to hold his attention. He felt he was about to build on a new beginning. Silas's words had made an impression. He would clear his debts at the Assembly Rooms, make some discreet enquiries about trustworthy surveyors, and discuss the matter with Masters.

He glanced up as a distant clock chimed three of the afternoon. The swirl of a dress caught his eye. An enticingly dressed young woman was meandering her way between the tables towards the back room. He called softly.

"May I buy you a drink, Miss?"

She turned towards him with a haughty air, which turned instantly to a simper when she saw he was a young man of rank.

"Thank you kindly, Sir. That would be most welcome." She approached and sat at his table as he signalled for attention.

"You are even more beautiful face to face than you appeared as you swept through the room," he said.

"You are most handsome yourself, Sir, and discerning, if I may say so."

The barman approached with two glasses. "Your usual choice,

Miss Demelza, if I may." He placed a glass in front of her. Richard caught the wink and grin in return, "and for you, Sir, another brandy. The private rooms are free at the moment, Miss Demelza," he added, without changing his expression.

The private room was more richly furnished than Rawdon's run-down brothel. Richard was impressed by the wall-hangings, the ornate wash basin and the rich linen bed coverings. Demelza explained that she entertained particularly handsome guests from high-class backgrounds from time to time to support her father's business. She prided herself on meeting their particular needs, strange though some of them were. As she began to disrobe, she described various acts that she could offer. Richard chose to complete the disrobing and engage her fully naked on the bed. She was highly skilled at pleasuring him and her charges were priced accordingly. He had been so transported that it was with great difficulty that he refrained from proposing marriage as they got dressed.

It was thus in a mood of exhilaration that he returned to the Assembly Rooms. He relished the sudden changes of expression from deep frowns, through relief and thorough going pleasure as he paid off his debts with a flourish. Such was the relief at his honouring the debts that he was invited to play a round or two before he left. He made modest gains to about half the cost of his visit to Demelza. He could not resist the temptation to revisit the Trelawney Arms. Perhaps she would offer favourable terms for a whole night together. She had clearly enjoyed their earlier encounter. He pushed open the door and froze. Rawdon stood, head bowed towards the barman who was talking into his ear. Richard allowed the door to shut without entering and returned to collect Caesar from the stables.

On the way home his resentment against Rawdon grew. Why did he always have to intrude? Rawdon was the cause of all his problems, especially now his own persistence and determination had eliminated that stupid little harlot. At least she had got what she deserved. Rawdon had better keep out of his way. He might meet the same fate. I am a new man now, he told himself. I shall not let that rogue ruin my mood. The day has gone well. I shall speak with Masters tomorrow and our new venture will be under way.

Next morning, Masters was sufficiently encouraged to mention the need for improved drainage and sewage disposal for the row of farm cottages where the majority of estate workers lived. The buildings had been variously patched, at their own expense, after the winter storms of the last two years but, with families of six or eight children in two-roomed houses with leaking roofs and damp walls, disease was rife.

"When they pay their rents we may be able to make a start," said Richard, "but I have a more immediate need which may help them greatly in the long run."

"Most of them do pay their rents, Sir Richard; they do have a good case."

"What do you know of tin and copper, Masters? If we could mine such metals on the estate, I am sure we could meet these demands, and offer employment to those idle men who waste their days at the Trewarren Arms."

"Sir Oliver commissioned a survey some years ago. Nothing of sufficient quantity was found to justify further expense. I feel we would do better to revive the seining of pilchards. The Trewarren Bay seine has gone, I know, but we have fishermen who have the skill to set up another with suitable investment. The market is buoyant, especially the Kingdom of the Two Sicilies, but the men no longer have the means. That would be my recommendation. Either attempt to repurchase the present Seine or set up a new one to compete. There is enough of a market with the right investment." Masters looked across at Richard, aware that he had said more in this short interview than in all their previous conversations.

"Nevertheless, I would like you to commission another survey with a surveyor using more up-to-date procedures."

"Very well, Sir Richard, but I ... "

"Let me know the results, Masters, that is all for now." Richard nodded and left the office. Masters shook his head at the folly of his employer and settled to his new task.

Richard had tried to resist thoughts of Demelza but, apart from the occasional ride around the estate, there was little to do until the survey was complete. At home his mother had little to say to him. She was deep in the depression she had experienced with the death of the girls. At times she could not bring herself to speak to him or spend any time in his presence. He took the opportunity of a lull in the winter storms to ride into Truro to see Demelza again. Over the late winter months, his visits developed in regularity and grew in length. Inevitably, he shared his plans and frustrations. She seemed to show an intelligent interest, asking questions worthy of a fellow businessman at times. When his passion was satisfied, and she continued to delight in this regard, she would act as an outlet for his other concerns. She listened, admired his boldness and shared his frustration at the inadequacies of others.

* * *

Silas resisted the temptation to invite Richard to Nankilly to discuss his business plans. Rawdon kept him informed through his arrangement with the barman at the Trelawney Arms. He had thought to advise against the tin and copper project, but Richard must rely on his own judgement if Silas was ever to consider a joint venture.

XVI

"You did not seem surprised, Uncle, at our seeking your permission to marry," said Sophia.

"I have not known and cared for you these last years without being able to sense your feelings. Your mutual attraction was obvious to anyone who knew you," smiled Silas. "I hope that this time the choice is the right one and you have years of happiness ahead of you."

"George is the kindest, bravest, handsomest man I have ever known. I only hope he survives this terrible war."

"And you have known how many?"

"Oh, you know what I mean."

"You are in love, my dear, and I am very happy for you. I do think George is a sound choice. He knows that life in New England will be very different, not to say plainer than you are used to. He sought my opinion and explained the situation very honestly before he sought your commitment. That is the way of an honest and caring man."

"I know it will be different; part of me cannot wait to be there, while a part of me fears it greatly; so strange, so far from home."

"I shall miss you terribly, but I am sure you will be carried along by your youth and strength and, above all, by the love of your new husband."

"Oh I hope so, Uncle, I do hope so."

***

When George arrived in Falmouth towards the end of March, he collected a note from New England. It was brief and to the point.

January 10, 1800. Cold winter, father taken ill, help needed on holding. Betsy Rainer, (neighbour).

George took a coach to Truro in the hope of finding Silas and passing on the news. He left a message with the butler at the town house. Two days later he was in Portsmouth, seeking long leave without pay or to be relieved of his commission.

Silas broke the news to Sophia as gently as he could but she was immediately in turmoil. Would he go without her?

She couldn't go with him if they weren't married, could she? Would she have to follow later? Could she do the journey alone? Would they marry there? What about Uncle Silas? George arrived at Nankilly a week later.

"I am at a loss," he said, his face drawn with fatigue and concern. "The Admiral refuses to accept the resignation of my commission. I must see my father if he is nearing death. My dearest wish is to spend the rest of my life with you. Yet I must go now. I am on my way to the Falmouth Packet."

"I will come with you," said Sophia.

"Sophie, you cannot go. You are not married. It is unheard of."

"Your uncle is right. Much as I would love us to go together, it would stain your good name. I will return for you as soon as the situation at home is resolved," said George.

"Have they granted you leave? How long before you sail again?" she said.

"I have no official leave. I am sure they have more important issues than chasing me."

"But you will be classed as a deserter! You will be at risk as soon as you enter British waters again. They do not view desertion lightly," said Silas. "I will arrange to have Sophie escorted once we have word that you are ready to receive her, and that marriage arrangements are in hand."

"You are right," said George. He turned to Sophia and held her arms. "It breaks my heart to leave you thus, but it is the only way. I will send word at the very earliest opportunity. Now I must fly. The tide turns in an hour and the packet leaves at nine of the evening." George looked for a long moment into Sophia's eyes, turned abruptly, mounted his horse and galloped off at speed. Wiping away her tears, Sophia retired to her room.

She sat staring at her own image in the mirror. Am I to let this ruin my life? After all our plans, all our patience, Uncle's great costs to Richard; am I to be a victim of cruel circumstance? I cannot bear it. She crossed to her dressing room, packed two strong travelling bags with essentials and dressed for riding. She wrote a brief note for her uncle and went out to the stable. Ailla was quickly saddled up and she set off as if going for her usual ride. Out of view, she spurred Ailla to a gallop and rode as she had not ridden since Richard's injury all those months ago.

As she rode through Falmouth, down the hill to the dock, she heard the single stroke as the church clock struck the half hour after eight. Darkness had fallen gradually during the last few miles. At the dock she asked an old mariner where the packet sailed from. He took the clay pipe from his mouth, paused for a tantalising moment, and pointed her along the quay.

"'Bout a furlong'll do it, gal."

"Thank you, Sir," she said, and trotted along until she was in the midst of the bustle and noise of a ship preparing for departure.

"Do you have a ticket for the passage, Miss?" said a man

in uniform by the boarding point. For a moment she panicked. Why hadn't she thought of that? Looking up, she caught sight of George moving along the deck and into one of the stairwells.

"My horse," she said. "Will you accept my horse as payment? I shall not be returning."

"'Tes not normal, Miss, but you seem in some need. Very well, get aboard. We'll be casting off directly."

She turned to Ailla, held her head in both hands and whispered in her ear. "I'm sorry my darling Ailla, I must leave you," adding to the guard, "you will care for her, Sir? Assure me, Sir."

"I'll care for the filly, indeed I will, Miss. Now embark, if you will. We are about to cast off."

Sophia boarded the packet, stood by the rail and turned to watch the man lead her beloved Ailla away. As the sail was run up she turned, and went in search of George and her new life.

XVII

Richard read with irritation the survey report and the notes Masters had attached. Masters, it seemed, was being far too cautious. There were signs of copper ore at the extreme edge of the estate land. The geology suggested that this was a small outcrop of copper-bearing rock. Only some miles beyond the estate was there enough of the rock to offer profitable production. A mine of sorts was already working there in a desultory fashion. Masters explained this by the rise and fall of the copper price. At its highest, the mine was profitable. Once the price fell by a few percentage points, there was nothing to be gained from extraction.

Richard was determined the risk was worth taking. He took note of the surveyor's use of the word 'appear'. Masters explained that, in the surveyor's view, there was an outside chance of a lode branching off, but there was little evidence of such. A survey to be completely sure would be prohibitively expensive, given the current copper price. Be bold where others feared to venture, thought Richard. Hadn't Silas said something similar? Masters was only interested in pilchards. He had drawn up plans for working with the Polperro lawyer to create another seiner team, thus doubling production. Once the quantity was there, they could provide the pilchard palace that Sir Oliver had turned down. Silas too had been keen on the idea during his early discussions with Oliver. It was cunning of Masters to mention that, thought Richard, and it did have a certain appeal. No, the mining concept was the more modern idea. The demand for copper could only increase rapidly as industries developed.

The end of the six-month period Silas had suggested for Richard to restore his finances and show better judgement approached. The comprehensive survey showed that, although some poor-quality ore could be extracted, it was not a profitable possibility in current conditions. There was some indication, however, that, at a deeper level, immediately below this there may be a lode of copper-rich ore. The costs of digging out the mine, setting up ventilation systems and associated lifting and pumping devices for a mine at this depth would be prohibitive unless huge profits were guaranteed. There was an equally strong chance this was a false hope based on a rogue rock movement. Richard had used all but a few guineas on settling debts, easing rents, the two surveys and enjoying Demelza's company. If he could rebuild his investment funds to a hundred guineas, he would convince Silas to fund the project. He was sure of that.

Masters was against the project; no point in seeking his guidance on rent rises, sales or loans. His mother left matters entirely to Masters and she rarely spoke to him now. Uncle Francis would not risk his small income on what he would consider an ill-advised scheme. He rode into Truro for his weekly visit to Demelza, deep in thought.

"You are distracted, my handsome hero," she said, when he climbed up to her rooms. "I suspect another beautiful woman has caught your attention."

"Of course not, my beauty. Who could possibly be more beautiful than you? I have things on my mind, business things; I need to raise money for a project I wish to undertake."

"Come, pleasure me, hero. I am sure we can resolve all your problems over a brandy or two when you are sated and relaxed." She stood very close to him by the bed and placed his hands on her waist.

Afterwards he lay on the bed, relaxed and disarmed. He shared all his frustrations over the estate, lamented the lack of business insight around him and gave increasingly precise details as she sympathised and encouraged him.

"There is a big meet in the old cockpit next week," she said. "It may be a sure winner could be found. I will make discreet enquiries. We cannot be seen together, of course, so you will have to come to visit very early if we are to complete all aspects of our business together."

"There must be certainty in the matter, if I am to place my hopes on it. I have been robbed in that way before."

"But you were not advised by me on that occasion."

"It must be certain. I vowed never to stake anything on such again."

"Does my handsome hero not trust his lover?" she said, detecting a hardening in his tone.

"Of course, but I would not want you deceived on my behalf," he said, as he stood and assembled his clothes.

"I would not advise if uncertainty remained," she said, sitting up and drawing her bodice around her.

***

The following week he arrived as agreed. She had two sure winners for him: one in the first fight, the other in the last. He treated the first with caution, placing five guineas at four to one. He collected his twenty guineas after a brief decisive encounter and felt he could trust her source. As the final bout approached, he scanned the noisy, drunken rows at the ring side for any sign of Rawdon. His presence would preclude any further wager. Devoran Dandy's owner was from the tinner community, a trade in which Rawdon had little involvement or interest, as far as Richard was aware. He felt secure enough to place all twenty guineas on the battle-hardened bird. He would still have his original five if he lost, so would be no worse off than at the start. The Dandy had a proud strut about him, a result of many hard-fought but ultimately successful bouts. His opponent, Bodmin Boy, was less experienced but an impressive bird nonetheless. The Master called both fighters to provide a worthy end to a great day's sport.

The Dandy spread his wings and rose imperiously, but found himself facing an equally imperious Boy a yard off the ground. Both pecked and scratched as their wings flapped vigorously and feathers from both fluttered to the ground. Dandy landed first and the Boy fell onto his neck biting into him, but the experienced Dandy twisted and turned away with only superficial injuries. Richard was nervous now, fearing that Dandy would tire first. There was much drunken cheering and cat calling as Dandy rose again, this time only a foot from the ground and thrusting metal claws at the Boy's chest and throat. The Boy was ready and lost only a few small brown feathers in the skirmish. Thus, the evenly matched birds fought on, wounding each other superficially. As both birds tired, the Dandy feinted to turn, deceived his opponent, and clamped an iron claw onto his thigh. The Boy uttered a high-pitched screech, swung all his weight against his adversary, and held down his other claw with his good leg. He was now able to peck viciously at his opponent with no response. The exhausted Dandy sank to the ground, pecking ineffectually at his triumphant foe. Richard's stake was lost.

He returned to the tavern to confront Demelza but, when he saw her tearful face, he did not have it in him to blame her.

She entertained him to a fine supper in her rooms and insisted they comfort each other in her copious four-poster. Afterwards she lay in his arms with her head on his chest while he slept.

XVIII

"I'd like us to have somewhere to live, somewhere of our own, when Josiah comes home," said Martha, as they stoked up the oven.

"But you ain't spliced yet. He'll never agree, being the strict Methody an' all," said Molly, putting in the last of the logs Thomas had chopped for them.

"I'd just like to have somewhere ready, is all. So when we get married we've somewhere to go. Somewhere he'll like; convenient for working here with you. Is there anywhere in the bay, do you know?"

"He be an officer; he'll be needing somewhere suited: can't expect him to live in some labourer's cottage."

"We shall only need a cottage, he ain't got pretensions. I'd like a nice 'un though, with water pump and clean privy." Martha stood straight and stared along the curve of the bay. "When we've got the orders in, we could have a look along the bay, over the far side there. What do you say?"

"We can; it's a fine day. We can walk for an hour or so; see what's a doing."

A wide cart track led up a gentle slope along the coast. Although grassed over between the wheel ruts, which were gravelled, the track was well used. The usual rows of fishermen's cottages fronted on to its lower levels, but beyond them and some storage sheds stood some individual houses. They seemed randomly placed, at varying distances from the track, some substantial two- or three-floored buildings, others simple cottages. All appeared occupied.

"Such as these would suit," said Martha, as they reached the top of the track and the low cliff curved away to the east.

"They look full o' fisher folk and the like, or those with a bit more to 'em," said Molly. "But they're Treloggan land, I'm minded. I'd leave such matters to Cap'n Carter. That be your right course."

"Maybe, yes, I suppose. I dream too much. It's all the waiting." Martha smiled, as they turned and walked back to check on the oven.

***

Josiah returned three weeks later, having felt the slow passing of time almost as acutely as Martha. He had seen no action, and very few warnings of enemy shipping. They had a quiet wedding in a makeshift Methodist chapel, Molly giving Martha away and a fellow officer and Methodist, Tom Pickerval, as Josiah's right-hand man. Three fiddlers led a jig along the harbour and across to the Rosevine Inn where a feast was served and much ale drunk, by all but the strictest Methodists. A room had been prepared for bride and groom. A great four poster decorated with roses and lilies. As they entered the room the fiddlers played outside the door, with songs praising their fertility. Laughing together and close to exhaustion, they lay in the bed, with one lamp giving a dim light. The marriage had removed any remaining inhibitions they may have felt. The hunger they felt for each other, hitherto suppressed, was released and, with renewed energy, they satisfied it with an intensity both had privately dreamed of.

Next morning they came down to take the coach to Truro. They made their way through the revellers, many of whom lay half on chairs or on the floor, where they had fallen as the celebrations had ended in the early hours of the morning. The landlord, a burly cheerful fellow, wished them happiness and helped them through to await the coach. They rode to Truro without incident but, as they crossed the Market Square, Martha held Josiah's arm, nervous of the proximity of Rawdon. They saw no sign of him, however, and were soon safe in Josiah's lodgings.

In the few days before Josiah returned to his ship they lived in their private world together, talking, laughing and making love. Martha raised the issue of where they would live and talked of the houses and cottages on Treloggan land. On a rare visit to town, Josiah identified Treloggan's agent and arranged that he or his wife would be notified of any vacancy in the houses on the far side of Trewarren Bay. Martha went back to her room at Molly's house when Josiah returned to his ship. Should a house become available, Josiah had left an envelope containing the likely six-month rental.

"Must you leave me, now we are married?" she said, when he was about to depart.

"You know I must, Mrs Carter; it is as painful for me as for you, but duty is duty." He reached for her and enfolded her in his arms. The carriage arrived and he was gone. Life resumed its old pattern, baking bread, mending nets, preparing for the pilchard season. Six weeks later, she was stacking the oven as usual when she felt a sudden surge from her gut.

"I be struck by some sickness," she said, as vomit spurted from her and she bent over, gripping her belly.

"Sit on that log over there, you'll feel fine shortly," said Molly. "You need to take it quieter," she added.

"Do you not feel it? We ate the same, I think."

"Fit as the fiddlers at a wedding, and so be little Henny. Have you felt it before?"

"Not any so bad, no; perhaps a little these last few days," said Martha.

"You be with babby, if I'm not mistook," laughed Molly. "That Cap'n Carter did his work well and no mistake."

"No! Can it be so? Why we only have a week together as man and wife."

"One night be enough, if the Lord shines down. That's what the Cap'n would say, I should think. Anyways, you'll know for sure in a week or two."

"Well if 'tes so, I hope he be back afore too long. I can't believe it yet awhile."

Keith McClellan

"You'll have your own place over the bay afore long, no doubt."

"Well the offer is there now. I suppose I should take it, but ... "

"Is it the Cap'n as worries you?" asked Molly, and she sensed rather than saw Martha's hesitation. "He left you the wherewithal. He wouldn't do that if he didn't want you to grab the chance, would he now?"

"I suppose, " said Martha, still hesitant.

"It is a fair rent he's asking. Not like that scoundrel, Trewarren. May the Lord frown on him for what his poor tenants do suffer."

"Well I'm out o' his grasp now. The Lord be thanked for that at least. Oh the thought of him's brought on my gut wrench again." Martha bent double and writhed from the stomach but nothing more would come.

"Here, drink this," said Molly, passing her a tankard of well water.

XIX

"Prayer is not enough, Francis. The house echoes with memories. Of hopes lost and regained, lessons not learned. I need more than prayer to save me from the depth of despond I inhabit."

"My dear Elizabeth, do not turn away from our Lord. Talk to me of all your troubles and then let us pray together. I am sure we may rely on God's guidance."

"I had such high hopes for Richard with Sophia. I thought her qualities would bring out the best in him; temper his thoughtless, foolhardy schemes where his father and I could not. Now his cousin George has stolen her away. Absconded from his ship and dragged her, unmarried, to the godless world across the ocean." Tears of indignation welled up from Elizabeth's eyes.

"So I've heard. But the father was dying, so he will claim his inheritance. They will not be without means."

"Much good may it do them. Poor Richard is devastated. At least Silas was generous in recognition of the breach of promise. Richard was in no state to make wise use of the money. It has all gone, Masters tells me."

"He has cleared his debts, I am sure," said Francis.

"But are there new debts? And there is this mad scheme for a copper mine. Masters tells me it is a profligate fantasy. He is in despair at the waste. Have you heard much of this mining idea?"

"Nothing. Richard never speaks to me now. His church attendance is irregular at best, so I have little chance to ask him about such things."

"He never speaks to me either. I rarely see him. I only hear from Masters. I think he hopes I can dissuade Richard from ruining the estate. He has ruined my life, why should he listen to me now?"

"Come, my dear, do not distress yourself so."

"Face the truth, Francis. I have to. As I wander round that great manor house alone, that fresh, light-toned decoration I was so proud of mocks me; mocks my presumption that we could ever be happy again." Elizabeth finally gave way to misery and sobbed without restraint. Francis said nothing until she quietened and looked up at him through her tears.

"I think you should move into the rectory here for a time. There is a guest room and dressing room you could make your own, and you would have sympathetic companionship to share your concerns." Francis smiled gentle encouragement.

"I don't know," said Elizabeth. "It is so tempting. I thank you for your kindness. Can I really leave Richard to himself?"

"Quite frankly, he pays no heed when you are there, and he will know where to find you should he feel so inclined. It is time to think of your own needs. You need someone to care for you and, if he will not, then here is the best place for you."

"I suppose you are right; it will be a great relief; that I am sure of. Thank you, Francis. I'll arrange for my things to be brought over first thing tomorrow." Her wan smile gave Francis some comfort as they sat in companionable silence until the light began to fade.

***

Richard had Pollard scurrying back and forth to his wardrobe. It was important to look the part of a prosperous businessman if Silas was to be impressed. In the end he chose a fustian jacket which was perhaps two years old. It smelt satisfyingly of stale cigars. He owned several white linen shirts and chose the least stained and his smartest breeches. He rarely wore a wig; it was not the image of a modern business man.

"Brush me down, Pollard. See that my coat lies well on my back and shoulders."

"Certainly, Sir Richard. You look the proper entrepreneur, if I may say so, Sir." said Pollard, who had been waiting for an opportunity to show off the word he knew would impress his master.

"Thank you, Pollard. Clear these away, will you?"

"Certainly, Sir."

Caesar was waiting as he descended the front steps. His papers were placed in the saddlebag and he set off at a trot.

At the town house he handed Caesar to the stable lad with an affectionate pat, drew his papers together, and strode confidently up to the entrance. No doubt Silas would be impressed this time. The project was forward-looking, a little risky but with lasting rewards if it succeeded. He was shown into the drawing room and reordered his papers, reminding himself of the strong points to emphasise. The room began to darken as the sun sank towards the west. He heard a noise from the hall. After what sounded like an animated discussion, the door opened and Silas appeared.

"Ah, Sir Richard, what an unexpected pleasure. How can I

be of service? Come through to the office, Come through; let's have some light." He offered his hand, which Richard accepted with a greeting before following Silas through to his office. Silas seated himself at his document-strewn desk and indicated a chair to Richard.

"I was sorry to hear of Sophia's kidnapping, Silas. I must admit that, in spite of our quarrel, I did not expect such utter lack of honour from Cousin George."

"It was no kidnapping, I assure you. I would be obliged if you would correct any rumours of that sort. George's father was taken ill, and he felt he had to go to him. He could not get leave and so absented himself without permission. He promised to return for Sophia when he had established the situation at his father's home. Sophia obviously felt she could not wait and chased after him. I knew nothing of this until they asked me at the stable if her horse was expected back here or in Nankilly. I was distraught, but there is nothing to be done. I have sent messages on the packet, but I have no way of knowing if they will reach her."

"It saddens me that she allowed herself to be seduced by such an unreliable person: a seduction for which you have had to bear the cost and the pain, Silas. I hope my visit will bring some recompense." Richard reached for his papers.

"The purpose of your visit is not yet clear to me, I confess. Perhaps you will explain, briefly if you will: I have important business to complete before tonight."

"The six months you gave for me to devise a joint project for us has now elapsed and I am pleased to say that I have found an ingenious route to a profitable enterprise. It involves some risk, but that is the challenge good business takes on." Richard shuffled his papers again, preparing to share their content.

"As I said, Richard, I am short of time. If this is that foolhardy copper mine venture then we need waste no more of each other's time." Silas stood.

"But Silas, you haven't heard the detail yet."

"I am well aware of the detail. The whole idea is foolhardy in the extreme."

"How on earth could you know the detail? I have only now pulled all the documentation together. There must be a misunderstanding. Please let me take you through this. You will see that I am right."

"I am sorry, Richard. This will not work. I have kept myself informed of your progress throughout the time since our settlement. If I am to make an investment, I need to be sure of its viability. This has none." Silas began to move towards the door.

"I still don't see ..."

"Richard, you remember the three criteria we discussed? Judgement was the first. No other person you have consulted supports this scheme; neither Masters nor the surveyor think it is an option. Secondly, finance: you have cleared your debts, enjoyed yourself at the Trelawney Arms and gambled a little in the cockpit. You have very little capital available to invest. If I were to come in with this, the risk would be entirely mine. And, thirdly, trust; the situation as I have described it does not inspire trust. It signifies to me that you live in a self-regarding fantasy land. I will not trouble you further. Remember me to your mother." Silas held the door open. Stunned, Richard rose, threw the papers on the desk and moved to the door.

"Tell me one thing, Silas, and I will ask no more of you. How did you gain such detailed information?"

"Think who you shared it with. I pay someone to research possible clients so that I am prepared. That person has licence, short of violence and theft, to acquire vital business information for me. I will say no more. Good day, Richard."

"Rawdon! Rawdon the scoundrel!" he shouted.

"Good day, Richard." said Silas again. Richard left the building without looking back. A stable lad brought Caesar to him. He mounted and trotted down to the tavern. At least he could console himself with Demelza before he returned to Trewarren.

He went up to the bar to enquire for Demelza.

"I am sorry, Sir. Demelza no longer wishes to see you. I would be obliged if you would leave the premises," said the man at the bar.

"That is nonsense, man. I demand to see her."

"I'm sorry, Sir." he took Richard's arm. Richard tried to shake him off.

"I'm not leaving until I've spoken to her," said Richard. The barman called for assistance. Two burly men Richard recognised from managing the cockpit crowd emerged from behind a curtain leading to the living quarters and grabbing an arm and a leg each, carried Richard to the door. The barman opened it and Richard was thrown down some yards beyond the entrance. A crowd gathered round, shouting insults. He stood, brushed himself down and walked up to Caesar, unable to recover his dignity.

He galloped away at a furious pace but slowed to a steady trot once clear of the town. Rawdon, he thought, he's the cause of all my troubles, always has been. A picture flitted across his mind. That day in the Trelawney Arms, he'd seen him then with the barman. That's why Demelza wouldn't see him. Yes, she was the only one who he'd discussed all these plans with. She knew every detail. She'd been so supportive, so encouraging. Rawdon must have dragged it out of her. She was too ashamed to face him. What had that brute done to her? She was the only human being he was close to in this whole hostile world. Rawdon had even poisoned her. Life would be unbearable until that evil demon was removed from this world forever. He would bide his time. Say nothing, the chance would come. He would take it, whatever the consequences. In the meantime, at least his mother there. He supposed he had neglected her of late.

XX

The September sun was low over the sea; white sails tacking to or from Falmouth were barely visible against the dark silhouette of The Lizard. The plaintive calls of the circling seagulls were the only sound above the soft hiss of the sea, as they sought their last feed before settling on their nests in the cliff face. Martha sat with Josiah, one hand in his, the other stroking the growing curve of her stomach. They had wandered up the cliff path, beyond the scattered remains of her old hut, to the shelter of the rock where she had so often sat in contemplation in earlier days.

"You are determined then?" said Martha.

"It is my duty, my dearest; much as I would love to watch over you in your confinement. We agreed before the marriage, did we not?" said Josiah with a pleading smile.

"Aye, but I did not think on it being so hard. I treasure every minute together but 'tes far less than I expected."

"I treasure it too but duty must be honoured. To resign my commission would take many months to work through and not stand me in favour for future employment."

"Duty is duty, 'tes true, but I live in dread of a second widowhood. A widow with a babby is a hard life indeed."

"I'd never wish that for you but, at the worst, there is some modest provision. Before I leave, let us brighten our thoughts. What names have you in mind for our child?"

"Well if'n is a boy, I s'll name him after the kindest man in my life, who is my Josiah," said Martha. "But he be your'n too, so what do you say?"

"My great inspiration is John Wesley, the greatest minister that ever spread the word of the good Lord, so I would name him John."

"So how shall we settle him?" said Martha.

"Why, give him both. John Josiah Carter. How does that sound?"

"One each! Now if it's a girl, my choice would be Molly. She has been the saviour of my life."

"A good Cornish name: Demelza? Demelza Molly Carter?" He caught her frown. "Rebecca then. Rebecca Molly Carter. What do you think?"

"Molly Rebecca Carter will be perfect. Now we must return and give her some rest." She rose, still holding his hand, and they walked together back towards their newly acquired cottage at the far end of the bay.

As they approached the quayside, the sound of a horse at full gallop grew louder behind them. Josiah glanced over his shoulder. He drew Martha aside as horse with rider bent low sped down the track and along the quay. There's something familiar about the rider, thought Martha, but it was difficult to tell in the falling light. Along the quay they saw that the rider had halted. A body lay on the quayside.

"Wait here," said Josiah, approaching to assist the fallen man.

Rawdon lay, still as death. Richard dismounted, the more easily to curse the cause of his downfall.

"I trust you have enough life in you to know I wish you

337

dead, Rawdon."

"Does he need help?" asked Josiah.   Richard turned, distracted.

In an instant, the prone Rawdon came to life, and heaved his whole weight against Richard's legs causing him to plunge awkwardly into the deep water at the quayside.   Josiah stepped across but looked in vain for any sign of life in the water.   The gentle lapping against the quay was the only sound. He turned back to Rawdon, who was now sitting on a boulder at the water's edge.

"Say nothing, man, for both our sakes."

"But you just killed a man, the lord of the manor," said Josiah in disbelief.

"He'll paddle his way, no doubt."

"But there's no sign of him; see for yourself."   Josiah turned to survey the water again, but the darkness now restricted his view to a circle of only a few yards. "There is no sign," he repeated. "We must inform the authorities."

"But you was party to the act," said Rawdon, with his customary sickly smile. "You is as guilty as me, unless it were accidental from the both of us. Besides," he added, as he registered Josiah's horrified expression, "methinks you has motive enough, after what he did to that wench o' yours."

Josiah looked back for Martha, but could not see her. Horrified by Rawdon's presence, she had kept hidden behind a fisherman's storage hut.

"But I only came to your aid."

"And that you did, Cap'n Carter, for it is you I see now. That you did, and I am mighty grateful for it. You gave me the chance, and I took it, for the both of us, and for that wench o' yours an' all."

"I don't believe this. It is a nightmare. Martha will vouch for my good intentions. She witnessed me rush to your aid."

"She be your wife, Cap'n, and she have every reason to see the end of the blackguard Trewarren."

A loud neighing interrupted them. Caesar was tossing his head and stamping his forelegs.

"What are we to do with him?" said Josiah.

"Leave him here and clear off. They'll think he threw him. There's brandy in them saddle bags, I've no doubt. Trewarren is a drinker, 'tes well known. That'll be the answer." Rawdon, somewhat recovered, attempted to stand. Josiah offered his arm. Rawdon grasped it, steadied himself and limped off.

Josiah was at a loss. He looked over into the harbour again; nothing. He noticed the boulder as he turned. Where Rawdon had sat he saw a small patch of hair stuck to the edge of the stone with blood. Sir Richard must have been unconscious as he hit the water, but why did he not float? Caesar neighed and stamped and tossed his head. Martha emerged into view.

"Horrible, horrible. Oh Josiah, I wish you were not leaving so soon. Rawdon will haunt me in our cottage."

"We will go to the constable now," said Josiah. "We'll explain what happened and give the horse over to his care. He is the one to inform Lady Trewarren and organise a search for the body. I do not understand why it did not float."

***

A month later, Rawdon lay in the squalor of Bodmin Gaol. The Judge had seen no reason to doubt the evidence of the constable. Rawdon's attempt to claim an accident was scornfully rejected. Without the body for evidence, the judge was not prepared to sentence a hanging, but he was anxious to be on his way and had no doubt that Rawdon was a conniving knave best kept out of harm's way. Elizabeth Trewarren fainted at the news of her son's disappearance, yet held out hope that the lack of a body might mean that he had survived. Francis consoled her as best he could. He feared for her sanity. As she refused to return to the manor, Francis felt that Elizabeth's continued presence at the rectory would cause gossip among the labouring classes.

"I am very fond of you, Elizabeth," he said, "and I feel our continued residence under the same roof provides food for gossip and does little for The Church in the face of the puritanical Methodists. You would make me very happy if you would agree to be my wife."

"Oh Francis, you have made me feel valued as I have not felt these many years. I shall be delighted to marry you, and feel free to show my true affection for you," she replied.

Francis suggested that they should entrust the running of the estate to Masters as he had proved an effective and loyal manager to Sir Oliver.

***

Martha settled into their cottage, glad of Molly's help in gathering firewood. Josiah had brought his small collection of furnishings and Thomas had constructed a basic truckle bed. As winter approached, Martha found it more and more difficult to manage the baking oven and to help with the pilchards. Late catches were still coming in. Molly had been so helpful that Martha felt she owed it to her sister-in-law to share the workload. Thomas returned from the tavern one cold night claiming to have seen the ghost of Sir Richard Trewarren.

"He were stridin' along the waterfront, staring straight ahead. He do not see me. I be glad o'that, for sure."

"'Tis the drink talking, Thomas. There ain't no ghost. I've heard tell he's gone to America," said Molly.

"'Tis true Josiah could see nothing of him in the water. Wherever he is I'll not let him trouble me no more." said Martha. "My babby'll be here soon. I don't want him troubling her."

"You've a husband now, and a good un. Trewarren'll not trouble you now, dead or alive," said Molly.

"If he be here to care for me," said Martha.

***

In early January, she was busy removing loaves from the

morning bake when she felt her stomach contract. Molly sat her in the house and called the midwife. Soon a little girl was crying in Martha's arms. The midwife was happy with a flagon of oil as payment. At Molly's insistence, Martha stayed with them for the first week and she was still there when her husband returned.

"You've a little beauty, Josiah! Ain't she a lovey? Say hello to Molly-Rebecca," said Martha, smiling a welcome.

"She is indeed, Martha, but you are the one in my thoughts all these months."

"I hope you be staying some. She'll want to know her father."

"And I want to know her, Martha, and to spend time with you. I am sure our cottage needs much work to make it fit for our family. For I am sure Molly-Rebecca will need a playmate. When you are ready of course," said Josiah, suddenly aware that he knew little of a woman's condition after childbirth.

"You must stay home a month or more, Josiah. After I'm healed we can try often as you like." She laughed. "We got lot's o'time to make up."

Notes

Some true events have been placed out of sequence for the purposes of the story.

The movements of the Navy are not based on fact.

The pilchard season runs from July through the autumn. The huer usually has a hut on a cliff top from where he shouts, "Heva, Heva," to alert the seining crew. He then directs them towards the shoal by large white flags or brushes, which he uses in a kind of semaphore signal.

The seine net is a very long net manoeuvred by a group of boats to surround the shoal. They are under the direction of the lead boat.

ABOUT THE AUTHOR

Keith McClellan is a retired head teacher. A play he wrote and directed for the Kenya Schools Drama Festival was televised and later published by Longman. Various other articles on educational matters were published in the local and national press. He has performed an autobiographical sketch on local radio and written and performed various pieces at Oxfringe. He has had a lifelong interest in amateur dramatics and belongs to several writing groups. He is currently engaged in researching the life of his father, an influential public librarian in the second half of the last century. He is married with two adult children and two grandchildren.

8069406R00190

Printed in Great Britain
by Amazon.co.uk, Ltd.,
Marston Gate.